song of renewal

emily sue harvey

THE
STORY PLANT

The Story Plant
The Aronica-Miller Publishing Project, LLC
P.O. Box 4331
Stamford, CT 06907

Cover design by Barbara Aronica-Buck

ISBN-13: 978-1-61188-002-1

Visit our website at www.thestoryplant.com

First Story Plant Hardcover Printing: July 2009

First Story Plant Paperback Printing (expanded):
February 2011

Printed in the United States of America

dedication

In memory of Angela Sue Harvey

1962 – 1974

To Angie, my daughter, you are the reason I write. You were my first experience of loss and perseverance to rise above the clouds. Through God's grace, I've been able to share renewal through my stories' characters, and perhaps give others hope. You remain special, dear Angie, and are an inspiration to your family. Your memory remains vibrant and alive even to your nieces and nephews – those you left too soon to meet – w ho, on special occasions, send up colorful balloons to you in Heaven and share stories passed down about your unsinkable spirit of fun and your compassionate heart. We miss you.

And to Leland, my quintessential hero, the wind beneath my wings, lifting me above the mundane, inspiring me to be more than I ever dreamed or hoped to be. Your applause means more than any other. Your love, so unconditional and passionate, makes me a woman among women, fulfilled beyond measure. One of your greatest gifts to me is our beautiful children, who crown our love with beauty and glory. The other is that you allow me to be me. For that, my love, I honor and cherish you.

And to my beloved remaining children and their spouses, Pam and David McCall, David and Susan Harvey, and Angel Callahan, with all my gratitude and love for the amazing people you are and for all the joy you've brought me. And for celebrating with me the good times and empathizing during the bad. Your compassion and respect are sterling gifts. May your years unfold with grace and ease. May you find joy, serenity, and love. And may all your dreams come true. I wish for you happy endings, over the rainbows, and all the good and lovely things life offers. I wish for, between you and your spouse, the freedom to be yourself, with all the wonderful love, passion, tenderness, and respect that I have with my life's love. Daily, strive to be happy. Take kindly the counsel of the years. Nurture strength of spirit to overcome adversity. Be at peace with God. Remember that, despite rough places, it is a beautiful world. Thank you for grandchildren who are as wonderful as you are.

And to God Almighty, the author of life, who has blessed me with these.

With all my love,
Mama/Mimi/ESH

acknowledgments

Song of Renewal grew from a lifetime of revitalization experiences. It is a novel fraught with seemingly insurmountable odds to overcome, that grew from a network of family and friends who loved and validated me, despite my human frailties and failures, and then rejoiced with me in renewal.

I am especially thankful for The Story Plant. Publishers Lou Aronica and Peter Miller's unwavering belief in me enabled me to pen the Wakefield family's amazing renewal journey.

Lou, you are an awesome editor and mentor who allows my stories to remain my own, only better. For this, I am eternally grateful. Peter, you believed in me from the first, and that confidence has remained steadfast. You and Lou both see my highest possible goals as doable and reachable. You two are God's blessing to me.

Angel, my youngest daughter, is truly an angel. During the writing of *Song of Renewal*, she brainstormed with me during plot-stuck times and maneuvered her tech-challenged mom through the mazes of cyberspace research and such. Having studied classical ballet, Angel also tutored me on the finer points of related technique and terminology.

To authors and professors Brian Jay Corrigan and Dr. Dennis Hensley, who separately brainstormed with me at last June's

SWA Workshop during my synopsis formulation – your insights propelled me in the right directions. You both have my heartfelt gratitude.

My grandchildren, Kristin and Russell Smith, Chelsea McCall, Kaleigh, Lindi, Ashley, and Trey Harvey; Peyton, and Jensen Callahan all served as muses for the story's young adult characters.

My son, David Harvey, and oldest daughter, Pam McCall, celebrated each phase of my writing project with, "Mama, I'm so proud of you. I knew you could do it!" Thank you!

To my best friend, Charlene Holubek, and siblings, Patsy Roach, Karen Bradley, Roger, Mike, and Jimmy Miller, you blessed me with unfailing validation and resounding, "It's time!" declarations.

Thanks to Dr. George Helmrich, my medical counselor friend, and to the real "Nurse Brenda," Brenda Boiter Duncan, RN, my old high school friend. Your skill in medical procedures with comatose patients truly got me through. What you didn't know, you found out. Thanks also to the staff at Spartanburg Regional Medical Center and Spartanburg Regional Restorative Care for your counsel on long-term medical care. Any mistakes made are entirely my own.

To Lori Shillingburg, my other "Angel," the most courageous, beautiful young woman I know, who shared her own post-accident experiences to enrich Angel Wakefield's journey to recovery. Be blessed, dear Lori – I so admire your generous spirit.

Deep appreciation to artist, Jim Baird and wife Frieda, long-time, extraordinary friends. Jim's specialty is not only in portraits and paintings, but also in commercial graphics. Thanks for being on call for my endless questions. Your expertise, patience, and helpfulness aided me beyond words.

To Gerald Ballenger, talented artist and his wife, Othello – family to me – whose contributions are constant and supportive, thank you!

To my parents, I hope you see this milestone from Heaven. Without you giving me life, it would not be.

To the James F. Byrnes High School 59ers and the Blue Flower Literary Club, you are a warm, vital constant in my life and I appreciate each and every one of you for supporting me during this creative odyssey.

To all my writing pals in Southeastern Writers Association, former presidents Pat Laye and Becky Lee Weyrich, who encouraged me from my early beginnings, who celebrated with me each rung up the success ladder. A big high five, especially to Debbie Brown and Meredith, Harry Rubin, childhood friend Eleanor Payne Mitchem, Holly McClure, and all my fellow members on the SWA Board of Directors: my husband, Lee Harvey, Sheila and Tim Hudson, Lee Clevenger, Charlotte Babb, Chris Wilkerson, Adrian Drost, and Amy Munnell.

A special acknowledgement to my late writing buddy, gorgeous, brilliant author Nelle McFather, who unflaggingly nurtured me all through the years, encouraging and supporting my writing dreams. I miss her unconditional love. I miss her. I really do.

So many of you, too many to mention here, are woven into the tapestry of my life, rendering it even more vibrant and colorful and beautiful. Those of you who celebrate with me my victories and grieve with me over my losses – you know who you are – I give my undying love and appreciation.

And thanks to you, dear reader, without whom all my efforts would be fruitless.

Keep peace in your soul. Enjoy.

"The only things that stand between a person and what they want in life are the will to try it and the faith to believe it's possible."

Rich DeVos

prelude

Even before the baby was born, things began to turn strange. Everything seemed too brilliant. Too vibrant. As Liza nested in preparation for the brand new life nestled deeply inside her, she felt that invisible Strobe-like emissions warmed and lit her entire world. The Wakefields knew it would be a girl because the ultrasound declared it so.

She and Garrison had been watching videos and studying parenting books for months now in anticipation of one of the most important roles of their lives. They discussed at length their philosophies on parenting and family life.

"I want to be a stay-at-home mom," Liza resolutely insisted from the first. "Those childhood years go so swiftly. Once they're gone, we can never get them back."

Garrison readily supported her sentiments. "I wish my mom had spent some of those years with me," he said a bit too mildly. Liza knew just how hard he worked to tamp down his emotions regarding that time of his life when his parents didn't always have time for him.

This slice of time was reshaping them for brand new responsibilities. They would nurture and care for their own little creation.

Baby showers had filled the new nursery closet and chest. Tiny bunnies decorated the door and drawer surfaces, compliments of the artist father. When building the manse, Garrison and Liza had been intent on providing hallowed space for their future children.

"Six," Liza insisted.

"Four. Two boys and two girls," Garrison laughed as his paintbrush added touches to Oz-Dorothy's pigtails. "Hell's bells, honey, I am but a poor, struggling artist."

So they laughingly settled on four.

The entire pink room sported Garrison's vision of baby paradise, with everything from peeking cherubs to Seven Dwarfs to Cinderella, to a prima ballerina who looked remarkably like Liza in her role as Giselle, all tenderly inclined toward and watching over the baby's crib.

What fun they had decorating. It made it all more real.

They made love a great deal in those first months, celebrating their accomplishment. That's what they considered it – an amazing, miraculous triumph – their making of another life. Their appetite for each other was insatiable, as though they must somehow imprint each others' souls and bodies on themselves in a quest to never lose that sacred connection. The excitement of creating a family was at once agony and ecstasy.

Would it change things? Would the *us* alter?

It seemed that they must hurry and pack in all the *us* they could. It wasn't a spoken thing. It just happened, everywhere, in new places, the slow, intense way of first discovery, in ways unforgettable.

This continued until the last month. The pressure in Liza's abdomen grew painful in those final weeks, so they abstained, instead showing inordinate affection in every other way possible.

Liza loved all of Garrison, heart, mind and soul. Even his melancholy idiosyncrasies. And his physical beauty, his leanness and hawkish features turned her knees to mush and her senses into a flailing mess. Theirs was a blissful, blessed lust. Good. Right.

While she was pregnant, Garrison was happier than she'd ever seen him, singing in the shower, whistling as he worked. He made lists of things to do when the baby came, including ridiculous trips to Disneyland or Six Flags. Liza indulged him, thinking how lucky she was to have such a man.

"Can't plan too early," he insisted, cleaning his wire-framed glasses as he leaned over the lists spread across the kitchen bar. "Why, the way time flies, she'll be a year old before you can say 'scat.' She'll be old enough to enjoy all the fun." He was deadly serious, which tickled Liza pink, but she hid her goofy grins, not wanting to dampen his palpable enthusiasm

The only thing that slowed Garrison down was his lack of painting commissions. He'd advertised in both the daily and weekly papers. Liza had spread the word in her ballet circles and had reaped a few commissioned portraits. However, with insurance and mounting utilities expenses, the money ran out quickly. Liza shared Garrison's frustration. She had been tempted at times to take on a clerical or typing job, but a difficult first two trimesters had knocked that notion out of her head. She had, in fact, been forced to rest much of the time.

"Stay off your feet" had become a refrain she detested, especially when she felt the longing to dance. Feeling the baby's fluttery movements had compelled her to obey, though. More than anything, she wanted this baby.

The huge, luxurious manse had become both blessing and curse. Blessing in the sense of comfort and space for a growing family, and curse in huge utility bills and mortgage payments. The big house pulled heavily on electricity for heating and cooling. To cut costs, they took to closing off the upper floor during extreme temperatures.

"It could be worse," Garrison conceded during one of his morose, dark spells. Artistic Melancholy, Liza labeled it. "If I hadn't had land to sell off to pay more up front, the mortgage payments would have tripled."

Characteristically, Garrison soon segued from gloom to gratitude to seventh heaven. "I feel like I could conquer the world," he exulted one night in her last month as he gathered Liza's bulk to him ever so tenderly.

"You can, by George!" she agreed, then began to feel awkward, and huge, and disgusting. "I feel like a water buffalo," she muttered glumly.

Garrison switched to Rhett-dialect. "Dah-ling Scarlett, you ah many things but a watuh buffalo you ah not. Nevah evah, *evah*." He kissed her then, passionately, yet holding her as though she were made of delicate china.

Liza's heart felt as though it would shatter from the wonder of their love.

In the next moment, something did shatter. Garrison felt warm liquid splash and cascade over his bare feet as he and Liza stood together, locked in each other's arms.

"What?" He pushed back and gazed down between them at the pool still slowly gathering on the floor. Liza's eyes were wide, her expression stunned.

"My water just broke," she murmured, and in the utterance he heard both awe and dread. He knew she feared the unknown, had told him so.

He pulled her to him once more and embraced her with all the love in him.

"It's gonna be okay, sweetheart," he whispered, hand clasping her head to his bosom, willing his strength to enter her, to carry her through this ancient rite she now faced. And he knew generations of women had survived it. But with Liza it was different. She was part of *him*. He felt her terror.

"It's not fair," he said through clenched teeth. "I should be able to share this with you more…not just with words but with my own body experiencing the labor –"

He felt her quivering and shaking. *Oh no he was making her cry.*

Garrison pulled back to peer into her face. "Honey, I'm sorry."

Then he saw that she was laughing. Hard. He frowned, thoroughly perplexed. "What's so funny?"

"Men," she said and burst into fresh laughter. "If you had to do one hour of labor pain, there'd never be any babies."

He watched her double over in a fresh upsurge of laughter and shook his head. Amazed as always at her great sense of the ridiculous, the humor hit him.

Yeah. She got that right. He did not do pain. Period. Not at all. His lips curled up at the corners and he began to chuckle along with Liza, who by now was somewhere between hysterical and manic in her doubled-over mirth.

Then, just as he began to scratch his head in comic relief, her laughter stopped. She slowly tried to straighten up, arms gripping her swollen belly. Her mouth rounded and her face began to contort.

"Garrison," she hissed. "Get me to the hospital."

They did a Caesarian section the next morning. Then, when complications set in, they did a hysterectomy. Liza cried. Garrison was slack with shock. He would never have a son.

But it was her tears that tore him up. He pulled himself together for her sake. He sat at her bedside holding one cold, clammy hand.

"Honey, you're more important to me than a house full of kids. Besides, we've got our Angel." As if on cue, the baby, nestled in the crook of Liza's arm, began to stir, puckering her tiny rosebud lips as she stretched delicate little arms and flexed fingers so small the fingernails appeared transparent.

Garrison leaned to kiss the small face, nuzzling its silken softness, then gazed upon it in worship. "She's so beautiful," he rasped hoarsely, blinking back tears. "So perfect. Like her mother."

Liza felt as if her heart would break. No more children. Tears coursed down her cheeks. "I'm sorry," she whispered.

Garrison gently blotted her face with a tissue and leaned to kiss her, stopping her flow of words. "You have nothing to be sorry for. We have us. And now, we have Angel." He grinned, warmth spilling from mahogany pools. "She's part of the *us* now. We are blessed, Liza. Blessed."

She gave him a wobbly smile and nodded. "Yes. We are, aren't we?

"Darned right."

He kissed her again.

"Mmm," she murmured, "I felt that clean down to my toes."

Eight weeks later, Garrison's vision blurred as he went over the monthly bills. He could hear Liza bathing little Angel in the nearby bathroom. Charlcy, Liza's older sister, was visiting, cooing absurdly.

"Stop crossing those eyes at your auntie, you little stinkpot," she teased gruffly. Then with syrupy sweetness, she crooned, "You are one cool chick, Angel-Pooh."

Liza chortled. "Come change this diaper, Auntie, and you won't be so enthralled."

"Not me, sis. You had her, you do poop duty."

Garrison swiped his hand across his eyes, tired beyond words. In the next instant, he heard Charlcy changing the diaper.

"Phew," she exclaimed, then laughed. "How can anything so precious smell so disgusting?"

"That's life," Liza quipped.

At those words, Garrison felt a rush of something foreign. It shot through him like a bad caffeine overdose.

Life.

He felt it sweep over him again, the freakish adrenaline OD. The strangeness.

Garrison swiveled and slid off the kitchen barstool. He climbed the stairs to his study and burrowed into an easy chair, propping his feet on a matching leather ottoman. The disquiet inside him refused to budge, even when he reasoned that he was simply exhausted from the second job he'd taken on. In desperation, he'd gone to their next-door neighbor, Rocky Bailey and asked for part-time work at the Baileys' dairy farm.

Rocky Bailey was near Garrison's age, thirtyish, tall, and rugged, with a shock of black hair and astute dark eyes that spared him from ever being called ordinary. His two-year-old son was a reflection not only in looks but in stride and mannerisms. Touchingly so. It drew Garrison.

Garrison stooped to eye level with the boy the first time he met him. "What's your name?"

"My name Twoy." The dark eyes surveyed him, curious. A touch shy. Trusting.

Garrison smiled and stuck out his hand. "Nice to meet you, Troy." Something in his heart grieved that he would never father a son, but he quickly, shamefully, doused the thought.

The boy peered at the outstretched hand for a long moment, then reached to take it, a grin splitting his face, stealing Garrison's heart forever.

Garrison stood and saw the father's proud look resting on his son.

"How about it, Rocky? Think you could find something for me to do around here?" Garrison recapped their earlier conversation, heart in throat, hoping, praying.

Rocky Bailey immediately reached for Garrison's hand and grasped it firmly.

"Well, Wakefield, I sure could use some help around here. And you living so close and all. It would be perfect. When can you start?"

From that point on, Garrison woke at five a.m. to rush over and help with the morning milking. He repeated this late afternoon for the evening milking. He still had enough time to do commissioned work, such as it was. Little was forthcoming these days.

Never quite enough. He'd been out of the art circles too long because his freelance commercial work took too much of his time.

Garrison's gaze swung to one of his early paintings hanging on the wall. It had been done before the house was finished, depicting his idealized vision of the manse and the grounds. He huffed a dry laugh. Reality was a far cry from the canvas-vision.

Like his dream of an art career.

He stood suddenly, shoved his hands in his slacks pockets, and moved to gaze out the window that overlooked the Wakefield property.

Landscaping sprawled in myriad phases of development. Money was scarce. Labor was expensive. It wasn't hard to do the math. The year before Liza had conceived, she and Garrison worked from sunup to sunset for months to seed zoysia grass over an entire acre of land. They'd dug flower beds and created picturesque berms. The two of them could only complete so much, though, without help.

Now with the baby taking much of Liza's time and energy, and Garrison working at the dairy to fill the gaps in his sparse art schedule the yard work had come to a stand still.

Though her figure had quickly returned to its elegant shape and suppleness, Liza refused to even discuss returning to the ballet. Garrison admired her devotion to full-time motherhood, even understood all the love and fears that drove that passion. But right here, right now, he needed help.

He needed Liza.

They'd resumed marital relations several weeks ago. But Liza's former energetic approach to life – and lovemaking – had done an abrupt to-the-rear march. He prayed that it was merely a post-surgery childbirth thing that would, in time, reverse itself.

She was busy being a mother. And he was happy about that. But at the same time, he missed her undivided attention. He missed her being…his Liza.

His alone.

Hell's bells. He threw back his head and raked impatient fingers through his hair. *How selfish am I? Huh?* He plopped back into the easy chair, disgusted with himself.

Torn.

God only knew how much he loved his little Angel. He was not jealous of her in the least. Or was he? Heaven help him, sometimes he didn't know for sure. Sometimes he seemed to be two people. One the devoted daddy. The other, a narcissistic jerk.

He just wished that Liza could spread herself enough to cover his hunger for her – his hankering for the days when their marriage was like a fantastic romance movie with the proverbial happily-ever-after. When, for no apparent reason, he would invade her upstairs ballet practice, sweep her into his arms, and break into silly dance steps. She would improvise and they would end up clinging to each other, laughing so hard they couldn't stop.

Then they would make love.

Now, the baby's crying took precedence. Diapers. Feeding. And it should.

But he missed it all. He missed the little rented house and few bills. He missed the once-in-a-lifetime passion of young love.

Most of all, he missed his dream.

chapter one

sixteen years later

"What do you remember most about your wedding day?"

Gwen's question, posed across the Wakefield dinner table, brought Liza's inner pendulum, one that swung lazily in a lulling motion that soothed and deluded, to a screeching halt.

The innocent query stunned Liza. Not because it was inappropriate, though the redheaded, inquisitive Gwen was adept at prickly probing, but because Liza had to force herself to switch her brain into romantic memories. She had to reach way, way back inside herself to dig them out. For long scary moments, they eluded her. To what dark, unfathomable place had those momentous vignettes fled?

Sixteen-year-old Angel's return from the bathroom to the seat beside her mother gave Liza a short reprieve. Angel leaned over and whispered, "Mama, please pass me a roll and the butter."

Liza raised her eyebrows. "Think that's wise?" she whispered back. "You've already had one."

Angel sighed, rolled her blue eyes, and gave a terse shrug.

"Suit yourself," Liza said, relenting only slightly. Angel was a ballerina and ballerinas needed to be light on their feet. But heck, at the same time, Liza wanted her daughter to enjoy life. "You feel okay?" she asked, suddenly alarmed at the pasty pallor of the girl's skin. "You look a little pale." Feeling guilty, she placed the breadbasket and butter dish within Angel's reach.

"I'm fine, Mama," Angel insisted in a flat timbre. Liza saw her daughter's hands tremble before she quickly shoved them into her shorts' pockets.

"You sure?" Liza whispered and was rewarded by a *you're embarrassing me* grimace.

Liza observed that her blond lithe daughter didn't get another roll but instead informed all present, just as the doorbell pealed, "Troy's taking me over to his family's house tonight." She slid her father a sharp glance. "We're gonna just hang out and watch a movie together. The whole family." She turned on her heel and, chin leading, marched from the room.

Liza noticed that Garrison didn't rise to Angel's pointed use of "family" and "together." After all, the two families were friends, and Troy's father had helped Garrison by giving him work at their dairy farm during tough financial times. Still, Liza caught Angel's message.

"Be home by ten thirty," he called after Angel, who met Troy outside the door before he had time to pop in for niceties,

Angel's relationship with Troy Bailey, her first boyfriend, had developed pleasantly in recent months. Angel was spending more and more time with the Bailey family. Liza's heart did a funny little dip that Angel seemed so anxious to get away, that her familial affections had, somewhere along the way, done an abrupt left flank.

Gwen, their dinner guest, whose architect husband Ron was out of town on a job, had for the past hour entertained them with stories of her own hilariously disastrous wedding day. Now she nudged Liza back to the topic.

"It's still your turn, Liza. Your most vivid memory of your wedding day?"

Liza's first impulse was to duck and run. That in itself gave her pause. But in the face of Gwen's own generous revelations, Liza couldn't refuse to be as open. She swiveled her head in her husband's direction. He stared at her, waiting, an uncertain look in his dark eyes. Was it anticipation? No. Sadness? Probably.

Her gaze skidded past his shoulder to a far wall where, suddenly, she stared at herself on canvas. She snatched the lifeline. "When Garrison presented me with his wedding gift, a portrait he'd painted of me." The words, poured out in the open, released some mystical sentiment curled deep inside her and for just an instant, moisture gathered behind Liza's eyes and pleasure, rich and sweet, oozed through her. "He worked on it all that last year at USC. It was the most romantic thing I've ever received."

"The one on the den wall? Over there?" Gwen asked, her gaze following the direction of Liza's. At Liza's nod, she arose and moved to the den niche of the large open living/dining area for a closer look. "It is absolutely breathtaking, Liza. What ballet are you dancing in it?"

"*Don Quixote,*"Liza said, her voice thick as emotions rippled through her. At one time, no one could have convinced Liza that she'd ever leave the ballet. She pushed that line of thought aside.

"Garrison, wow." Gwen's voice was soft, reverential. "You are one talented guy." She slowly shook her head. "I didn't have any idea. The graphic work we do doesn't show your real stuff. Why aren't you taking commissions for portraits?" She moved back to the table and reseated herself, her astounded gaze piercing Garrison.

"It's called survival. Regular income, family, that sort of stuff." Garrison blushed a bit as he smiled in acknowledgment. "Thanks, Gwen. But the real honor goes to the subject I had to work with." He looked at Liza and the undisguised appreciation in his eyes warmed her. It came so seldom lately, the glow in the mahogany depths. "She was my inspiration." Liza almost gulped at the naked adulation in that statement. Pleasure splintered through her, a feeling so alien these days that Liza felt momentarily drunk on it.

Gwen's amused voice shattered the moment. "Hey, you two. Wait till I leave, will you?"

Flustered a bit by her own agitated emotions, Liza arose and reached for the iced tea pitcher on the buffet to refill all their glasses.

"What about you, Garrison?" Gwen said. "Your best wedding memory?"

Liza witnessed Garrison's transition while filling his glass. Saw his body tense and the warmth fade from his features. Felt the awareness between them evaporate and awkwardness settle upon him.

The old familiar sinking feeling returned, making her insides heavy and her spirit sag. Liza reseated herself, fighting a niggle of irritation at Gwen's insistence on reminiscing. Why was this bothering her? Maybe it was how Garrison hesitated, as though thinking back on those days taxed his brain. That his initial response to the question mirrored her own wasn't relevant.

Gwen was Garrison's right hand. She assisted Garrison in his commercial graphic arts company. Liza instinctively glanced at the colleagues' bundle of accounts, piled high on the buffet, screaming for attention. Following dinner, they would spread them out over the table to mull, dissect, and manage.

Gwen snapped her fingers at Garrison's tentativeness. "Wake up, Garrison. Your favorite memory of your wedding day?" Then she laughed from the belly. "Except for *that*, of course."

Liza couldn't help but laugh when Gwen cut her a sly wink. She also couldn't help the thrill that shot through her, summoned by the allusion to her wedding night's passion. It had been an extraordinary honeymoon.

Garrison blushed, grinned, and shifted in his chair. "Uh, I don't know." He frowned in concentration for a long moment. "I suppose it was the excitement of slipping away, finally married, from the reception in that ridiculous little black Skylark with words, not nice words, mind you, big as boxcar type slathered on with shaving cream"

"The words were *suggestive,* compliments of my sister Charlcy," Liza said, brimming with memory.

Gwen laughed uproariously. "My kind of gal."

Liza looked at Garrison. Memories and sensual nuances from those vibrant young years invaded her. "We were finally alone. I remember the buzz of not having to leave you that night."

Oh God, how the memory stirred her. How she yearned to reclaim those intensely loving moments.

"Yeah," he murmured softly, eyes suddenly sad as they locked with hers. Liza knew that feeling. She, too, felt it. "Remember how we couldn't wait to get to our home?"

She smiled, remembering how, instead of leaving immediately for their beach honeymoon, they'd spent that first night at their own little rented house. They simply couldn't wait to initiate their loving claim there. Their present home, much grander, came more than a year later when Garrison sold off some of the property to finance it. At the time, however, the small cottage was an enchanted love nest.

Liza closed her eyes, remembering. "We wanted to cook dinner together."

Gwen snorted incredulously, blue eyes skewer them with comical disbelief. "You cooked?"

"Of course," Garrison said, feigning indignation. "And it was great. Steaks grilled to perfection and Liza's heavenly potato salad. Nobody can do it quite like her."

His gaze locked with Liza's. For a long moment, his tender smile reached down into her heart, stirring up emotions long dormant. His darkly chiseled features spoke eloquently of that long-ago time when just a look from him sent her senses into a heated gallop. Her lips slowly curved in response.

Liza's cell phone, hooked onto her slacks belt, vibrated and burst into a loud, syncopated Latin rhythm, scattering the magic. Darn! She'd meant to turn it off. "Excuse me," she murmured and left the table when she saw Betty Branch's name on the screen. The Women's League committee chairperson had some information Liza needed for their upcoming charity bazaar.

By the time she finished the phone conversation, Garrison and Gwen had lapsed into business talk at the table. Disappointment speared her. A phone call had assassinated a breathtaking moment of young love. That starry-eyed awareness so seldom surfaced now that, when it did raise its head, she wanted to cling to it. One look at Garrison, however, put that notion to rest. Immersed in commerce, he'd gone off into that land far removed from her.

Liza efficiently gathered the dishes and, refusing Gwen's polite offer of help, took them to the kitchen, scraped them, and deposited them into the dishwasher, her indisputable best friend these days, what with the seemingly endless committee meetings and charity causes.

When Liza returned, business papers and two laptops dominated the dining room table. "Coffee?" she asked, drawing detached, negative nods as Garrison and his assistant delved single-mindedly into fathoms beyond Liza's understanding.

She went into the den to catch a movie. An old Alfred Hitchcock thriller was playing on American Movie Classics, but Liza, who usually adored them, couldn't harness her concentration to the storyline. The discussion at dinner of wedding day memories kept hauling her mind back.

She closed her eyes, laid her head back, and remembered the beautiful night following their wedding.

"I want to hang the portrait right here, over the mantle," Liza said.

"Anything you want, my darlin' Scarlett," Garrison said in his oft-used Rhett Butler drawl. He swept her up and into his arms, kissing her as thoroughly as Rhett kissed Scarlett while carrying her up the staircase on those vintage *Gone With the Wind* movie posters.

Soon, he lowered her feet to the floor, lips still locked in a new, rampant pursuit of consummation. Oh, they'd had heated sessions all during the past year at school but they'd agreed to save this for marriage. Now, all the frustrated hormones swarmed into frenzy, catapulting them to the marriage bed in an unforgettable tangle of limbs and flesh and unbridled coupling.

Never in Liza's life had she begun to imagine the pleasures Garrison would bring to her. Nor had she fathomed the words and phrases he murmured in her ear during those following months and years.

And fatherhood. Aah. Garrison leaning over mother and infant daughter, tears of joy puddled in those splendid dark eyes, murmuring, "I've never loved you more than at this moment, Liza. Thank you for the most precious gift I've ever known."

Liza luxuriated in the memory until the sound of voices sprang her eyes open.

"How about some coffee, Gwen?" Garrison asked.

"Sure." Liza heard Gwen's chair scrape as she rose. Muffled banter and soft laughter brought her nerves to a fine edge. Her ears keened to discern the words. The affinity between Garrison and Gwen triggered an icy curl in Liza's abdomen. Liza sat there, listening to the sounds of Gwen moving about, searching for and finding things in Liza's kitchen. Water running. Liza felt frozen to her seat, one step removed from this cozy, domestic scene.

Tense moments later, during which Gwen and Garrison talked softly, comfortably about things common to the two of them, Liza inhaled the aroma of freshly perked coffee. Her alarm grew as she rose and found Gwen in the kitchen, pouring for them.

She grinned tiredly at Liza. "We changed our minds about coffee. That good food makes one groggy. Let's see, Garrison's is black. Where's your sugar, Liza?"

Liza silently got the sugar bowl from the cabinet and a spoon from the drawer.

"Thanks." Gwen efficiently placed the steaming cups on saucers and stirred in her sugar. "Say. There's enough for another cup there if you'd like." She smiled and returned to the dining room, depositing Garrison's coffee before him and taking her own seat at her laptop. Quiet conversation turned once more to shared business items and graphic designs they conspired to perfect.

Liza blindly wiped the counter clean and felt a jab of something dark, pungent, and visceral. Jealousy? No. Not exactly, but something akin to it. A sense of being stranded seized her.

She was a left-behind thing. She knew Gwen's taking over Garrison's coffee tonight wasn't an intentional slight. After all, Liza wasn't normally a part of the Gwen-and-Garrison equation.

But when had Garrison stopped depending on Liza for small comforts?

Garrison had not asked her, Liza, for coffee. He'd asked Gwen.

Truth was, Gwen had become more a wife to Garrison than Liza.

chapter two

The summer rain came in a sudden burst. The Wakefield manse's tin roof became an acoustic conduit for the percussion, especially in Garrison's upstairs office. It was a luxury he had anticipated when building this elegant country home for his young bride eighteen years ago. This evening, in his precious solitude, he propped his elbows on his studio desk, anchored chin in hands, and closed his dark eyes.

For long moments, he listened. Rain danced across the metal roof like a thousand snare drums, lulling him, relaxing tense shoulders and arms. Its cadence spiraled him back to his grandparents' rural South Carolina farm, where he'd spent youthful summer vacations and indulged his love affair with painting, easel ensconced in meadows, beside creeks, and facing sloping hills. His oils and chalk art dazzled his family, and later, a much larger audience.

The *Greenville News* hailed him "the next great artist of our time." Even the *Charleston Post and Courier* touted, "Garrison Wakefield is a phenomenal talent whose arrival is a heads-up to the art world."

Today, he looked at his logo, Wakefield Creations, which specialized in commercial graphic art and thought about how destiny had other ideas. His tired mind ambled back to last night's scene in the den, to the portrait of Liza dancing, and again he experienced the slow evaporation of hopes and dreams. He blinked back fatigue and adjusted his designer glasses, ones that lent his features austerity, casting him as an ageless Hitchcock Cary Grant. At least that's what Liza had told him during their courtship days, when she was principle of the city ballet. That seemed eons ago.

He recalled last night's conversation at dinner. Gwen's question about wedding memories had opened up a real hornets' nest. He'd known that marriage could morph from hormonally charged tumult to lesser degrees of passion. But for the first time he realized just how far apart he and Liza had grown in recent years. He knew, too, that she felt it.

Yet for one moment last night, he'd experienced the magic bliss of their wedding day. How powerful, their passion. It had burst upon and through them and swept them up for years. But now it was like the portrait on the wall. At first, the sight of it had thrilled him beyond comprehension. He continued to pass the same painting, day in and day out, glancing its way and feeling the depth of their romance. How long had it been now that he'd walked past it without really seeing it?

He shook his dark head to dispel the bleakness and gave attention to the project spread before him on the mahogany, glass-topped worktable. He rarely came home empty-handed. The Vanhauser account loomed before him on the horizon. The courtship involved design samples on his and his assistant's drawing boards. He needed to get this right. If so, it would put him over the top financially.

Another new account was a famous restaurant chain for which he needed to complete the promotional art and advertising layouts. Sometimes, like tonight, he had mixed emotions about his business. More and more, its demands depleted him, left him feeling stretched out on a medieval torture rack.

Focus! he commanded. His brow furrowed and he attacked the project with renewed vengeance. Beneath the rain, he almost didn't hear the muffled knock on his door.

He frowned and called, "Come in."

Angel's face poked tentatively around the door. "Hi, Daddy."

He swiveled in his chair, aware that he did a poor job of hiding his impatience. He tried to soften his voice. "Hi, Angelface." He spotted Troy behind her. Garrison had a special place in his heart for the boy whom he'd known first as a little towheaded tyke, chasing behind him when Garrison had worked at his dad's dairy farm. Though he'd nearly tripped over him at times, Garrison had never ceased to be charmed. "Hi, Troy," he said warmly. "Come on in, you two. What's happening?"

Troy gave Garrison a big grin. "Hi, Mr. Wakefield." He stepped forward and extended his hand. Garrison grasped it in a hearty handshake. "Sorry to disturb you."

"S'okay," Garrison said politely, though it wasn't okay at all. He had a deadline to meet. He turned his attention to his daughter, who seemed fidgety, a sign that she was about to dump some unwelcome agenda upon him.

Angel's fair hair shimmered in the light of the desk lamp. The cloudy day had brought an early dusk, rashly dimming the chamber. Her blue eyes, so clear one could almost see through them, held a note of pleading, which made him feel, suddenly less than he wanted to be. But he was, after all, working.

"Daddy," she drew the word out into four syllables, her appeal dialect. "Today's Troy's birthday. I baked him a cake. We just cut it. Here, I brought you a piece." She placed the plate on the desk corner and shot her boyfriend a quick grin. "So...may Troy and I go to the concert at the Bi-Lo Center? The Vines are a group we really, really want to hear. He has tickets."

Garrison inhaled deeply, and then tiredly blew it out. "Happy birthday, Troy. Eighteen, is it?"

"Yes, sir."

Garrison shook his head in disbelief. "Amazing how time flies. Eighteen, huh? That was a good year," Garrison muttered, a lopsided, weary smile grazing his lips. He addressed Angel then as his mouth settled into a grim line. "Thanks for the cake, Angel. I'll eat it later. As for the concert," Garrison's head moved from side to side decisively. "No. I'm sorry about the tickets, Troy, I truly am, but no." The denial was abrupt and final as his chair swiveled away.

"But why-y?" Angel pealed, instantly distraught.

"Why?" Garrison spun around again and glared at her as though she'd lost her senses. "Listen to that rain, Angel. You don't go out in weather like this. It's dangerous."

"Daddy," Angel whined, "you're being overprotective."

"Maybe so," Garrison said over his shoulder. "But my job is to keep you safe." He hated to say no to Angel, but this time his refusal was justified. Was he overprotective? Maybe. That he and Liza could not have more children was not even in the equation. If he had ten children, he'd still say no. Garrison returned to his sketching, the one thing he did enjoy about this work. The creation.

Long moments passed. A rustle of movement at his elbow startled Garrison.

"You're so talented, Daddy," Angel said.

He turned and squinted up at her, annoyance filtering through. "I thought you left. Where's Troy?"

"Downstairs." She smiled a bit nervously, licked her lips, and gazed appealingly at her father. "Daddy, please, please let us go to the concert." She stooped suddenly and hugged him tightly, kissing his cheek. "Please, pretty please! I'll wash the Jag four times in a row and cut the grass for a month if you'll just —"

He disentangled himself, not unkindly but firmly, then slowly removed his glasses. "Angel." He rubbed his eyes tiredly. "You sound like your mother trying to get her way when it's not exactly kosher. You don't need to be on the roads tonight." He looked at her then, his face empty with fatigue. "Sorry, honey, but the answer is still no."

He swiveled in his chair once more and resumed his work. A moment later, he heard Angel leave the room, shutting the door firmly behind her.

"Mama, you know how much I want to see the Vines." Angel jiggled her propped sneakered foot against the bar stool, her mouth pouty. "It starts in just a couple of hours."

Mama looked over her shoulder from where she stood at the kitchen sink. "What did Daddy say?"

"He said no. Just that. No." To her way of thinking, that was the bottom line.

Mama looked thoughtful, then sympathetic, and resumed putting away leftovers from their earlier dinner of cold cuts and salad. Troy couldn't make it for dinner but he'd come over later for cake to celebrate his birthday with Angel. Secretly, she'd banked on Troy's presence getting her dad's permission. So much for that.

In fact, after Daddy had refused to give her permission to go, Troy had cautioned her against pushing her dad too hard. "You've got a super father, Angel," he'd said. "Don't underestimate his wisdom."

"But Troy," Angel argued, "If I don't push, Daddy would never let me out of the house." Troy had simply shrugged and gone off into the den. She knew she'd exaggerated her father's stringency, but tonight was special and she wanted to go to that concert more than she'd ever wanted to do anything in her life.

"Why doesn't Daddy want me around?" Angel asked morosely, swiveling the seat back and forth at the kitchen bar while her mother rinsed off supper dishes and loaded them into the dishwasher.

Mama turned, hands dripping. "Darling, your daddy *does* want you around. He simply works all the time and isn't always there for you. He doesn't mean it to be that way."

But it is. The thought, unspoken, hung silently between them as her mother continued to tidy things.

"Mama, you sure I can't help?" Angel's voice was listless.

"No, no. You sit right there. You prepared the meal so I'll do clean up."

"Thanks." Angel replayed her father's rebuff of her affectionate hug. Did he have to be so…so cold? Tears of rejection and shame pooled in her eyes. She wondered, not for the first time, what had drawn her parents together. She knew her father had not always been so aloof. What gentle, explosive rudiments made their marriage work? Their signals were, at least in recent years, almost always mixed, perplexed. At one time, their passion had been a palpable thing, though at the time she'd not, in her innocence, been able to name it.

Angel just knew they adored each other, and it spilled over to include her. At least at one time it had been so. In her earlier years. She remembered the looks that had passed between them, so charged with ardor and sensitivity to each other that she'd felt guilty at witnessing them.

Sadly, she reflected, that awareness didn't seem to visit the Wakefield home very often anymore.

If it did, it was quickly doused by arguments over money. Her daddy's mantra these days was, "I'm the one who keeps this ship afloat, so please be considerate. Turn out lights when you leave the rooms and don't use the credit card like a wish list."

In response, Mama would insist that, "I can't cook without buying groceries," and go on about the cost of chicken and beef.

Angel dreaded when Daddy balanced the checkbook and got the credit card bill. Then there were the utility bills that seemed to climb higher and higher each month.

Again, she wondered what sinister or magnanimous forces kept her parents together. A real mystery. Would she figure out how love manifested itself between her and Troy, how to engage in it without pain and disappointment? Lordy, she hoped so. She certainly knew that Troy would never be as cold to their child as her father was to her.

Nearby in the den, Troy watched an Animal Planet special on bears in the wild while wolfing down a huge second piece of fresh strawberry birthday cake, his favorite. "This is delicious, Angel," he called to her. "You're a great cook."

"Thanks." Dismally, she pulled the crystal cake pedestal toward her and sliced off another big hunk of the luscious pink, sugary fruit concoction, scooted it onto a small plate, and picked up a fork.

"Ah ah," Mama said, lifting a dainty finger of caution. "You've already had a slice."

Angel's breath came out in a whoosh. "Mama! It was so thin it got lost between my teeth." Her fork clattered to the countertop's granite surface, echoing Angel's morale.

Mama looked indecisive for a moment, then waved a dismissive hand. "Oh, don't mind me." She nodded her okay. "Go ahead, honey. This is a special occasion. You do well with your weight, anyway. Not like me when I was your age with ol' Tarishka calling me Miss Piggy in ballet class!" She crossed her eyes and assumed an awkward, knock-kneed waddling execution, arms at a grotesque angle, eliciting a sudden, rolling belly laugh from Angel.

"Aw, Mama," Angel said, gurgling with laughter, "you were never fat."

Mama rolled her eyes, then laughed with her and gestured to Angel's heaping plate. "Have at it, darlin'."

Angel tucked into the cake, from which carb comfort, within seconds, swirled through her willowy yet supple body. *Why does everything I look at turn to fat?*

She knew what she needed to do. She excused herself to go to the bathroom and quietly, succinctly made herself throw up. There. That would take care of Karinsky's in-class references to her "chub" and her ballet coach's snide remarks like, "been laying into the French fries and milk shakes, have we, Angel?"

The upchucking always left her feeling weak and downtrodden. Unreasonably depressed.

Needy.

Angel shuffled despondently to the bar stool, rejoining her mother. "Would you have had me if you hadn't retired from ballet?" she asked.

Mama dropped her dishcloth and moved swiftly to place her hands on Angel's shoulders and gaze into her eyes. "My darlin' daughter, you were destined to be. There was never a question in my mind that you were what I wanted in life. "

Angel slanted her a searching look. "No regrets?"

Mama laughed, a joyful, exuberant, celebratory sound. "None whatsoever." Then she kissed Angel's tilted nose and returned to her cleanup.

Angel gazed at her mom at work, awed anew by her strength. She knew of her mom's difficult childhood, of her being emotionally abandoned by Angel's sick grandmother, a woman Angel never knew.

It still warmed Angel to hear her mama's fervent insistence that she preferred spending her life as a stay-at-home mother. Not many friends of hers could say that. Many of them came from broken homes and had custody issues. She didn't know what glue held her folks together, she was just thankful it did.

Suddenly, Angel's sugar high crashed, leaving her feeling more morose than ever. "Daddy doesn't love me anymore," she proclaimed, believing it in that instant.

"Don't ever think that, Angel."

Mama moved quickly to give Angel another warm hug. She looked into her daughter's moist eyes, fingers gently pushing back a stray tendril from Angel's forehead. "He doesn't mean to shut you out, honey. He's just got a lot on his plate right now, several new accounts, which is good, but it takes so much from him. Right at the moment, he has deadlines to meet. Soon, things will even out. Just wait. You'll see."

She kissed Angel's cheek, gave another snuggly hug, then moved back to the sink and dried the counter. Angel watched her mother move about with a dancer's lithe grace, looking elegant even doing household chores. Angel gave a little huff and shook her head of shoulder-length wheat-streaked hair. Unlike her, Mama had balletic poise, beautiful muscles, and turned-out legs. Even walking through the mall, Mama couldn't help it – she stood lifted and tall.

She retained her distinctive "duck foot," the turned-out stance of ballerinas, where toes lined up with outer hip bone. Once absorbed, Angel knew that these ballet technique fundamentals remained with dancers for life. At least, with most of them.

Her mother kept up by cross training with a variety of tools including Pilates, resistance training, and even Yoga. Frequently, Mama joined her in her dance studio upstairs, her coaching providing them time together. Doing stories together to dance and music gave Angel great pleasure. She especially loved to watch her mother do mimes with her expressive arms and hands, a thing that could turn comical in a heartbeat, throwing

Angel into stitches, and sending her rolling on the floor. Then just as suddenly, the same appendages would shift her emotions to tears. She loved to watch Mama improvise to her favorite John Barry movie themes, movements especially poignant and moving.

"Daddy's right," Angel said. "You do look like her, y'know? Margot Fonteyn? Dance like her, too. I saw her in a ballet movie video last night, one I rented and took to show Troy's mama. She loves ballet and wanted to see it with me. I was curious because Daddy always said you looked and dance like Fonteyn. And you do." She turned toward the television. "Doesn't she, Troy?"

"What?"

"Mama looks like Margot Fonteyn, the famous ballerina – except Mama's blond. Remember the '70s ballet movie we watched over at your house last night?"

"Oh! Yeah, you do look a lot like her, Mrs. Wakefield. Really."

Mama tossed a big ol' grin over her shoulder. "Muchas gracias."

"I wish I could get lost in dance like you," Angel said pensively, meaning it.

"Hey! Don't sell yourself short. You're coming along fine." Then Mama grinned over her shoulder and sing-songed, "I'm so proud of my little ballerina."

Angel sighed wistfully at the oft-repeated praise, one that had become their private little humor thing, a sentiment that both pleased and perplexed her. "I'm glad somebody's proud of me."

"Honey." Mama turned to gaze at her, face solemn, "Your daddy *does* love you. With all his heart. Working so hard leaves him...weary and somewhat distant. He just needs to get over the present hump. He'll soon be different toward you. Trust me." Angel heard the note of uncertainty in Mama's declaration and knew that at times she, too, felt Daddy's remoteness.

"I doubt that, Mama." An uncharacteristic snort burst from Angel. "I've been waiting for years now and it seems the older I get, the more he shuts me out. For example, he knows how much I want to go to the Vines concert tonight and he flatly refuses to let me go. Troy's even got free tickets, for cryin' out loud!"

She waited for her mother's reaction, which she knew would be well considered and wisely weighed. Mama was always there, no matter what. She always did the right thing. But tonight, Angel wasn't interested in what constituted right. Her dad's rebuff still stung terribly. The hurt nudged her toward recklessness.

"Why can't he be like you? He acts like an old fart, fussing about the rainy weather and all. Mama, you know how Daddy is. Always looking on the dark side."

Encouraged by her mother's lack of rebuttal, she continued. "Know what he said? He said I sounded just like you, always conniving to get my way! Just because I hugged and kissed him. Is that not kinda paranoid?"

She saw her mama's body tense and rise to ballerina full mast. Angel quickly lowered her lashes, convinced that her mother could look into her eyes and know.

"He said that, huh?" Mama stood stock still for a long moment, hands on hips.

"Yeah." Guilt gnawed at Angel. Daddy had said something to that effect, hadn't he? Yet she had obviously embellished on it. But she couldn't back down now, with Mama getting all stirred up. Besides, she did deserve this one night out. Didn't she? She'd done well on her schoolwork and danced her tail off in ballet classes. Her chin lifted. Yes, she did.

"So he said that, did he?" Mama wiped her hands on a dish towel. Her patrician nose flared delicately and her blue eyes narrowed to slits. "Well, you two just go on to the concert, honey." She marched over and gave her daughter another sound embrace. "And have a good time."

Angel dashed to get her purse before Mama could change her mind or Daddy came downstairs. An hour had passed quickly as she'd talked with Mama. So they would have to scuttle to get there by eight. She and Troy hurried out the front door into the downpour, from beneath the dripping wet umbrella, she glimpsed Mama, peering out into the night, her lovely brow furrowed, just before she cried out, "Be careful, now. Y'hear?"

chapter three

Liza poured herself a cup of coffee, took it into the spacious den, and lowered herself onto the overstuffed cream, soft-leather sofa. She'd just finished making some calls upstairs for a parent-teacher meeting and wanted a few minutes of off time.

She took a scalding sip and admitted to herself that her rush to busy-ness was mostly to detract from the sting of Garrison's callousness toward Angel. Never mind his smart-ass reference to Liza's being manipulative. She rolled her eyes; that was another thing entirely.

Her gaze settled on a mantle portrait of the elder Wakefields.

At that moment, she hated Garrison's parents for what they'd done to him in his youth. They weren't truly bad people; exemplary citizens, actually. They just hadn't wanted children. Garrison – the proverbial *accident* – had messed up their dreams of an unencumbered lifestyle of travel and leisure. During much of his youth, they'd pushed him away or shuttled him off to his grandparents when he threatened to intrude upon their intimacy.

Garrison, the end product, was a storehouse of contradictions. He had a level of sensitivity that could take away one's breath. He was the most protective, noble and giving of men.

Yet, to him, giving meant materially and physically – not emotionally. Not anymore. Once, it had.

She pushed away the pity that always ambushed her when she thought of Garrison as a young, lonely boy. She couldn't allow it to cloud her judgment when it came to Angel.

The next sip of coffee tasted bitter. Needed sugar.

What was it with Garrison? Why did he allow history to repeat itself in his father/daughter situation? Liza knew Garrison loved Angel, but couldn't he handle her a bit more gently?

Liza took another hot sip, made a face, and firmly deposited the coffee on the glass-top. Had she done the right thing tonight in overruling Garrison? After all, he was being protective.

Yet....

She cocked her head and scrunched her forehead. Where exactly did paternal safeguarding end and neuroticism begin? At times, during his gloom-doom moods, Garrison seemed – to Liza – inclined to overkill, both on finances and fathering. Did everything have to be so life-and-death grim?

She knuckled her pulsing temples and closed her eyes, feeling like the pot calling the kettle black, for crying out loud. It was just that she couldn't bear to see the crushed look on Angel's young face when Garrison so blatantly rejected her overtures. Didn't Garrison realize a girl's need for her father's acceptance and validation? The girl deserved some fun in her life.

Liza clicked on Fox News. A young woman was missing in Georgia. A college student. Her picture flashed across the screen. She was blond and had a big smile that reminded Liza of her own daughter. How sad.

The doorbell rang. She frowned as she uncurled her legs and headed for the door, wondering who it could be.

☙

Garrison shifted in his chair and stretched his tired back. He stood and glanced at the antique mahogany wall clock, surprised that well over two hours had elapsed since he had begun working. He paused. Was that the doorbell? He couldn't really tell over the rain, now a soft nettling hum against the tin.

Tonight's progress pleased him. One logo, for a new dentistry clinic, read "Gentle Dental Care...Gentle Care for Sensitive Patients" in elaborately prepared script. Another logo, for a restaurant, read "WASABI...Traditional Japanese Cuisine." Above it loomed an imposing Samurai warrior with signature topknot and kimono topped with kamishimo, sword raised high, ready to engage in battle. Under the logo, in intricate script, appeared the line "Chefs experienced in the art of tableside knife tossing and salt and pepper juggling."

He shrugged. Not exactly a masterpiece or particularly challenging, but accounts like these put a roof over their heads and provided all the comforts of life. As long as he remained busy.

Garrison straightened his work and clicked off the desk lamp. The dampness outside left him with a chill. It was a good night to be inside.

Descending the stairs, he heard voices, soft at first, then Liza's rising in alarm.

"No! Nooo!"

He spanned the last steps two at a time. At the open front door stood two uniformed highway patrolmen. Alarm blasted through him. The smell of rain wafted inside.

"What?" He rushed to Liza's side and turned her to face him. Liza's face was pasty white.

"What?" The word burst from him and he knew he really did not want to know what caused her to look like this. But he had to know.

"My God, Liza. What's wrong?"

Her lips struggled to move, but tears trailed down her cheeks and the words choked off. He spun to face the two officers. "What's going on here?" he demanded hoarsely.

"There's been an accident and you're needed at the hospital."

Garrison's brows drew together in confusion. "But…who?"

"Your daughter, sir. And the young man with her."

"No, no. You've got the wrong house."

He looked at Liza, brow furrowed. *Then why is she crying?*

"But they're here," he insisted, confusion and desperation emanating from him like atomic discharges. His voice dropped to a whisper as he gazed at his wife. "Aren't they?"

She gulped, swallowed, and replied in a voice barely above a whisper, "No, Garrison. No, they're not."

The ride to Spartanburg Regional Medical Center was silent, except for Garrison's oft repeated, "Why? Why did you let them go?"

"Oh my God – what have I done?" murmured Liza. She struggled to breathe as the world crashed in upon her. *How could I have been so stupid? Reacting in anger, impetuously. How could I not have known how dangerous –*

Near panic, she turned to her husband, whose hands gripped the steering wheel with knuckle-whitening intensity. "Garrison?" she whispered.

Help me, please. Tell me it's going to be okay, her heart cried out.

If he heard or sensed her desperation, he gave no indication. His face appeared cast in gray stone as he parked in the Emergency parking area and helped her from the car, not meeting her pleading gaze. Her legs felt rubbery and when she swayed with dizziness, his arm slid around her. He impelled her swiftly through the warm misting rain toward the entrance and inside, where air conditioning slapped her damp clothing and flung her into chills.

Garrison relentlessly propelled her along the white corridor of the ER. There, a doctor ushered them into a small consultation room and seated them at a table.

"I'm Dr. Abrams, head of Neurosurgery and –"

Garrison sprang to his feet in one frantic motion. "Where's our daughter?"

"Please," the doctor said quietly. "I know this is difficult, but try to be calm."

"Is she…." Liza's voice was a mere wisp of sound as she convulsed with chills.

"She's alive, but barely." The doctor ordered a passing nurse to get a blanket for Liza. "I want to be up front with you." The man's features and manner painted a grim picture. "Your daughter has sustained terrible trauma to the brain and is unconscious. At present, she cannot breathe on her own. We've inserted a breathing tube and hooked her to a respiratory machine. Right now, we know that there are injuries to both her back and legs. We'll need more tests to show the extent of her internal injuries.

"The prognosis is… not good. I think you should prepare yourselves for the worst. Naturally, we'll do everything we can to save her, but at this moment, I can't promise anything other than to keep you informed."

"What –" Liza licked her dry lips. "What about Troy?" Another chill assailed her. The nurse entered and quickly wrapped Liza's shoulders with a blanket.

Dr. Abrams was silent for a moment, head lowered, then he looked at her. "I'm sorry. He died instantly. The car hydroplaned before leaving the road and crashing into a tree. The impact was profound."

"Oh my God!" Liza sobbed and buried her face in the blanket's fold.

Garrison looked at her, his eyes dazed. "Does Troy's family know?" he asked the doctor. Dr. Abrams said that they did and that they'd informed the staff that Troy was an organ donor. They wanted to honor that, to give someone else life. They were currently preparing for the organ procedures, as well as making arrangements with a local funeral home.

"Is your daughter an organ donor?" asked Dr. Abrams.

"No." They both spoke at once. Then Liza said, "We – I'm not ready to –"

"Right," Garrison confirmed abruptly.

"I understand," said Dr. Abrams.

Organ donor. Liza squeezed her eyes shut. *The nightmare grows.*

The doctor leaned and took Liza's icy hands in his. He spoke soothing words to her, then turned to Garrison and asked, "Are you all right?"

Garrison shook his head. "No. I'm not."

Liza heard the anger in his voice and withdrew even more within herself. *Will I survive this?*

"Is there anything I can do for you?" Dr. Abrams asked.

Garrison's white lips tightened into a thin line and he looked at Liza, his eyes black as onyx. "Yes. Undo tonight."

Liza gazed down into her daughter's still, ghastly pale, swollen face and despair slammed her, sucked the breath from her. Tubes protruded from the young body in Frankenstein fashion. Seeing the hose down Angel's throat nearly gagged Liza. Did it have to be so big and intrusive? How must that feel? *Oh God – my baby.*

Had she not known who Angel was by her wheat-blond hair alone, she could never have ID'd her. *How can I live with this?*

I caused it all. She swayed and then caught the mattress edge to steady herself.

Reality slapped her again. She could not depend on Garrison right now. The poor man now paddled his own canoe as hard as he could. Upstream. Over rapids.

Liza, too, would have to paddle hers alone.

Standing on the opposite side of the hospital bed, he'd not so much as glanced her way since their arrival in the antiseptic, dimly lit chamber. *Will he be able to forgive me?*

Shock. Some people react this way. Liza felt an overwhelming sympathy for Garrison and resolved to be stronger. To face this thing. She must.

Much later, at three a.m., on doctor's orders, they drove home to get some rest. The rain had let up. A dismal fog replaced it. "You won't be of any use to your daughter or yourselves if you don't get some sleep," Dr. Abrams had pointed out. "Besides, you can't go back to the ICU until morning."

What he said was true. It only made sense to go home and pray that no call came through the night.

She turned to Garrison in the car. "Garrison, I wish they wouldn't keep bringing up the subject of organ donation. At least two different physicians have broached it."

Her husband grunted assent, looking so tormented that her hand automatically reached to touch his cheek. But he recoiled discernibly, turning his face to avoid contact. Taken aback, she faced the front of the car again and forced herself to calm down and not react. When they arrived home and he opened her car door, she didn't flinch when he averted his gaze from hers and again evaded her touch.

Oh God, how she needed his arms around her. She pulled her feeble strength about her and put one foot in front of the other. Garrison simply needed to work things out in his own way. She knew he would soon adjust to the situation, as she was struggling to do. In time. After all, their daughter's survival was their top concern. Patience. That's what it would take. And hope. Much hope.

chapter four

"How bad is the head injury?" Garrison asked Dr. Abrams and braced himself as if against a Hoover Dam burst. A long pecan-wood table and matching chairs centered the consultation room in which he and Liza met with the physician.

Garrison felt a tiny bit more inclined to face the truth after sleeping a restless three hours. He'd awakened to the smell of coffee at six o'clock to find Liza, gaunt and pale, huddled on the sofa, ignored coffee clasped in both white-knuckled hands.

Her sunken eyes had appealed to him, but he'd turned away and gone to shower, dress, and attempt to face the day. He felt gourd empty – except when sporadic anger and pain seized him. He tried to hold it at bay. Looking at Liza brought it on, so he avoided doing so. His emotions felt numb one moment and inflamed the next.

How could she have gone against his wishes? His insides coiled tighter.

Dr. Abrams leaned against a corner desk, arms crossed. He looked world-weary with his receding hairline, thick black-rimmed glasses, and craggy features. "Our team spent most of the night battling tooth and nail for Angel's life. We did all we could to stabilize her. But it's still touch and go."

"When will we know if – ?" Garrison's voice trailed off and he blinked back moisture and a rising tide of dread.

Dr. Abrams cleared his throat. "I know it sounds cruel and uncaring to say that we'll just have to wait and see, but in essence that's what we have to do. I try to be up-front with my patients' caregivers and you'll be no exception. I can't predict whether a particular head injury will cause death, though in Angel's case, that's not the only danger she faces.

"The initial critical period in the recovery of a head-injured patient is the day or two after, when the injuries may be so overwhelming as to cause death in the face of the most intensive treatment. That's where your daughter is right now."

Liza gulped back sobs, her shoulders shaking. Garrison stared at her, seated across from him at the long table. He shared her anguish, but he was unable to let go the way she did. His throat ached to bursting, but the tears shored up against the back of his eyes, making his head throb and his heart feel as though it would explode from his chest cavity.

"Please, I know this sounds trite, considering these circumstances," Dr. Abrams said kindly, handing Liza a box of tissues, "but try not to upset yourself, Mrs. Wakefield. I'm not saying there's no hope. I'm just preparing you for the reality of what lies ahead."

"What are her chances of survival?" Garrison's voice husked as he arose and paced to a window, one that overlooked a busy hospital parking lot. He took a deep, apprehensive breath and glanced at Liza, who looked like death warmed over. No, on second thought, not warmed over at all. She looked like the walking, breathing dead. Exactly the way he felt inside.

Dr. Abrams spoke solemnly. "We're doing more tests to determine the extent of her head injury. There's a chance the spinal cord may be involved. We already know that she has other bodily injuries, but we need more X-rays to determine exactly what they are. We already know that there are several back and leg injuries."

"Spinal cord? She won't —"   Liza took a deep, unsteady breath, looking for the world as though she'd faint at any moment. "She won't be paralyzed, will she?" Then she burst into tears.

Garrison swiped his hand through his hair and moved his neck around to loosen the tension.

"Paralysis?" Dr. Abrams shook his head. "Let's not go there at this time. We're trying to get Angel through this present crisis. To keep her alive. It'll take all your strength to get through this, so take it an hour at a time. Okay?"

He started to leave the room, then turned back to face them. "If your daughter survives tonight, just remember that this will likely be a long, drawn-out process. Try to be patient. I know that's easier said than done, but patience is important right now. I can't overemphasize that. The next forty-eight hours are crucial. And her other injuries complicate things."

The doctor dropped his head for a moment, then looked at them, expression grave. "If you're praying folks, it's time to get down to some serious business."

Then he was gone.

Suspended...weightless....

Angel could see men in white gathered about the young girl on the table below. Doctors. That much she knew...but where was she? Floating overhead...yeah. Strange. How did she get here?

The activity below hooked her attention, held her spellbound.

They worked frantically and she wondered who it was over which they labored so...so desperately. She floated down a bit for a closer look. Dear God! The patient looked remarkably like her, though the features were beginning to swell and turn all shades of blue and purple. Hard to tell, though she herself felt not a twinge of anything. She couldn't be there and here, too, could she?

Of course not. One of the men took a strange-looking instrument with paddles in each hand. He pressed both of them to the young woman's chest and gave an order.

"Surge!"

Immediately, Angel felt a gush of agony so immense she could not bear it. She began to swirl downward as the pain spread and spread, catching her on fire, plunging her into blackness....

Nothingness...gray mist surrounded her...light spilled through the school cafeteria window...Troy eating with her... "Here, eat more than that," he said, grinning, forking over his extra roll.

Angel shook her head...her mouth watered for the bread, but Mama wouldn't like it...fog descended...blackness....

Ballet music pulled her to her upstairs studio...her feet wouldn't move....Mama won't like it if I don't practice...her teeth ground together in agony, but her feet and legs refused to budge...Mama won't like it! HELP ME MOVE MY LEGS!

Blackness.

The hours merged and melted into one another. Liza felt that the long night away from Angel was the worst. "We nearly lost her," Dr. Abrams told them the next morning. "But she's stabilized. For now." His reservation terrified Liza as she groped for something to cling to.

Time passed in a blur of panic one minute and hope the next.

"Mrs. W.?" a small voice quavered. Liza looked up from her seat in the ICU waiting room on the vigil's second day. Garrison had gone for a walk and some coffee.

"Penny?" Before her, quaking with teen angst and grief, was Angel's best friend and fellow Byrnes High cheerleader, Penny Johnson.

Liza stood and opened her arms. The girl fell into them, bawling like a three-year-old.

"Shh," Liza soothed and consoled until her bosom was moist with tears. Only then did the spiked dark head lift.

"H-how is she? Is she —?"

Liza nodded and forced a smile. "She's holding her own, thank God."

Penny snatched a tissue from a box and blew her nose soundly. She then joined Liza in the wait for the next visiting time window. The girl sat quietly, contemplative and nonintrusive. Liza reached out and took her hand, gently squeezing it. "I'm so glad you're here." Penny was a part of Angel's world. Suddenly, Liza didn't feel quite as alone.

Penny smiled, her red, swollen eyes lighting up a bit, her fingers returning the squeeze. "Me too." Her near-black spiked hair added drama to her pale features.

Several others on the Byrnes cheering squad drifted in and out during the next two days. Teachers and administrators came and went, expressing care and support. Liza tried to allow them moments with Angel during the brief visiting-time span. It became a finely tuned balancing act, loosing Angel's young world upon her while carving out a tiny slice of space for Garrison and herself as well.

"Perhaps, just perhaps," she told Garrison on the drive home one of those nights, "having the people she relates to around her will somehow bring her back. It can't hurt."

Garrison was silent as he drove. She thought he wasn't going to reply at all, but he finally said, "What hurts is seeing all those kids moving around, laughing, living...like she did before. Why —" His voice choked off.

Liza felt her heart splinter again. She didn't have to clarify the question he was asking. She knew. And she knew not to offer consolation just then because he would not receive it from her.

This would be another long, lonely, restless night.

Liza followed the path her mother had taken up the hill, her steps quickening as she lost sight of the tight green slacks and white tube top. Small fingers clutched Barbie's blond ponytail as tears trickled down Liza's cheeks. Swiping her face, she snuffled hard and her mother's Armani fragrance ambushed her nostrils, making her cry even harder.

Oh, how she missed Mama when she set out on these treks, ones that separated Liza from her for days, even weeks at a time, and ones that left her daddy pale and gone off inside himself and explaining fervently how sick Mama was to do such a thing.

Treks that made her thirteen-year-old sister, Charlcy, blazing mad and cursing and bitter.

Liza took off again, dashing toward the last place she'd glimpsed the glitter of Mama's ear and wrist accessories. Trash littered the trail into the woods, beer bottles strewn like dead leaves. Liza's foot caught on a protruding root and she tumbled face-first hard onto the ground. She lay there for moments, dazed — then remembered the reason for the chase. Mama knew all the routes to the bus stop. Daddy had taken her car keys long ago and only relinquished them when her mind intermittently leveled out.

Hurry. She must hurry and catch Mama before she tumbled headlong into that black hole outside her family, one that seduced and sucked her in.

She scrambled to her feet, clapped the dirt from her hands, and snatched Barbie up from the weeds to clutch to her chest, a gesture that somehow comforted her, but as she cast her gaze about in a frantic search for some sign of her mother, the emptiness, the absence of the familiar maternal presence, howled at her.

"Mama?" Liza croaked tentatively. The silence was deafening, bouncing like Ping-Pong balls against her eardrums and making the fine hairs on her arms take on a life of their own. Mama's fragrance no longer wafted to her on the breeze.

Liza slowly turned, her gaze lifting to scan the trees, whose limbs suddenly morphed into monstrous black fingers that linked together as one to block out the sunlight. Liza shivered and looked around for the trail.

Where is the path? She turned around and around, growing more confused by the moment.

"*Mama!*" Her scream pierced the air. "Where are you, Mama?" She sobbed, collapsing into a heap, face buried in her hands, Barbie forgotten.

Daddy always excused Mama's lapses, insisting that she must take her medicine every day. When Mama failed to comply, Daddy seemed to take full responsibility for her actions. This infuriated Liza's big sister, Charlcy. Liza had not yet figured out why Mama was so sweet most of the time, enjoying Liza's blossoming ballet talents and making ridiculous desserts such as bunny cakes with silly hats and then, lightning-fast, became this other eerie creature, who frightened yet beguiled Liza to search beneath that bizarre coating for the Mama whom she adored and who adored her. Her weeping revved up.

"Liza!"

Liza didn't register the summons, so great was her grief. "Liza! Thank God!"

Charlcy burst through the undergrowth like a volatile genie and scooped her into her arms. "You scared me half to death!"

Liza bawled as her sister plopped onto the ground, pulling her onto her lap, holding her close with frenzied care.

"Shh." Charlcy stroked a bit heavily, kissing the top of the tow head. "What were you thinking, Liza? You can't just go running off like that, scaring the daylights out of us."

Liza looked up at Charlcy then, swiping tears from her face with the back of her hand. All at once, she felt unaccountably self-conscious and disoriented. Where had Mama vanished to this time? She scrambled off the comfortable lap, one that didn't hold her as often lately. After all, she was six and no longer cuddly sized. She stood awkwardly as her big sister arose.

Liza could not hold the searching, concerned gaze of her sister. She dropped her head. "I-I'm sorry," she whispered, guilt-ridden. She looked up into worried eyes and snuffled hard, shuffling her feet. "B-but I w-want M-Mama." Tears splashed over and ran down her cheeks as she tried unsuccessfully to gulp back the sobs.

"I know, baby, I know." Charlcy gathered her again to her. Liza could feel tension gather beneath her sister's budding bosom. Knew when she ground her teeth together to suppress the rage that always came with their mother's frolics. Charlcy didn't cry for Mama anymore. Rather, anger braced her up and got her through these crazy times. Even in the midst of it, Liza felt Charlcy's love, knew that she, Liza, was not the target of that rage.

"Stupid woman," Charlcy hissed into Liza's hair. "Who in God's name throws away pills that keep 'em from going nuts? Huh? Her, that's who. Stupid, stupid, *stupid!*"

Liza shifted to loosen the arms that began to squeeze a little too tightly. All the emotions flailed at her, pummeled her.

When Liza's grief welled up anew, Charlcy quickly back-tracked and soothed. "C'mon, honey. It'll be okay. Daddy'll find her and bring her home." She snorted and muttered, "You can count on *that*."

Finally, when Liza quieted, Charlcy matter-of-factly took her hand and tugged her back through the thick foliage. Liza gazed around one more time over her shoulder, this time glimpsing the distant, phantasmal figure of the woman who'd birthed her, who loved her except these times when she slid into this hellion persona who disregarded everybody and everything dear to Liza.

Only now, long white chiffon billowed about the thin figure whose lovely gaze cast away from Liza to some faraway world "Mama!" Liza yelled, tearing her hand loose from her sister's to dash back into the forest. As she drew nearer, the shimmery white phantasm appeared to lift into the treetops, growing more and more transparent until only the face, transfixed intently on some point in space, remained.

"Mama!" screamed Liza, fresh tears cropping and spilling over as she reached out with both arms.

Somewhere in the distance Charlcy called "Liza! Come back!"

Before Liza's eyes, that dear face turned toward her, slowly morphing into gray skeletal features whose black sockets stared but did not see.

Liza screamed ….

"Ahh!" She bolted upright in bed, hands to damp face, mouth wide open.

❧

"Liza!" Garrison, startled from his own restless slumber, gazed blearily at her.

"Nightmare," she gasped, gulping in air then taking long, dragging, calming breaths to slow her frantic pulse. Garrison was accustomed to her bad dreams and knew of her deep fear of abandonment.

Only this time, he did not take her in his arms until the monsters eventually slinked away. Rather, his reaction was that of someone placating an addled stranger. She rocked slowly, arms anxiously hugging herself, immersed in a black realm of ghoulish, bone-chilling portent. The brush of Garrison's hand on her arm stilled the frantic motion.

"Try to get some rest," he coaxed in his most polite tone. Her jerky nod seemed to satisfy him because he turned over and pounded his pillow before sinking into it.

Thanks, Garrison. But in that instant she had not the lucidity to muster up umbrage.

Still reeling, she turned over to face the opposite wall. Nightmare-hangover images of abandonment assailed her. Pummeled her. Tonight she felt as vulnerable as she had at age six. She'd decided long ago that she would never do that to a child. Liza recalled too vividly why she'd decided to leave the ballet to be a full-time mother to her daughter.

Her daughter.

A daughter who now faced possible death. *At least,* she swiped a tear from her cheek, she didn't have to feel guilty on that count. She had never abandoned her child.

Would never, ever abandon her. *Please, Angel, come back to me.*

No regrets there. But the guilt wrenched from her fateful decision that rainy night was enough to cover a multitude of sins and saturate several lifetimes. Liza quietly wept as she watched daylight drive back the night.

Liza and Garrison lunched on hospital cafeteria sandwiches with Garrison's Floridian parents, who'd flown in the night before. Then they returned to the ICU waiting area for the two o'clock visiting window. The older Wakefields were, to Liza's relief, perfectly sympathetic and subdued. The usually talkative Ruth had little to say beyond offering compassion and assistance. As soon as the ICU door opened, Liza and Garrison rushed to their daughter's side. The grandparents acquiesced and waited outside until the very last moment.

In the small cubicle, on opposite sides of the bed, Liza and Garrison gently held their daughter's horribly swollen hands. Liza despaired at the near lifelessness of the once vital girl lying there, one unrecognizable in her injuries.

Dr. Abrams appeared in the entrance doorway. "Angel nearly left us through the night. Again." The doctor rubbed the back of his neck and then faced them squarely. "Fortunately, we were able to bring her back. We're running tests to try and determine why her blood pressure dropped so suddenly." He shrugged tensely, shaking his head. "But the bottom line is that she's a critically injured girl who's holding her own so far, beating all odds of survival." He gave them a terse smile and disappeared.

Liza felt Ruth's hand gently squeeze her arm in empathy. She and Tom had slipped in quietly as the doctor talked. Twenty brief, silent minutes ticked away and visiting time ended.

"It's plain heartless," Liza grumbled to Garrison on their way out. "We shouldn't have to leave our girl at a time like this." The elder Wakefields walked a distance behind, allowing their son and his wife privacy. But then, Liza thought with a touch of resentment, that was their style. Distance.

"Yeah," Garrison concurred darkly. "I don't like it, but it's a necessary evil."

"I know. I just wish your folks could stay longer." The senior Wakefields had to leave the following morning. But Garrison needed them. She needed them.

"Yeah, me too."

Family. Liza was just now realizing how crucial familial connection was at a time like this.

Liza had been sixteen when her own mother died from breast cancer. Fortunately, Renee's erratic behavior had been less difficult to control in her last years. Partly because Liza's father learned to crush and slip her pills into her religious morning mocha coffee and partly because as her cancer progressed, she was too sick to resist his loving oversight.

Ironically, Liza now admitted, her mother's declining health had gifted Liza with the most precious of memories. It bore the double comedy/tragedy drama mask. On the one hand, Renee became the icon of motherhood, bestowing upon her girls the one thing they had missed out on in their short years with her — constancy.

The tragic side of the mask bore the imminency of separation. This time, permanent separation. How Liza had clung to those days. Charlcy, true to character, held herself more aloof, though Liza knew it was a survival thing with her sister. Plus, Charlcy had married during her mother's long illness, providing more acceptable, guiltless distancing.

Liza suspected that Charlcy's desperate sequestered deportment was to vaccinate herself against the demons of her mother's illness, ones that could reappear at any given moment.

Hers was a position earned by her hellish odyssey from such a young age. "Battle scarred" was Charlcy's bantering label.

Liza's father, an Alzheimer's patient in an assisted living home, was not accessible. Even Charlcy, her joined-at-the-hip sister, was halfway around the world right now. How she missed Charlcy's snug presence at that moment.

Yeh, along with Garrison's distancing, Liza felt the aloneness closing in on her.

"I guess I just plain need family," Liza said, barely controlling her voice and emotions as she looked at Garrison. When their gazes collided, his slid away. Her heart dropped even lower. He wasn't buying in to her need.

His distancing stung even more right now. Once he would have sailed like a scud missile to her. Long ago. He'd never have held her at arm's length when Liza keened to fall into his comforting embrace while their daughter lay at death's door.

Thanks, Garrison. She would get the hang of going it alone, even if it killed her.

&

"When will Charlcy be back?" Garrison asked Liza the next evening after they'd gotten home from the hospital. Their dinner had been a hamburger and fries again, half of it dumped down the garbage disposal.

"Charlcy's month long European cruise has three more weeks to go before her ship comes in. She knows about Angel, but I told her under no circumstance is she to shorten her trip and fly back. There's nothing she can do. I can keep her informed by e-mail and on rare occasions by phone. She carried her laptop." She was aware of her nervous prattling and reined herself in.

He shrugged and moved to the den. Liza felt hurt at his lack of real dialogue. Lately he'd grown more and more taciturn. She could no longer read him. Nor his body language. She followed him into the den, where he flipped on Fox News. She curled up in her chair while he slid onto the long sofa. Did his little shrug mean he censured her not summoning Charlcy home or that he simply did not want to talk?

She decided to elaborate. "Charlcy's saved for this vacation for a long time and it's not fair to her to cut it short. Teaching isn't the most lucrative profession."

Garrison's eyes remained glued to the screen, where Bill O'Reilly declared the "Patriot and Pinhead of the day." "My mother was a teacher." His voice was empty. Flat.

In other words, *shut the heck up.* Hurt swirled and tossed about inside her, bouncing like boulders against her vitals. Her already wounded and raw emotions flamed high, like an out of control wildfire. Desperation clawed at her nerve endings.

He wants Charlcy here so he won't have to endure my presence as much.

Suddenly, Garrison arose and asked Liza politely, "Can I bring you anything from the kitchen? I'm going for some ice cream."

"No, thank you," she replied, perplexed, jerked around. Just when she thought there was no hope left for them, he turned on his blasted manners.

Liza credited Ruth for that. His mother's long classroom experience enabled her to teach Garrison the finer points of behavior. She had done a great job there.

Except for teaching him about *being there.* And forgiveness.

Liza shoved away that line of thought. She would survive. With or without him.

Chapter Five

Angel floated in nothingness...bits and snatches of sounds wafted in and out...voices...Mama...Daddy...others not familiar...words reverberated in a strange way, echoing, running together, seamless, Loveloveloveyoucheckbloodpressure...Penny's voice...she's crying...why?...Laurie and Ginger, "She'ssosopalepaleale...lookslookslooksbadbad...cheerleading squad...Chuck and Buddy, "wha's'supupup, Angelgelgel?"

I've gotta get outta here! Can't move!

"Byebyebye, Angelgelgel. Seeseeyouyoulaterter."

Wait! I'm going, too! Don't leave me!

Floating...floating...*why can't I move, dang it?* ...tightness like a coil, intruding on the blasted nothingness... coil pulls pulls pulls....

Snap!

Blackness.

The ten a.m. visit to Angel's bedside ended. The Wakefields returned to the waiting area with Penny and five other Byrnes cheerleading teammates of Angel's trailing in their wake. All seven of them had managed to rotate in twos and threes, the visit quota max, and spend a few moments with Angel.

Garrison's parents had left for the airport after the morning visiting slot and Liza already sorely missed their consoling presence. Liza liked them despite their lapses in Garrison's young years. They did try to be good parents; they just didn't have all of the parenting skill ingredients together in the right measure and order. She had to admit that their presence had assuaged some of her desperate neediness, a primal, clawing thing now.

The timing of their departure sucked.

"The staff was quite understanding," Garrison muttered to Liza on the walk back down the wide white corridor. "They absorbed all the moving about quite well."

Liza nodded. "They did."

The tension she felt with Garrison had let up somewhat during the visit to the ICU. But then, that was only natural since their minds and emotions centered on their daughter. Whatever, she appreciated the daily respite.

How Liza missed bygone days when her and Garrison's hearts were so finely tuned together that they could finish each others' sentences and divine each others' thoughts. Even their silence, in those days, meant peace. Fulfillment.

Four of the teens departed with promises to come back another day. Penny remained with Liza and Garrison as they found chairs in the waiting area. Garrison, seated several feet away, spread open the *Spartanburg Herald* newspaper and buried himself in it.

Penny smiled past the sadness etched into her young features. "I'll bet it's hard not having Angel's grandfather here with you now. I'd miss my daddy, too, if I were you."

Liza felt a pang of longing all the way to her toes. She nodded and sighed. "Placing Dad in a nursing facility was tough. But it was also a blessing. We don't have to worry about him anymore. He's safe." Liza ached that, just when her father could enjoy life without the agitation of managing a hellion bipolar wife, he had lapsed into early onset Alzheimer's. Not fair.

But then, whoever said that life was fair?

"Yeah. I guess your sister feels the same way, huh?"

"Yes. She does. We rotate visiting days with him. With Charlcy gone, it's not possible. Some days his mind's clear as a spring. Others, he doesn't know anybody. I just hope he's not aware of our absence." She shrugged and smiled sadly. "Charlcy doesn't think it's a problem."

Penny grinned, her turned up, freckled nose tilting even more. "Charlcy's cool."

Liza chuckled. "Yup. She is that. My big sister has the family corner on wit and cool. Well, almost. Angel's no slouch there."

Penny giggled. "Got that right. And neither are you, Mrs. W."

Liza raised her eyebrows and crossed her eyes. "Ya think?"

Full belly laughter erupted from Penny, reminding Liza so much of Angel's exuberant laughter that it took her breath.

In that moment, everything in Liza longed to wake from this nightmare and engage Angel in droll, silly nonsense over the crazy dream and laugh until they rolled on the dance studio floor, until tears filled their eyes then trailed down their cheeks.

Dr. Abrams' appearance in the ICU waiting room was, as always, with strobe-light haste. He got right to the point. "Your daughter has just had a seizure. I just happened to be there when it happened."

"Oh, God, *no*," Liza moaned, her eyes misting. Penny's hands shot up to her mouth, eyes round as donuts above them.

Garrison's paper rustled as he tossed it aside, shot to his feet, and strode across the floor, his features tense and pale. "What does this mean?"

"It means her brain is swelling. I'm sorry. For the moment, we're using Dilantin to control the intracranial pressure. It's a very strong drug and hopefully it will do the trick. We'll monitor her constantly to see how this works. In the meantime, keep doing what you're doing; take it a minute at a time."

In the next instant, he was gone.

Liza looked at Garrison, who stood gazing at the empty doorway, frozen as a video pause, as if a three-hundred-pound linebacker had slammed into him and he needed only to topple. Feeling as though she were in a slow free fall to hell, Liza glimpsed Penny's pasty face just as the girl burst into tears.

"Oh, Mrs. W," she sobbed, "what's gonna happen?"

Liza, numb as a Novocained tooth, gathered Penny in her arms. "Shh. It's gonna be okay. We have to believe that."

Garrison turned, a gaunt zombie as he faced her. "Yes," he murmured in a voice as desolate as she felt. "We must believe that."

Garrison awoke early, glad there had not been a call from the hospital during the night. *No news is good news.* He showered and dressed in a navy blue Armani suit and paisley tie for the difficult day ahead. Liza now finished her own grooming upstairs.

He picked up a mail package on the foyer table and turned it over. He hadn't checked through the mail since the accident. The package was addressed to Angel. From Troy. Surrealism descended in a horrific avalanche.

Will she live to open it? Doubt nearly suffocated him. He clawed against it and shoved the package angrily onto the foyer closet shelf next to his briefcase. Troy's memorial service lay before them on this lovely warm day. Wouldn't you know the blasted sun would be shining? Yet he knew rain would be worse, with clouds and mist darkening an already unbearable situation.

Neither he nor Liza wanted to leave their daughter's bedside, but for the moment, her condition remained unchanged. Penny had arranged to stay at the hospital and vowed to call Garrison's cell phone immediately in the event that anything happened.

We owe Troy's parents. Garrison couldn't get past that fact. June and Rocky Bailey were good, hard working people who'd lost their only son.

Troy's dead. Young, vital Troy. How can it be?

Angel, please don't die.

That possibility hit him like a sonic blast, right in the heart. He closed his eyes and collapsed against the foyer door, face burrowed in hands. *God, Liza. Why did you let them go? I did all I could to protect Angel. And it wasn't enough!* The pain inside him roiled and swelled to bursting. *Daddies are supposed to take care of their children. I tried, Angel. I tried in my own way to protect you. Maybe not always like you thought I should. But I always had your best interests at heart. With everything in me, I wish I could have prevented you from going that night. Troy would be alive. You would be moving around. Well. Whole.*

In that moment, a vision of a small toddler boy zoomed in. "My name Twoy." Little Troy, grinning from ear to ear, shaking Garrison's hand on that long-ago day when Rocky Bailey had hired Garrison at the dairy farm, bailing him out of a penury existence.

Troy. Dead.

Troy was being laid in the ground today because Liza had overruled his judgment. And Angel lay at death's door. Why? Anger blazed through him like a wild inferno and he threw his head back and clenched his teeth to stem a roar like a thousand cannons.

"Aargh!" He burst into sobs, and that's how Liza found him, slithered to the floor, head between knees, in the grips of unholy, masculine weeping.

Liza dropped to her knees beside him, and he felt her reach to console him. Instinctively, his arms flew up to ward off her touch. When she persisted and attempted to embrace him, he curled himself away from her. The movement was primal, the survival kind.

"Oh, darling," she sobbed, rocking back on her heels. "I don't know what to do. I've caused all this suffering. I'm...so... sorry."

Then she cast her arms outward and raised her face to the ceiling, tears coursing down her face. "What have I done? Please, God. Forgive me."

Garrison heard her heartrending cry, knew she needed his forgiveness, his comfort. He tried to open his mouth and say it, but he could not. God help him. He could not. That place inside him, where mercy dwells, was as empty as an ancient, deserted cave. He had nothing left to give.

While birds sang outside their window, the two of them pulled themselves to their feet, and together, yet far, far apart, they did the right thing. They honored Troy's memory.

After the memorial service Garrison drove them straight to the hospital. They'd exchanged a few comments along the way, though to Liza, it was like gouging out molars to engage Garrison in conversation. She still gave it her best attempt.

The only exception was when he pulled his cell phone from his suit coat pocket. "I forgot to turn it off vibrate. Looks like I missed a call from the office." He snapped it shut and put it back in his pocket. "I'll call Gwen from the hospital. Traffic's heavy."

Encouraged by that small concession, Liza said, " Troy's mother asked about Angel. Know what she said?" Not even expecting a response, she went on. "She said, 'he loved her, you know.'" The divulgence had touched Liza's soul. "I know how hollow she and Rocky feel inside, but they are so brave." Liza had merely wept with the grieving mother, whose pain matched – no, surpassed her own. June had no hope.

Liza still clung to it.

Garrison was silent for long moments as their black Jag swung into the ICU parking lot. He cut the motor and looked at Liza and her heart leaped from her belly's cold floor to her throat. Lightness flooded her, hope fluttered.

Then he said quietly, "It hasn't hit them yet." He got out of the car, slamming the door behind him, echoing her heart's thud. Liza felt the weak, warm stinging of tears in her nose and throat but with great effort pushed them back.

He came around and opened her door, a courtesy from which his Southern gentleman upbringing wouldn't release him. Even now, when Liza knew it was the last thing he would choose to do, he practiced civility. Walking through the hot, humid, ninety-three degree July day and through the entrance doors, she noted that he dodged even the tiniest brush with her.

She sighed and murmured, "At least they don't have any regrets."

"What?" Garrison asked with a ring of annoyance, walking briskly, forcing her to hasten her pace.

She shrugged. "Troy's folks. At least they won't wrestle with regrets."

He gave a tiny huff of exasperation. "Regrets? They buried their son today. Yeah. I'd say they regret having to do that." His sarcasm cut her deeply, as did his implications.

Regrets. She carried enough of them for Troy's parents, Garrison, and the whole danged world. Humor had always gotten her past dark times. Had enabled her to wheedle and tease Garrison out of his sporadic artistic melancholy, occasions that culminated with them rolling on the carpet, laughing like doofuses.

Garrison had once told her, "I love your sense of humor. It's one of the things that drew me to you from the first. There's something so *pure* in it. So spontaneous. I love that, like you, it's so real and uncontrollable, even in the most serious of times."

This time was different. A hovering Death specter obliterated humor, disarming her of the one weapon to which Garrison might respond.

Inside the ICU waiting area chatting with Penny was Garrison's redheaded assistant, Gwen. She embraced them both, murmuring, "I'm so sorry about all this. Is there anything I can do? That is," she apologetically pulled an envelope from under her arm, "besides getting your signature on these forms?"

Penny said, "I'm going to get a snack in the cafeteria. Want me to bring you something?"

Liza smiled tiredly. "No, but thanks. I'm good." Her rumbling stomach reminded her that she and Garrison had not eaten since early that morning. With the midday funeral, emotions had run high, driving back appetites. Vaguely, she watched Penny, dear Penny, leave.

Garrison's smile was warm and welcoming as he sat beside Gwen on the sofa and, heads bent together, they went over pertinent data. He signed each of the documents.

"Thanks, Gwen," he said softly, gratitude and apology vibrating from his deep voice. "I'm afraid I'm not much good at handling business right now."

She shook her head. "No problem. I'm at your beck and call 24/7."

Then she smiled encouragingly at Liza, who'd taken a chair across from them. Gwen apologized for intruding and Garrison apologized for his phone's inaccessibility. Liza noted his open-ness and camaraderie with his assistant, and everything in her heart and soul keened for even a morsel of it. Aloneness at-tacked her anew.

Shut out. I'm shut out. The awfulness of the thought hung there, palpable and terrible. *I…am…shut…out.*

Penny returned, carrying a bag and drink tray. She placed the drinks and sandwiches, Wakefield favorites, beside their re-spective tables.

"Thank you," Liza said, her eyes moist. In that moment, Penny's *being there* elicited a primeval, surging gratefulness, one that brings one to one's knees. "Here." She reached for her purse.

"No," Penny insisted. "Please, Mrs. W., let me do this. I've saved most of my allowance lately. No big deal."

"But Penny − ."Garrison, too, reached for his wallet.

"No," Penny persisted desperately. She shook her head. "Please, I want to do this. There's so little I can do." Her voice broke. "Don't you see? I can do this."

"Excuse me," Garrison murmured to Gwen and moved to sit on the other side of Penny, his gaze tangling with Liza's in a moment of affinity. "Of course you can do this, Penny. We appreciate it from the bottom of our hearts, don't we, Liza?"

"You bet," Liza agreed.

Garrison spoke gently. "It's just − look, can't I repay you at least?"

"No." Penny looked at him and her tear-brimmed green eyes seemed bottomless. Liza's heart nearly broke when she saw Garrison's moisten, too. "Please," Penny whispered as a tear rolled down her cheek and her trembling hand swiped it away. "I want to do this. You see," two more huge tears spilled over, "it's like I'm doing it for Angel."

Garrison gave a big, watery smile. "I get it." He reached out to hug the thin shoulders and rasped, "Thanks, Penny."

"You're so thoughtful," Liza added, blinking back tears. "Thank you."

Liza peeled the wrapper from the sandwich and took a couple of obligatory bites. She watched Garrison walk Gwen down the corridor. At the elevator, they talked intensely for long moments and then Gwen stretched up and hugged Garrison. The gesture was warm and Garrison's arms returned the embrace.

Liza rewrapped the remainder of the sandwich, appetite gone. A tiny alarm shrilled inside her and a memory corked to the surface. She'd recently dropped by unannounced at the Wakefield Creations office, needing Garrison's consultation on a benefit seating arrangement. Upon entering, she'd seen Garrison at Gwen's desk, leaned over her shoulder in a conspiratorial way that seemed, in Liza's wifely estimation, a bit too cozy. But working on graphic designs brought them into close contact, didn't it?

So why did she feel so threatened now?

Because today was different. She felt vulnerable. Alone.

It wasn't the chaste embrace; it was the spontaneity that tore at Liza's heart. Why did Garrison behave so affectionately with Gwen when he refused even to tolerate Liza's touch? To hardly ever even look into her eyes?

But she knew the answer.

Anger. She headed for the ICU to be with her daughter. *Garrison blames me.*

In the unit, Garrison joined her. "I don't believe her face is as swollen," he said hopefully.

Liza watched him lean to kiss the ashen cheek. "I think you're right."

He straightened quickly, peering intently at the inert form. "Did she flinch?"

"No, she didn't. The doctor said that the Dilantin puts her even deeper into the coma. She won't be moving at all, much as we want her to. This protects her brain from further injury. Gives it time to heal."

He gazed into space, that glimmer of something building in the dark depths of his eyes. He looked at her and she saw that it was despair.

"She's going to come back," she said with compassion, and saw the darkness in his eyes shift. Lift. Then she leaned and softly murmured in Angel's ear, "You're brave and strong. Hang in there. You can do this."

They knew, quivering on the perimeter, the Grim Reaper hovered.

By silent consent, they agreed upon one thing: they would pay it no heed.

chapter six

Voices…Mama… "You're brave and strong. You can do this."

What, Mama? What can I do? Not ballet, please…. *Nonono.*

Troy sat beside her on the golden pine needle carpet floor… the hue of him seemed to blend with the gold as he murmured, "It's okay, Angel." His arm slid around her and it felt so good. She felt so safe. "You don't have to do anything you don't want to. Not now."

She looked into his dark eyes, so gentle in their regard of her, so…concerned. He could read her thoughts and she could read his. "How do you do that?" she asked without saying it aloud. "How do you know what I'm thinking?"

He smiled and joy, like a tidal wave, washed up in her throat. Love flowed into her, a love so powerful she thought it would consume her. Yet it was not like anything she'd ever felt before. It was pure and peaceful and gripping all at once.

"It's this place." The thought flowed to her in his velvety voice. "Here you simply are. There's nothing to prove, Angel. You simply be yourself…at peace."

In the distance, Mama and Daddy sat on a rustic, sun-bleached, silver-gray wooden bench beneath the pines, talking quietly. They watched her as they chatted. She couldn't hear much of what they said, only caught snippets of conversation, but somehow she knew it involved her. "Drug helps sometimes …Penny said the team… Dr Abrams says she…."

Angel couldn't wrap her mind around any of it. Right now, whenever now was, she would simply *be*. With Troy. She smiled at him, snuggling closer.

His eyes gave off a golden aura as they plundered hers. "Angel…be yourself." The thought slid into her heart like heated honey.

Then the atmosphere began to shift from beneath her.

Fog moved in…gloom spread…darker…the warmth of him abruptly left her and she shivered. *Nonono*. Icy fingers clutched her as peace shattered in a million directions…Angel tumbled headlong into darkness.

❧

Silence separated them. Liza grew to detest its noiseless silken hum.

Through the day, while Penny was there at the hospital with Liza, it wasn't as bad. At least Penny's chatter kept the insufferable silence at bay. And the loneliness. Because even with Garrison nearby, he wasn't truly there.

She missed Charlcy. Needed her. *Suck it up, Liza. Get tough.* That's what Charlcy would tell her. It seemed that this was Liza's calling now; to get over it. Never in her life had she felt less adept to do so.

Later that evening, as she and Garrison sat at the kitchen bar picking halfheartedly at Bojangles Fried Chicken, the damnable quiet got to Liza.

"Who the heck said that silence is golden had rocks for brains." She viciously speared a French fry and slammed it into her mouth. She glared at her husband as she chewed vigorously, challenging him to differ. Oh, how she spoiled for a fight. All the pain and frustration of recent days boiled over.

Garrison narrowed his dark gaze on her, no doubt surprised at her uncharacteristic combative stance. "What?"

Liza felt a spurt of pleasure that she held his undivided attention. At last. "Silence. It stinks. And tastes like crap. You've been force-feeding me for days now and I've had it up to here." She slashed a finger across her throat. Then, ceremoniously, she lifted her Coke glass to him and took a dainty sip.

His face remained closed and she wondered if what she said even registered. *I may as well dump the whole load. What the heck?*

She leaned forward, elbows on table. "Get this, *dude*…I actually miss the hospital equipment's *bleeping* and *whishing* cause even that's less lethal than this. Now I know how Angel felt, trying to get you to talk to her. And all those times you pushed her away."

His eyes flickered, then sparked. "That's hitting below the belt, don't you think?"

"Ha! So now it's inappropriate to cast stones, huh? How does it feel, the shoe being on the other foot?"

"Like you're fighting dirty. It's just not you, Liza." His voice vibrated with offense as he rearranged his frame in the chair with one tense shift.

"No," she agreed, suddenly incensed. "It's not. But then, this angry, judgmental character who's treating me like a criminal just isn't you, either, Garrison."

Suddenly his fist slammed the countertop, causing her to jump. "Liza! I can't help what I feel. Can't you get that through your head?" His dark gaze glittered with indignation. She gaped at him. *The audacity, after all he's put me through.* Liza felt a sudden, irresistible desire to strike him. Her hands curled into fists and for long moments she glared at him and fought against the same violence she'd witnessed at the hands of her mother in those early years – slaps that struck like a rattlesnake when she'd moved too slowly – reliving her screams as she watched Charlcy step in and ward off blows and endure profane indictments when her dad wasn't instantly there to protect them.

No. I cannot do this.

Liza knew in that moment that she must banish her mother's ghost – the evil one. She also knew that, face to face with her current tormentor, she could not so easily dismiss the cruel treatment of recent days.

"It's hell." She narrowed her gaze on him. "That's what your silent treatment is to me just now. Hell! In case you haven't noticed, I have a daughter lying at death's door, too."

She cupped her hands at her mouth. "Helloooo?"

"I know that!" he snapped, clearly agitated.

"Oh? Sure could've fooled me." Her voice broke and she swallowed and took a moment to regain her composure. "You're not the only one suffering, my noble Mr. Perfect Who-Never-Makes-Mistakes."

Head high, she arose to full height and looked steadily into his black, black eyes. "I shall conclude my thesis on the evils of silence." A sad little smile appeared, then vanished as abruptly as it came. "I find your silence abominable because, in it, you are unconscionably cruel and unmerciful. And in it, I'm exiled to a place that's frightening." A tear slid down her pale cheek and she angrily swiped it away. "It's frightening because you're not here." She patted her bosom and whispered, "With me." She struggled again to compose herself.

"Yeah," her lips twisted in self-derision, "I'm imperfect. So shoot me. What was it Jane Fonda said in that movie? Oh yeah…they shoot horses! They put 'em out of their misery. And hey! I'm miserable. You couldn't have made your rejection of me more flagrant had you jumped up and down atop the hospital roof and bellowed it to the world."

Garrison watched her, his eyes once more hooded, his features revealing nothing. "See? There you go back behind that blasted mask." She gave a sudden snort, half sob, half laugh, waving a hand at him. "But what did I expect? My husband is gone. Ever since the accident." She paused and then slowly shook her head. Her voice dropped to a sad husk. "No, longer than that. The man I married left years ago."

Garrison's eyes flickered with some unnamed emotion. "There are reasons."

She gave another harsh laugh. "I suppose I'm to blame for those, too, huh?"

His shoulders lifted in a noncommittal shrug.

That smarted. Liza's brows lifted as though in comical revelation. "Guess what? You're off the hook, Garrison! I will leave you the…heck…alone."

With that, head majestically high, she glided from the room, as graceful as her wobbly ballerina legs would carry her. When she extended a one-fingered obscene gesture over her retreating shoulder, she heard something suspiciously akin to a muffled curse.

Garrison soon discovered that Liza meant what she said. He also discovered that her words, spoken in anger, stung. In all their twenty years' relationship, they'd never engaged in such a heated, hateful exchange. Oh they'd had their spats but they would end with Liza humoring him out of his angst and into making up. Mild skirmishes. Nothing like this one. It was the closest they'd come to a legitimate fight. He'd always valued that rarity and he knew Liza felt the same.

It all seemed to be crumbling around him in bits and chunks…chipping away at something in their marriage that was once invincible. His self-control, near the bottom of his arsenal, was drowning as circumstances gushed in like icy waters into the doomed *Titanic*.

Decorum had gotten him through his early difficult years, when he'd felt emotionally abandoned. Even though his parents had shipped him off to his grandparents at the slightest holiday-travel enticement, they'd done so with impeccable, affectionate politesse. His and Liza's departure from civility left Garrison feeling gutted.

Gutted, mainly because of how true her words were. God help him. He regretted ever having pushed his daughter away. After all, he knew from experience how it felt to be nudged aside by his own parents, to be told, "What a big, brave boy you are." This when he cried on the occasions of being dropped off with his grandparents during their frequent school-break world treks.

"You are so grown-up and responsible."

They'd recited the words in that overly exuberant way of folks forcing their sentiments down your throat. They'd totally ignored his stricken-eyed response, and the puffed-up, feigned pride they'd gushed all over him had spawned in him tiny spurts of sympathy for their desperation. He'd forced himself to buck up for their benefit.

Training from his mother's militant insistence upon correctness.

Training or no training, it had still stung. He had not always felt grown-up. Or responsible, whatever that meant. Heck, he didn't have a clue in those young days.

He just knew that he felt tossed aside. Why had he forgotten that in his dealings with Angel? In his childhood innocence, he'd allowed his parents to turn him into what they wanted him

to be then. Just as he'd evolved into what they were later on –
distant and aloof. What was it the Bible said about the sins of
the fathers being passed down for generations?

He crawled into bed that night burdened with the culpability of having hurt his precious Angel. Why hadn't he seen that
she needed a firm but *gentle* hand?

God, if you'll just bring her back, I'll make it up to her.

The next Saturday morning, heat slapped him in the face
when he stepped outside the house for the newspaper. The gar-
den thermometer read ninety-three degrees at 8:35 a.m.

Things at the office, for once, did not scream for attention
so he would be able to spend more time with Angel at the hospital. He showered and dressed in cool khaki cargo shorts and a
blue, three-button Polo shirt. He needed his tan Dockside loafers. He couldn't remember the last time he'd worn them. Not
this season. Last summer? He scrounged around in his closet
and came up empty-handed.

"Liza," he called, impatience snapping at him. Oh, how he
resented having to ask her for anything. "Where are my Dockside loafers?" Silence. *Blast her hide!* He knew she was in the
dressing room, only feet away. He'd put up with her distancing for days now and it didn't sit well. Irritation sizzled as he
remembered the things she'd thrown in his face the other night
during their fight.

The terrible thing was that they were mostly true. But she
could at least be polite.

"Liza, where did you put them?" Garrison bellowed. When
no answer was forthcoming, he arose quickly and poked his
face through the door of Liza's adjoining dressing room, where
she calmly smoothed on light makeup and dusted powder.

"Didn't you hear me calling you?" he asked, scowling. She applied a soft pink lipstick and pressed her lips together before replying.

"Oh. Were you calling me?" She blotted and then daintily brushed pink blush onto her cheeks.

"You know I was. Where are my Docksides? I can't find them."

"On your closet shelf. In a box."

He glared at her. "Why didn't you tell me that before now?" She ignored him.

He shook his head in exasperation and returned to the closet where he found the shoes exactly where she'd indicated. He plopped down on the bed with a thud and slid his feet into them. His anger sizzled for long moments. Then slowly, in its place oozed sadness.

From the big mirror, his wretchedness reflected. Where had all the joy gone?

Will the two of us ever be able to regain what we've lost?

Thoughts of Angel. Her condition shocked him anew. How close his little girl perched on eternity's threshold. Resentment washed over him. Liza had even deprived him of that. His child. He tried – oh how he tried in that moment – to delete the thought and the emotions that rode its tail. He could not. God help him. He could not.

Liza proceeded to style her pixyish blond hair with a little help from a curling iron. Not that she needed it. In the near hundred-degree humidity today, the natural curl would regenerate on its own. The process merely kept her occupied and away from Garrison.

She heard Garrison's commotion and felt his annoyance as he pulled the shoes in question from his closet shelf, and she heard the bedsprings creak as he sat to slide his feet into them.

Even with walls separating them, his agitation pounced at her, snarling and snapping, but she didn't bat a long, mascaraed eyelash. Nor did she look at him when he returned to snatch up his own nearby hairbrush and flick it through his thick, softly waved mahogany hair, which like her own would disarray itself in time.

No, she didn't dare look or he might see the hunger in her eyes. Oh yeah. It was there. With anger's adrenaline rush came sexual awareness, an earthy thing with a life all its own. Liza swore that, in their chemistry concoction, anger and desire were first cousins. Garrison's maleness radiated, spontaneous and bold, awakening the beast she'd sent into hibernation.

It was especially difficult when she looked at him. He was classically handsome, with brooding, elegant features and body. The guy couldn't help it. She sighed deeply, tamping down passion. He was something else. Even in his icy remoteness, his features were all exotically carved planes and angles of masculinity. Fighting with him was especially threatening because he was magnificent at making up.

The brain was traitorous in its vivid sensual recall.

Beastly dependable.

Eyes carefully averted, she heard him spin on his heel and stalk away, muttering under his breath. From the vanity mirror, her eyes stared back at her, inordinately sad, bereft of things vital – things once sacred and unquestioned.

She walked into the bedroom, knowing Garrison's favorite fragrance, Givenchy's Ysatis, swirled lightly about her, and she saw his head lift like a jungle beast sniffing a kill. It was the only choice light enough to wear around a respiratory-challenged Angel.

She inadvertently glimpsed his face and the predatory glint in his eye. She quickly looked away, but not before awareness slammed her like a Mack truck.

God, he's gorgeous. His anger gave him a look of danger that, perversely, whipped her senses into a dither. She didn't dare gaze into those eyes, whose shade fluctuated from onyx to mahogany in a heartbeat, depending upon his mood. Once she did, she was lost.

It would be difficult, but she would numb out to him. True, a lot of their earlier passion had waned. Sadly. It happened in a lot of marriages, didn't it? Time alone could erode romance's sharp edge. But it didn't kill the spark. And after all these years of their being one in body, soul and spirit, she wouldn't bring about apathy overnight. It would take time.

She walked briskly ahead of him to the Jaguar, where he politely opened the door for her to slide in.

She ordered her heart to cease its pounding. Then she concentrated on distancing herself. For self-preservation. Yes, it would take time. But she'd gone this thing solo from the night of the accident, and knew she could go on with or without Garrison's reassurance or comfort, relying on her own self-parenting and survival skills.

With the help of the good Lord, she would stop caring.

chapter seven

Sunlight and shadow dappled Garrison as he strode down the wooded slope into the forest oasis. His black Reebok walking shoes crunched over golden pine-needle carpet as solar rays warmed him and drove back the chill of sadness and despair that dogged each step he took.

He'd left Liza at the hospital, telling her that he needed to go to the office for a spell. Actually, he'd felt overwhelmed to the point of suffocation and needed some time alone. Needed to chill – level out, to become one with creation again. So he'd found himself driving here. Perhaps being here, in his and Liza's corner of paradise, would somehow offset the stress of recent days and jar loose some positive, embedded recalls from his *remember when* canvas. He desperately needed something good to hang on to.

He lowered himself into the rustic wooden swing and began to push himself in a slow, lulling cadence. He inhaled nature's scents, a lush blend of sun-warmed pine trees, foliage, and water. With each backward motion, he closed his eyes and turned loose of *now*. During forward thrusts, he opened his psyche to *then*.

His head lolled back lazily, stirring memories that burst free and surfaced. Two in particular leaped at him.

The first was the day his parents visited the newlyweds in their little rented bungalow and handed them a clear title-deed to half the Wakefields' expansive rural properties. "We want you and Liza to have this. An added wedding gift." His father cleared his throat, blinked moist eyes, and added, "We thought about it and decided it was the right thing to do. If you wish, you may sell off some plots to help finance building a house." Garrison later did this.

"We're retiring to Florida," his mother gushed, overcome with emotion, realizing her lifelong dream of getting away from it all. The words had caused familiar hurt to well up, then churn, until Garrison reminded himself that, heck, he'd lived it all his life, that *pushed away* thing, interrupted by intermittent spells such as that day's memory. If only he'd had a sibling – as Liza had had in Charlcy – to buffer the lonely shipwreck of his life. But that would have been doubly distressing for his parents, since Garrison himself had not been planned. So Garrison had – like the brave, strong young man that he was – developed the fine art of self-parenting and meeting his own needs.

That settled, he had willed the inner hardness to snap back into place.

The armadillo shell that protected him was more and more his friend and sanctuary.

He now recalled that, after his father's presentation on that long ago day, exultation over the land gift had swept through him, transporting him from despair to a sunburst horizon. After all those years of jerked-around psyche, he'd become quite agile at springing back.

"We sold the other half to the Bailey family," his father explained. "Good folks."

"They plan to use it for a dairy farm," his mother injected, still visibly buoyed by the turn of events. Garrison, even
now, felt happiness for her, for his parents and their untethered
lifestyle.

Today, sitting in the swing overlooking the lily pond, he almost laughed at that term. He rolled his eyes – his parents'
untethered lifestyle was not, after all, a startling new entity. At
least not where Garrison fit into the equation. To their credit,
they'd given him a relatively good upbringing and education.
They certainly weren't abusive. They just weren't always *there*.

But in recent years they'd mellowed and seemed to reach
out to him more, to realize his significance in their earthly
jaunt. People could, after all, change. He'd decided to be more
forgiving and understanding, hadn't he? Liza had helped him
on that score. Her mercy was free and generous and, at times, it
splashed over and into him. She swore Garrison's parents loved
him. Measured against her own early hellish parental experience, he agreed with her that bottom line, his folks weren't so
bad.

Liza's constant reinforcement had been a soothing, validat-
ing balm. Sure, being the excluded one still stung at times. But
its ferocity had ebbed with time. It passed over him, sometimes
quickly, sometimes more slowly, like water over a shifting oil-
cloth. At times it puddled and loitered, but eventually Garrison
leveled his attitude and it drained away until the next tumult.

He stirred restlessly in the weathered wooden swing, hung
by chains from a bold oak limb. He pushed away encroaching
dark thoughts and beckoned the memory of that first walk.

That walk. Aah. The building site had been perfect for
their dream home, as was the lay of the land for Garrison's vision. But it was when he spanned the open field and entered the
forest that first time that his heart nearly leaped from his chest.

The little pond lay in the bowl of the great forest, beneath a late afternoon sun that filtered through tall pines, oaks, maples, and poplars. In that heartbeat, Garrison's artist mind saw it as it would be – expanded and covered with crimson and white lilies riding vibrant green pads. He saw that removing some of the trees canopied over the water would open up the sky. Sunlight would spill over the entire scene. Sun and water would become one in a glorious explosion of golden light, with the colorful bouquet dancing over its sparkling surface.

Garrison had drawn up the plans for The Oasis, as he and Liza eventually named it. Later, during the early stages of house groundbreaking, he'd arranged with his contractors to secretly clear out strategic forest trees and leave others until it was just right.

A covered shed was structured, one part for storage and the pavilion end open and available for dining or simply snoozing in the shade. A practical shelter, too, from sudden southern showers. Other picnic tables ambled over the golden forest floor, relaxed and welcoming.

The pond was enlarged and hardy water lilies added. The choice was low maintenance, one that thrived in the southern climate that segued from near tropical summer temperatures to mild winters that occasionally crisped to brief ice.

He opened his eyes today and saw it in its full beauty. Yet – his heart still sagged with heaviness, for what had been in those days and for what no longer was. He'd painstakingly hidden The Oasis from Liza all those months, wanting her discovery of it to be unforgettable. He'd wanted to blow her away with surprise and delight.

And he had. He squeezed his eyes shut, reliving the moment – the day of the picnic – when he'd allowed her to remove the blindfold after leading her down the forest slope.

"Open your eyes," he'd whispered, and when she did, those extraordinary blue eyes had rounded like a child's on Christmas morning discovering Santa's treasures or seeing a fireworks display for the very first time.

"Oh...my...God." The words conveyed and vibrated her sentiments all in one exhaled gush. Shock. Joy. Jubilation. Everything in her tone trickled along his soul's strings and he was certain he'd never experienced a more fulfilling moment in his entire life. She'd hugged him fiercely, speechless with bliss, clinging like a June bug for endless rapturous moments before spinning away and dancing like a pixie all over The Oasis until, breathless, she'd plopped into the swing.

Then she'd watched him sprint back to the car to gather the basket and picnic paraphernalia they'd prepared earlier for what she'd thought would be a trip to Paris Mountain State Park.

Garrison would never forget the picnic – the lovely meal Liza had spread for them the day after they moved into their new house. Nearly five months pregnant, she remained lithe and light on her feet and breathtakingly beautiful after having weathered the first trimester's siege of morning sickness.

Flapping open and covering the rustic table with a white tablecloth, and laying her best china and silver, Liza moved with a new sultry grace. Garrison drank in the sight of her, so serene and secure in her womanhood, breasts becomingly full, belly swelling with their child. *Theirs.* And his heart inflated till it nearly split his chest. He felt like a rooster crowing at the crack of dawn and not one whit ashamed of it.

That spring day, as they feasted on delicious southern fried chicken and Liza's sublime cold, zesty dill-potato salad, Liza's moist, bright gaze kept ambling back to the vibrant lily blossoms. At times, she wiped tears from her flushed rosy cheeks and shot him wide, wide smiles that plucked at his heartstrings.

He knew that, in a small way, this elaborate gift made up for his insistence upon penny pinching during those struggling days, ones that forced Liza to plunder consignment clothing shops and become a grocery coupon guru. Not that he was yet an exemplary provider, but he hoped that, soon, that would change.

Today, reality intruded and he opened his eyes.

He squelched thoughts of Angel's mounting hospital costs.

Angel's life did not have a price tag. He would live in a barn and subsist on bread and water if that would bring her back safely.

He blinked back the disheartening intrusion, frantically re-conjuring and clinging tenaciously to memories of the picnic. He needed the surge of sustenance it gave him. It had been one of the highlight of his life. One so embedded in his memory that it would never fade. For long moments he engaged the euphoria of it, marinating in it until he felt a certain leveling out.

Garrison sighed deeply and reluctantly allowed the memory to ebb.

He gazed up into the tall pines and saw a squirrel soaring in glorious flight from one limb to another. He smiled. Spotting Garrison, the tiny creature froze in attack mode and let loose a screeching clatter of protest. Garrison's smile grew.

Seeing Garrison's lack of rejoinder, the squirrel thrust into spread-winged flight to other regions of forest refuge. Garrison sighed, relishing the moment.

In the next breath, intruding on the golden moment, came a replay of the last picnic here together. Teenage Angel's visit that day with Troy's family had given Garrison and Liza solitude, a rare gift. A perfect setup for romance, right?

Garrison huffed at that line of thought.

Kaleidoscopic images of that outing swarmed in, merciless in their insolence. Liza's picnic basket had sported deli-prepared fried chicken and potato salad.

Garrison remembered how cheated he'd felt when she told him she was too busy with the charity drive to cook her own specialties.

"Isn't deli food pretty expensive?" he'd retorted, seeing her back stiffen, her fine nostrils flare ever so slightly as she laid out paper plates and plastic cutlery.

"Some things are more important than saving a few dollars," she'd snapped back.

Stung by her "skinflint" insinuations, he'd countered, "From where I'm sitting at the helm of this boat – that keeps us afloat, by the way – I'd put it right up there at the top."

She turned to him, eyes sad, and slowly shook her head. "Above my sanity and peace?"

He'd been the first to break eye contact, but his brooding did not escape her notice because she'd grown morose and then prickly.

They ate in silence. Birdsong and cricket chirrups broke it into bearable increments and the lily pond's shimmery surface provided rest and pleasure to the eye. But they didn't look at each other.

"Why didn't you dress comfortably?" There was a mean edge to her voice as she refilled soft drinks into iced cups, fizzing them over the sides and onto the tablecloth. "You're wearing a suit, for heaven's sake." She snatched wads of napkins to soak up the spills.

"I have an important appointment with a prospective client, so I'll have to cut this short." His clipped response came out cold, even to his own ears.

"I don't know why I even bother," she muttered, obviously pissed.

"Hey!" Garrison's temper flared. "Somebody around here has to work. Remember? Don't shoot down the golden goose."

Unexpectedly, she'd burst into laughter. Then, seeing Garrison's lack of amusement, she'd bitten her lip, turned away, and begun clearing picnic supplies, her fine features turning more solemn by the heartbeat.

Apathy and disenchantment seeped into the excursion, rendering them silent and distant with each other.

Passionless, he now admitted.

He recalled how she'd turned back to him and touched his arm, halting him in his fierce packing away of the picnic remains. "Garrison," she said quietly, entreatingly, raising his on-guard antennae, "sometimes I feel like an afterthought with you."

Challenge slapped him in the face, with gloves. "What more do you want me to do, Liza?" he'd asked sharply, exasperated, the words flooding his throat like bile. "I'm already giving blood. Can't you see that?"

The sadness pooled in her eyes still haunted him

She'd looked at him steadily in the cricket-chirping, frog-croaking quiet of the forest. For long moments she'd gazed into his eyes, searching for something he could not fathom. He felt her urgency, her need to reach an inaccessible place in him, saw disappointment gather in her features. He felt helpless and confused as she turned away, her eyes downcast, cheeks flushed, lips pressed together.

Flayed by needs he could not meet, Garrison clamped his teeth together, tightened his jaw, and, in stony silence, helped Liza repack their gear and leave. After all, he was only one man and there were just so many hours in a day in which to cram all the work it took to keep a roof over their heads and food in their bellies, and to perform the hundred and one other things indexed under "Garrison's Duties."

With his blessing, Liza had chosen to be a stay-at-home wife and mother. At times, though, in the earliest days of establishing his graphic arts business, he'd felt torn by her decision. Even with his parents' generous gift of land, making ends meet had been rough. An extra paycheck would have come in handy during that struggling time.

Today, Garrison jolted back to the present with a fresh shock of guilt. Liza had dedicated her life to being a wife and mother. And here he was resenting it. The thought hung there, obnoxious and taunting. Real.

Grinding his teeth together, he pushed the guilt away – adding one extra weight to the current self-reproach. "I can't do this," he muttered hoarsely between his teeth, scruffing a hand over his face and shaking his head as if to stave off the onslaught.

The life-and-death struggle now facing them had to take prominence over all other issues. Would any of them survive it?

"I've got to," he muttered, feeling the heavy plodding of blood through his veins and the weary drag of his heart. Despair slammed him, leaving him struggling for his next breath.

At just that moment, the pond's sparkling demeanor began to shift. Late summer storm clouds loitering overhead intercepted the sun's rays and scattered The Oasis's golden enchantment – turning the atmosphere gray.

Garrison felt the wind pick up, then begin to gust. He watched the strong air current whip crimson and white lily blossoms into flutters and curls and the water into angry little waves.

A chill passed over Garrison as he felt the first cold drops of rain.

Where? he wondered. Where had the magic gone?

Angel's condition remained alarmingly the same. The time-will-tell mantra rang more and more like a death knell.

"Isn't there any medication that can stimulate the brain to consciousness?" Liza asked the nurse checking Angel's vital signs. She was in Angel's curtained-off ICU cubicle for her bi-hourly twenty-minute allotted visit.

"'Fraid not, Liza." By now, the medical staff was on first name terms with the Wakefields. Other patients were in and out of ICU within a day or two. Angel's stay now stretched well beyond that, lending more familiarity. And the end was not in sight.

Nurse Brenda updated Angel's chart as she talked. "There are currently no medicines known that will shorten the duration of a coma. Remember, most actually deepen the state of unconsciousness. Others are used to paralyze the body temporarily. Both kinds are involved in Angel's treatment for seizures, so she's pretty deeply comatose." She shrugged and smiled sympathetically. "The effects of the medicine may have to be tolerated for the well-being of the patient."

Liza watched her leave and wanted to share the update with Garrison. He'd gone to the office. And though Liza found herself feeling a bit forsaken, she was not truly uncomfortable being alone.

Her committees and causes had disappeared behind a cloud of dust as she rallied for her daughter. The only thing she missed about them was the fact that they no longer diverted her from the reality of the widening gulf between Garrison and herself.

She did not regret for a second her choice to be a stay-at-home wife and mother, but after Angel reached wobbly, self-reliant adolescence and then boogied into her sovereign teens, Liza's Supermom image slowly eroded, then fizzled away.

Garrison, by then accustomed to Liza's full-time calling as a mother, operated under his own profound drive and ambition for excellence. The melancholy, artistic strain pivoted him in whatever direction he aimed, forcefully and full of steam. Wakefield Creations, his graphic arts company, had, by Angel's adolescent years, become his zealous focus.

Liza had not set out to neglect Garrison by taking on more and more good causes. He'd just seemed so fanatical in his business venture and not truly aware of their veering off in opposite directions. In self-help books she'd read that this was the way of career-building men, so she'd taken it in stride and given Garrison space to do what he had to do.

Through the years, she'd shed, layer by layer, the little things wives do for husbands. She squeezed her eyes shut, remembering that she'd not cooked his special dish of limas, tomatoes, and smoked sausages, nor bought him a new outfit for no reason at all, nor planned sexy weekend getaways – not in years. Shame washed over her in waves. And regret.

She called the Wakefield Creations office. No answer. She pushed back the disturbing fact of Garrison's inaccessibility.

Suck it up, Liza. You can deal with this.

Dr. Abrams came by the waiting room later. He remained, as with his earlier briefings, up front. "The longer she's in the coma, the lower her chances of complete renewal. But she's hanging in there." His abrupt departure left her reeling.

Liza felt the pierce of the double-edged sword.

Angel's friends, in awe of the tragedy, came quietly, one by one and in clusters. Liza recalled her own youthful sense of immortality and knew that to them Angel's prone, intubated, near-lifeless body was like a horrific dream that would end with everyone waking up to find it wasn't real at all. Ah, to have such notions now.

Of all Angel's friends, Penny most grasped the situation's gravity. Garrison needed to work for the better part of days now, or his business would go under financially. So Liza soaked up Penny's company. Her presence broke up endless waiting hours. The monotony and confinement relentlessly bore upon Liza. Yet she knew that it would be worse not to be there. *Suppose Angel wakes up?* The possibility incessantly loitered in her mind.

She wouldn't even consciously entertain the flipside of that coin. But of course, it was there, hovering in the dark periphery of her psyche.

The day-to-day suspense and tension bore upon Penny, too. "I miss her," she said as she and Liza sat in the cafeteria, eating a sandwich. "She *is* going to get better, isn't she?" Penny seemed, at times, somehow older, mellow in her youth. Emotions skittered across her lightly freckled face as Penny reflected. "I mean, she's so swollen and –"

Liza raised her brows. "But she does look better now, Penny. Remember how much worse she looked in the beginning?"

"Yeah. The dark bruises are faded and her eyes aren't nearly as puffed up."

"Oh, yeah. She's come a long way. And is she going to get better? I certainly want to believe that she will."

"Me too." Penny took a sip of iced tea and sighed. "Our Youth at St. Joseph's is holding prayer vigils for her every day." Her green eyes suddenly glimmered with hope. "And the kids at school are doing the same thing every morning before homeroom."

Liza's eyes gathered moisture. "Then she's in good hands, huh?" She lifted her tea glass. "To Angel's recovery."

Penny's glass lifted to hers. "To Angel."

"Charlcy?" Liza's cell phone reception wasn't the greatest at the hospital and the voice was breaking up. Her heart already sang just hearing her sister's voice. She moved out into the corridor and it cleared.

"Yeah, it's Charlcy, dodo. Who'd you think it was?"

Liza burst into laughter. This greeting was typical Charlcy. The more dire and murky the emotional register around her, the more levity in Charlcy's reaction. Charlcy adored Angel. Thus, she would avoid the gravity of the situation as long as possible. Liza understood that her sister simply could not abide heaviness except in infinitesimal increments, spaced out to kingdom come. She was an all-or-nothing misfit. And to Liza, she was absolutely beautiful inside and out.

"Where the heck are you?"

"In Greece."

"I always figured you'd end up in something hot. Grease is as good as anything."

"Corny, corn corn." Her sister snorted. "Seriously, sis." The gruffness left her voice. "What's happening there?"

"Nothing's changed."

A long silence ensued. Then her older sister said, "Wish you'd have let me come on home to be with you. If you need me, I'll fly out –"

"Finish your vacation or I'll beat your fanny. I'm good."

"You promised you'd call if –"

"I'll call."

A long sigh rippled over the line. "Okay. I'll be home at the end of the week anyway. Liza?"

"Yeah?"

"You okay?"

Another pause. "I'm good." A bold-faced lie.

Long moments of silence, of simply feeling and being there.
Then a deep drag of breath and exhaling. "Okaaay. See you in
a week, Duck Feet." She chortled. "Speakin' of duck feet, you
should see the new Louboutins I'm wearing. Oh, just wait till
you see all the new shoes I picked up in Milan. There might
even be a little gift for you somewhere in there. I don't know; I'll
have to think about that."

"I hear you, Dumbo ears."

"Hey! Don't knock 'em. They're great for tethering dangling diamond baubles." Then more quietly, "Hang in there,
honey. Love you bunches."

"Me too. Bye."

Liza rang off and wept. How precious was her sister's voice.

Garrison watched Liza lean to kiss Angel's pale cheek and
something clutched at his heart. They drove home in silence,
and during the meal of carryout cold cuts, she took her tray
into the den, kicked off her slippers, and turned on Fox News,
leaving him alone at the bar. Alone didn't sit too well just then.
He wasn't in the mood. He took his own tray to join her.

"You forgot your iced tea," he said and returned to the
kitchen. He placed her glass on the coffee table next to his own
and sat beside her. And he realized that he hadn't been so considerate of such small needs in a long time. Still, Liza never
glanced his way. Not even a thank you. That sniped at him a
bit.

For the next thirty minutes, they ate in silence except for
broadcasting clatter. Soon, the revolving news updates became
repetitious. Garrison switched to another channel. He wasn't
up to reality television – too intrusive. And *Cold Case* was too
heavy, too close to death.

"Anything you want to watch?" he asked Liza.

"No." She shook her head, staring blankly at the screen.

"Would you like some ice cream?" Garrison headed for the kitchen.

"No, thank you."

Disappointment swamped him. For some reason, having her eat with him tonight was important. He missed her optimism, her coaxing him toward hope.

But what about when my anger rises again? He'd gotten what he asked for, hadn't he? He aggressively scooped Butter Pecan balls into a bowl while his emotions warred.

His hand paused midair *Can I truly forgive her? And forget? Be honest, Wakefield.* Angel's prone figure and Troy's casket flashed before him along with the moment he'd told Angel, "No. It's too dangerous." His hand thudded to the counter, dropping the metal scoop with a splat into the stainless steel sink.

No. No, he couldn't say that he could. And yeah, he was a jerk to expect anything from Liza under the circumstances.

He rejoined his wife, this time seating himself across from her, his bowl of ice cream melting atop the coffee table. "Liza," he said. "We need to talk." He hooked an ankle over his leg and steepled his long fingers before him.

She looked at him, features empty. "So talk."

"Liza, I love you. Please, I want you to know that. With everything in me, I love you. But I can't shake loose from this anger inside me. I'm trying not to blame you, to accept that it just happened."

He shook his head. "But at this moment, I can't wrap my mind around it. You see, this tragedy has handed me a whole new set of emotions to deal with." Tears gathered in his eyes. His voice dropped to a husk. "And I don't know how." He shrugged and spread his hands in helplessness. "But I do know that I can't stand to see you suffer because of my attitude."

The expression in Liza's eyes shifted suddenly. Fear? Apprehension? Like she braced for something bad coming.

"Don't – please don't look like that," he said. "I'm trying not to hurt you any worse." His gut hitched. He had to release her from all this. "This anger – it's nestled deeply in my spirit and no matter how much I reason with myself, I can't shake it. At the same time, I miss your warmth." He rolled his eyes and spread his hands. "I know what that makes me. I know I've driven you away with my coldness."

He leaned forward, face intent, desperate for her to understand. "This anger is a new thing, something I've never dealt with before. It's like being gripped in a vise, unable to twist in any direction – standing toe to toe with these hostile demons. They torment and harass me. They woo me." He sat back and sighed wearily. "They conquer me, Liza. They're destroying our marriage."

If anything, Liza's face grew paler and more vigilant. He wasn't doing too well with this.

He shifted forward in the easy chair, clasping his hands together between his knees. "I'm going to move out for a little while. Give you some space. You have enough to put up with without my adding to your burdens."

Liza sat up straighter, perched on the seat's edge, peering at him with undisguised incredulity. "Now let me get this straight, Garrison. You're leaving me because you love me?" She shook her wheat blond head, eyes narrowing. "Am I missing something here?"

Garrison stood in one decisive motion. "Trust me, Liza; I'm doing this for you." Then he turned on his heel and strode to the bedroom.

"Trust you?" she rasped, then arose, following Garrison into their room, where he took a suitcase from the closet and began to pack. "What are you doing?" Her voice was whispery.

He looked at her white, shocked face and nearly backed down. No, this was for the best. If he didn't go, he would only hurt her more. He looked over his shoulder. She had her head bowed, eyes tightly shut. Face stark pale. He looked down at her slender hands clutching the bedspread, knuckles white. He started toward her –

The bedside phone rang. Garrison turned and snatched it to his ear. "Yes, this is he." He listened for long moments "What? What did you say?" He felt the blood drain from his head. "Oh my God! We'll be right there!"

He turned to Liza. "That was the hospital. Angel just went into cardiac arrest. Let's go."

Pain! Ungodly pain…crushing…grinding. *Oh God,* free me…spinning, spinning, swirling…blackness….

Lights so bright everything glowed. Angel floated above a room…hospital again. Same patient in bed that centered the white and stainless steel chamber with its many machines that pumped and whirred constantly.

Troy? Where's Troy? He stood apart from the doctors and nurses rushing frantically from one procedure to the next. The two paddles appeared. Angel felt something like dread hovering….

Troy! Help me! She could not speak but he heard and gazed up at her, his dark eyes appealing to her in some way that calmed her. As long as he was there, she would be okay. Somehow she knew that.

Another doctor entered the room. Angel couldn't see the face behind the mask and scrubs, but she detected that it was a female by the size and shape and the feminine way she moved. From overhead, Angel watched her approach the one who was about to administer the strange paddles. The others didn't seem to notice her. She seemed hesitant and unobtrusive. Once removed. But Troy watched her intently, as though he wanted to say something to her. Angel was now intrigued by Troy's interest, but just as she would have asked him why, the paddles pressed to the patient's chest and....

Wham! Spinning, swirling, swirling downward...fog....

Aargh! Pain...bursting with agony....

Blackness, welcome, blessed blackness swallowed Angel.

At the hospital, the medical team hustled them directly to the consultation room. There, they learned that heroic measures had revived Angel's heartbeat. The team's projection for recovery, however, remained grim.

"Why did this happen?" Garrison asked in a hoarse voice.

Dr. Abrams, the designated spokesman, seated them at the table. "It was brought on by an electrolyte imbalance that sent the heart into ventricular fibrillation, then heart failure. It was sudden, but fortunately, immediate CPR kept her blood flowing until defibrillation. Her condition is still grave. The next forty-eight hours are critical."

Dr. Abrams then pointed to some X-rays and explained the severity of Angel's injuries. "As for the head trauma, we're still on wait and see. There seems to be some bruising," he pointed to a slight shadow in the neck region, "right here, near the brain stem. Unfortunately, we can only guess the extent of the damage or the outcome. The spinal cord is intact and the bruising isn't directly on the brain stem. The affected area may or may not have long-term effects."

He pointed lower. "Next to the head injury, however, this is what concerns me most. The vertebrae in the lower back between the thoracic vertebrae, where the ribs attach to the pelvis, are the lumbar vertebrae. The sacral vertebrae run from the pelvis to the end of the spinal column. Injuries to the five lumbar vertebrae and similarly to the five sacral vertebrae generally result in some loss of functioning in the hips and legs."

He pointed to another X-ray "Besides these injuries, she has a fracture to the shaft of the left tibia. The bones pierced through the skin and the degree of resulting damage to the nerves and muscles are difficult to ascertain until the patient is recovering. Both legs are in casts, as you know."

He faced Garrison and Liza, his features grim. "Do you understand what this implies?"

Numb with overload, Garrison nodded and glanced at Liza, who sat motionless, white as chalk, hands spread limply in her lap.

Dr. Abrams continued. "Brain function recoveries are unpredictable – your daughter's brain may not regain all its potential. Then again –" He shrugged. "So far, she's holding her own. If she survives, the back and leg injuries will render her, at best, severely limited. It's unlikely she'll walk."

The doctor peered at Liza. "Mrs. Wakefield, do you understand? I know this is a lot to take in…are you all right?"

Garrison rushed to her, his features worried. "Liza? Are you okay?"

Liza? Are you okay?

For Liza, it was as if the words came from a far distance, echoing in her head, bouncing around. Spinal cord injury Spinal cord…if she lives…Angel won't dance again. Might not even live. It bounded about in her brain. And then *Garrison's leaving me…leaving me*…joined in the mêlée. Strobe images…shouts, "*Mama! Where are you going, Mama?*" Charlcy's screams…"*Please don't hit Charlcy anymore, Mama! Pleeease!*"

Where is silence when I need it?

Liza grabbed her head with both hands, squeezing, squeezing. *If only I can stop it!*

Then blackness.

"Liza?" Garrison's voice.

She cracked her eyes and his blurred features swam above her. She cut her eyes to the side and saw white. A hospital curtain. Her fingers sensed fabric. Sheets. She rolled her head over and realized she was in a hospital room…bed. *Garrison's leaving me but….*

Her voice came out whispery, wispy as spun cotton. "You… didn't leave?"

"No." Pain flickered across his features. "You passed out." His voice was gentle. She peered bleary-eyed at him, feeling extremely fuzzy. His deep voice soothed her. "You're all right. You're just sedated."

How he knew her. How he sensed her fears and knew how and when to reassure her. The thought lulled her. "Just rest. Doctor's orders. You're experiencing a little shock, is all. But you'll soon feel better. Sleep, honey."

Honey. She felt so exhausted. Drained. Her eyes closed… sleep….

"What have I done?" Garrison groaned. He watched Liza's still, pale face.

Why hadn't he seen it coming? Why hadn't he known? She'd been so brave through everything. She'd put up with his coldness. Had allowed him to jerk her emotions around. And then she'd felt completely abandoned tonight when he told her he was leaving. Why hadn't he remembered her fear of abandonment, remnants of her ill mother's lifelong disappearances?

Add to that Angel's cardiac arrest and the grim revelation of Angel's other injuries. He took her slender, icy fingers in his hand. They did not respond to his attempt to warm them. They lay there still, lifeless. She seemed so far away just now. Inaccessible.

"God, how I love you." The words slipped out, unbidden, from his very soul. And in that moment, he realized the depth of them. His throat ached as tears gathered and prickled behind his eyes. *How many times during this devastation have I pushed you away? How unconscionable, how cruel of me.*

"Liza...can you hear me?" He leaned in closer and saw her eyelids struggle to open as her breathing deepened. "Honey? I'm so sorry. Please...forgive me?" Her eyelids remained sealed as his wife's lovely features slackened into deep, deep slumber.

He laid his head on her bosom and wept. *Will you ever forgive me?*

Oh God, please...I don't want to lose her, too.

chapter eight

Liza insisted upon visiting Angel the next day. She couldn't bear not seeing her daughter. The strong tranquilizer Dr. Abrams prescribed to spring Liza from the state of shock had, at first, spiraled her down, down, downward through many stratums of anxiety – terror, fear, apprehension, disquiet, tension – all in a few minutes. The free-fall sensation was fierce and succinct.

The magic capsule then propelled her on a smooth, level ride of tranquility, where she remained oblivious to anything and everything cerebral. She felt mostly, for the next couple of days, languidness in her bones that, once she sat or reclined, lulled her to sleep. She could have, at any time or anywhere, slithered to the floor in a snoring heap. She didn't worry about anything because she couldn't remember anything.

For two days, she existed in the vacuum of otherness. "Dr. Abrams is testing Angel today for – what is it, Garrison?" She slightly slurred the words as she relayed an update to Penny in the ICU waiting room. Angel's friend watched her apprehensively and shot Garrison alarmed glances.

"Those tests were done yesterday, Liza," Garrison clarified gently.

"You told me about the tests two days ago, Mrs. W.," Penny softly reminded her.

"You sure?" Liza squinted at Garrison. She would have sworn that the doctor told her that very morning. Would have bet her life on it.

"Positive," he said and smiled at her. The smile, she noted, was indulgent.

She blinked away at the stupor, still doubting their version. "I don't like this," she grumped petulantly.

"It's helping you to heal, Liza. You need to heal."

"You need to heal, too, Garrison." The words slid over her tongue like melting butter, completely bypassing her brain. Childlike. The medication deleted her inhibitions. "It's not healthy to be unforgivin'."

Garrison shot Penny a look of appeal.

"Uh," she shot to her feet, "if you'll excuse me, I think I'll go get a Coke."

"Now, what did you do that for?" Liza drawled, her eyelids blinking in slow motion. "Sending Penny away?"

Garrison pulled his chair closer. "Liza, I'm trying to…be healed, too. It's just taking time. I love you. I know that beyond a doubt. And I want you well. I can't stand to see you like you've been."

Liza gazed blearily into his eyes for a long time. "H-how have I been?" she finally said, her tongue barely touching the consonants.

"Unhappy. Sad. And not just about Angel."

"Tha's 'cause you won' forgive me. You wanna leave me." She was being matter-of-fact, as open as a barn door. She looked more deeply into his troubled eyes. Delving, plundering. Then she slowly shook her head. "It's still there. In your eyes." The ingenuous statement hung in the air between them, heavy and dark.

"What?" Garrison husked, the hair on his neck rising.

Liza gave him a sad, groggy smile. "Con-dem-nation."

In that one moment of crystal clarity, she decided. "Don' need pills. I can do it myself, Garrison." She blinked slowly and sighed. "Won' depend on anybody." Her head tipped back and plopped softly against the wall behind the waiting chair. Her eyelids slid shut.

"Liza," Garrison leaned close and murmured, "Liza...you can depend on me. Don't ever forget that. I'm trying to work all this out inside. And I do know how very much you mean to me. Please, believe that." She didn't answer.

"You hear me?" He looked closer and saw that her mouth had grown slack and her breathing deep and even. Liza was asleep.

❧

Garrison handled Liza with the utmost gentleness in the following days. Though not happy with it, he grew accustomed to her eerie silence, one she maintained even when in the ICU with Angel. Dr. Abrams said it would take time for her to heal from the breakdown.

"Cut her lots of slack. She's going to need it," Dr. Abrams had cautioned. The good doctor was not happy with Liza's decision to go off the tranquilizer, but told Garrison, "She's leveled off and will probably be okay if she isn't exposed to undue additional stress."

So far, Garrison had managed to protect her. It wasn't easy. She'd become more and more prickly as time passed.

Garrison ran her warm bathwater one evening and added her favorite lavender bath beads. "I'm going to take a shower," she declared when she saw what he'd done, and promptly did so, though he knew she was not a shower person.

Later, he fastidiously prepared a lovely salad plate with choice meats, cheeses, and fruits he knew she loved. It was, if he said so himself, an artistic masterpiece. "I don't want salad tonight," she said and scrounged in the fridge for leftover Chinese noodles.

"You're crowding me," she said to him tonight, nudging him when he spooned against her back in bed, their customary position all through the years. She tugged his arm loose from around her waist.

He knew the cause of her reactions to him. *He* was that cause. He'd created a monster.

Garrison tiredly rolled over and sat up. "I'm moving my things into the guest room, Liza. You need space and I'm giving it to you. When you're ready to have me back in your bed, let me know."

So it was that he ended up in the attic later, after sleepless tossing and turning on the guest bed's uncomfortable mattress. Wide awake he plundered through photos and memorabilia. There, amid things of the past, he came across his artsy black-and-white prints, a bygone fad, and saw a photo of the three of them in happy days.

He remembered a summer picnic at The Oasis. The air was sweetened by the fragrance of water lilies and soft breezes off the water…sunshine on their skin and shade to cool them… their laughter as they munched Liza's fried chicken with her incomparable potato salad…little Angel's exuberance as Daddy carved her name on the Love Tree to join Liza's and his own….

He didn't know he wept until a tear plopped, then trickled down the photograph. He snuffled and returned the album to its storage shelf.

His venture continued and he discovered his easels, canvas, paints, and worn brushes. He even found his old, clean artist smocks folded neatly on a nearby shelf. *Liza's touch is everywhere.*

In a sudden splash of inspiration, he hauled his paraphernalia to Angel's large bedroom where, within minutes, his easel and canvas claimed an entire corner of the room, whose pastel walls and décor lent an aura of peace and tranquility. Here he felt close to his daughter. Here, he would do what he could to will her back to this world.

Tentatively, he began sketching. While doing so, he found himself transported back to when he and Liza met and fell in love. He'd walked past the University of South Carolina dance department late that afternoon and saw her at the ballet barre. God, she was beautiful…lithe and supple.

"Hi," he'd said boldly, though the butterflies in his stomach raged. "I'm Garrison Wakefield, an art major. Would you mind if I sketch you while you dance?" He smiled at her then, beguiled by her innocent regard of him, amused at the flicker of wariness from blue, blue depths. Long, thick, amazingly black lashes framed the entire pool of delight and he already, in his mind, mixed Prussian Blue with a small puddle of Ultramarine Blue paint for their extraordinary transition on canvas. "Uh, I need some sketches in the study of anatomy, for required credits."

When she still looked a bit guarded, he said, "You would be contributing to a worthy cause. It pays well. A Coke in the snack shop after I sketch you each time."

Then he saw it, the blush tingeing her smooth, porcelain cheeks. And his heart nearly stopped. Was the emotion that painted them anger? Offense? Had he been too pushy? Too presumptive?

She'd laughed then, a spontaneous peal of delight. Then, as though embarrassed at the display of emotion, she lowered her astonishing eyelashes and shifted her near willowy, yet supple frame.

"Would you mind?" he muttered in soft appeal.

"N-no…I suppose it'll be okay." Then she'd looked up at him and startled him with the direct honesty in her near translucent gaze. "But wouldn't you rather study rugged male muscles? I mean —" she shrugged.

He'd found her modesty incredibly appealing. He felt like he was drowning in the blue depths of her eyes. "To quote Renoir, 'Why shouldn't art be pretty? There are enough unpleasant things in the world'."

She smiled then. It burst across her features and lit up the place and tethered Liza doggedly to his heartstrings. That fast. That simple. And immediately, he'd started on a portrait of her back in his dormitory room. Each day, he'd go past the dance studio during her practice time and sketch her from all angles. Everything about her etched itself into his psyche and soul. Even her little mannerisms, like biting on a fingernail when in deep thought and rotating her neck and shoulders when limbering up, endeared her to him.

The portrait, entitled "Love Song," portrayed Liza dancing Kitri, from *Don Quixote*, whose love affair with Basilio lacked parental approval. Garrison had watched her dance the part, in awe, storing up the images for his final portrait. Sizzling moves in the final pas de deux with flirting fan, fouettes and leaps that drew gasps from him. It all culminated in the image captured by Garrison's brush on canvas: a stunning arabesque en pointe. From Liza's luminous smile glowed the message that love conquers all. Energy sizzled from her expressive arms and fingers, from her very pores. Her features, beneath hair pulled tightly from the center to beads locking it at her nape, showed a passionate joy of being.

He'd kept the portrait to himself all that year. Just as they'd saved themselves for marriage's glorious and mystical discoveries, he'd saved the portrait to be his gift to her on the day they wed.

In keeping with Liza's tradition of going to church with her family when her mother's mood swings periodically leveled off, he and Liza began attending services down the street from campus, finding there a sense of comfort and rightness. His own parents' churchgoing had consisted mainly of C and E – Christmas and Easter – so he'd enjoyed summers with his churchgoing grandparents because they avidly lived and loved as the Bible taught. Those were the times he'd felt truly accepted and valued.

After his and Liza's wedding, he'd presented the portrait to her with a flourish Rhett Butler would have envied.

How she'd exulted over it! "Are you sure I'm that beautiful?" she asked teasingly, flirtatiously, breathless with sheer joy.

"Absolutely," he'd replied, awash with the wonder of her… of them.

Tonight, he wondered, *where do I begin?* He mixed more paints and made the first stroke over canvas. Like a burst of sunshine, her face came to him. Liza. That's where he would begin. He would capture her again. Somehow, he would.

He set up his sketchpad and began. First, he sketched her hands from all angles, from memory. The tapering grace of the fingers was distinctly Liza's, even to the shape and size of the nails.

Next, he outlined the face and features, paying close attention to the eyes, lips, and hair. Especially the eyes. The eyes excited him, inspired him.

He mixed more paints and began to stroke life into the planes and angles. His hands gained momentum and his heart raced with exhilaration. His hands moved but he was in a spiritual searching trance.

Hours passed and he looked in wonder at his canvas. *Is this as good as I think it is?* The eyes, alight with joy and wonder, with fulfillment, gazed at him from the canvas, bringing tears of wonder to his own. The lips spread wide with laughter and sheer elation. The wheat hair texture made his fingers tingle with the anticipation of touch.

He continued. His level of creativity surpassed anything of his past. He wasn't sure of what it was or where it was going, but he was attaching himself to it in search of the young man he'd once been. Unsure of how it filtered into his paintbrush, he felt electrified in ways he had not in years.

He poured his heart onto the canvas as he began his soul-search for the man Liza married, the one true to himself.

Liza, angry with herself for missing Garrison's warm bulk snuggled to her, could not sleep. She was also angry that Garrison had left her bed again. With a heavy heart, she conceded that it merely proved he was not, after all, dependable. But then, she'd grown up with a mother whose least attribute had been dependability.

She squelched that recall, again cutting her mom slack for an illness she'd not asked for.

Even though she'd passed the nervous collapse crisis fairly well, aided initially by the strong, calming medication, she still experienced shifting doses of disquiet. Sometimes she felt weaker, like now, but only temporarily. Somewhere along the way that week, when loneliness, helplessness, and desperation had driven her to the Maker and taken her to a new level of self-discovery, she'd developed a mystical new inner strength from which to draw.

She didn't need Garrison to fix things for her anymore. Being stronger and able to deal with anything that arose made her feel good about herself.

Liza stretched and yawned. The only thing she couldn't resolve tonight was getting to sleep. She finally crawled from the sheets and headed for the one place in which she might find solace.

Upstairs, she opened the door to Angel's room, surprised to see the lights on. In fact, the place was lit up like Fourth of July and Christmas, overhead lights and all.

"Oh!" She jumped when she spotted Garrison. "Ah, I'm sorry." She slowly backtracked to the door.

"Wait." Garrison rushed over, paintbrush in stained hand. "Stay." His eyes, so sincere, enticed her, but she shook her head. Curiosity sprang forth as she eyed his blemished smock and brush. Nostalgia ran through her, triggered by the smell of paint and canvas. Long ago, those hands had created magic and –

She shook her head again, shaking loose of the memory's grip. She was still too, too ravaged with hurt, and didn't ever again need the pain of being so near him and yet so far away. She must be careful not to arouse the siren of need.

"No. It's better if I go to her studio." She left, closing the door firmly behind her.

Moments later, in the studio, Liza turned on some warm-up and stretch music. From the echoes of her mind came a signaled response to the notes' rhythm. The tempo inside her leaped to life as she found clean black leotards, tights, and ballet slippers in the closet and dressed. The snug contours of the costume hugged those of her body like a second skin, lending weightless aerodynamics to her movements.

She'd always kept a supply of her own dance costumes there because she made impromptu appearances to spend time with her daughter, dancing with her, coaching, and, at times, simply encouraging her.

Reliving young ballet days of her own.

Her warm-up today began with frappés at Angel's ballet barre, where floor-to-ceiling mirrors bordered the entire twenty-by-twenty chamber. Her hand rested gently on the wooden barre as she broke down ballet movements into their smallest, most elemental components. She allowed herself to indulge in the memories of Angel dancing, of their times together here.

Tonight, she traveled back in time to her beginnings, thinking of Angel as she went through the pliés, keeping her knees soft and articulating her feet, pointing them not just at the ankle but also through the toes and metatarsals; the area from instep to toe. Demi-pliés, grande pliés, and relevés, backward and forward, stretching to the floor, head between knees all served to increase her tissue temperature – like lubricating the joints.

It had been a long time. *Ah, Angel. How beautiful you are and how beautifully you dance.* Her heart felt near to breaking at what was no more. *All because of me.*

Liza felt tears gather, but she stubbornly pushed on, placing a tennis ball between and just below her ankles, helping her find her placement, knowing she was properly aligned before she did her first grand battement. It was a controlled throwing of one straight leg into full extension, distributing her weight equally on the other foot, all five toes turned out, the support leg stiff and straight, allowing her body to balance. She continued long minutes, alternating right and left legs.

Her body, now feeling warm, would be more receptive to dancing. Tonight, however, Liza didn't feel the patience for small controlled movements that would protect against injury. Anger's adrenaline launched her into uncharacteristic recklessness. She hung out in several static stretch positions at the barre and then segued into a sudden, big forceful a' la seconde straddle stretch on the floor.

That brought on *uh-oh* pain. The punishment seemed fitting. Penance.

If I can hurt my body, I won't feel my heart and soul coming apart at the seams.

Tears coursed down her cheeks as she went about stretching and flexing long unused muscles and limbs. She welcomed the exertion. She would glory in the next-day soreness, the pain giving her respite from her thoughts. Heedlessly switching the music to an allegro tempo from "The Sleeping Beauty Prologue," she spun to petit allégro in the fifth fairy's "finger" variation of a daunting series of pas de chats that go where men don't dare, taking off and landing on pointe.

Breathless, her senses heightened, she quickly switched music again, this time to *Don Quixote*, when Kitri replies to Basilio's, her lover's, leaps with a signature jump of her own, a grand jeté with her back leg bent to graze the back of her head.

She was astonished that she could still feel the brush of foot against occipital hair.

Emboldened, Liza switched the music to "Allegro Brillante." She escalated her turns in the same way the music built. Her first pirouette was a double, second pirouette was a triple, and so on. She lost track in the dizzying splendor of it all.

She employed *enchainement* to center floor dancing, a linking of various steps in combinations of movements, allowing her to move more freely through space. The combinations made her feel "dancier," more into emphasizing musicality and the expressive use of the head and shoulders.

Breeeeeathe, Liza had to remind herself more than once to keep from freezing in the air, thus ending the jumps. When she did so a couple of times, she doggedly recommenced, mentally challenging herself to breathe at regular intervals.

Soon, she soared, weightlessly, as free as a winged creature born into dance.

How she'd missed dancing. Was it wrong to enjoy it tonight, when Angel –

Guilt hovered, heaving and groaning like some ghoul.

Then Angel's glowing face flashed before her, like the times when she'd watched her mother dance. Liza still tasted and breathed the pride shimmering from her daughter's sweet features.

And it struck her anew just how much her dancing for the girl had meant to Angel. Impulsively, she switched "Allegro Brillante" back on and did a breathless series of pirouettes about the studio, just the way Angel loved her to do.

This time, she truly danced for Angel.

Liza knew in that heartbeat that Angel would want her to do just what she was doing tonight. Having Angel study ballet and Liza being on the local ballet board of directors, had kept her, to an extent, connected. Here tonight, she could feel Angel's presence and she prayed that soon that presence would be not just in spirit but in body as well.

Later, in the wee hours before dawn, she and Garrison went to their separate rooms, passing each other in the hallway. Their gazes locked for a long moment....

I cannot trust my heart to him.

Liza averted her eyes and brushed past him.

Angel's condition, with seizure control drugs, stabilized. She remained comatose.

"They're talking about moving her," Liza told Garrison one Sunday, his only full day off from the office. They ate a lunch of veggies and salad downstairs in the hospital cafeteria. "She's been here three and a half weeks. They only retain patients for a certain period before transferring them to Restorative Care."

"Where's Restorative Care?" Garrison wiped his mouth with a napkin.

"Across the road, behind the hospital. It's a fairly new facility, I understand."

They remained silent for long moments. "Do you suppose they're giving up on her?" Liza asked with trepidation.

Garrison peered at her, worry evident in his mahogany eyes. "I don't think so. I would think that they only send patients there who – well, those for whom they've done all they can. We'll ask Dr. Abrams about it when he makes his rounds."

Their later talk with the primary physician reassured them both that Angel's care would remain in good hands in the ICU annex. "They're set up to handle all that we do here. It's simply a longer-term care provider."

Two days later, an ambulance transported their daughter to Restorative Care. True to what Liza had heard, the facility was indeed new and the atmosphere caring and efficient.

"We could consider this as a step up," Garrison told Liza as they stored Angel's belongings in her room's corner locker. "We can at least stay with her throughout the day."

"Thank the good Lord," Liza agreed, refolding and stacking a pink pullover and matching pink socks atop jeans and white Reeboks, the clothing Angel wore the night of the accident. She then pulled a moderately comfortable chair up to her daughter's bedside. "These accommodations sure beat the old waiting room, with elbow to elbow visitors. And we aren't limited to seeing Angel only twenty minutes out of every two to three hours."

"Yeah," Garrison said, settling into his own chair on the opposite side of the bed. "That was the roughest part – leaving her."

In the new quarters, a wall-mounted cable television offered respite from boredom. "It's great to know," Liza observed, "that little has changed care-wise. She's still constantly monitored and the staff is here pronto when a light goes off."

Hovering, however, was the reflection that this move signaled either moving on to recovery or death. Daily, folks in RC died. Few experienced remarkable, quick recoveries.

Liza forced herself to think positive thoughts.

Pastor Steve Dill, from St. Joseph's Presbyterian Church, where they attended, came by around noon. "Everyone sends their prayers and thoughts," he said. "Angel is missed in her youth choir and Sunday school class."

Tears pooled in Liza's eyes before she quickly swiped them away and thanked Pastor Dill for the church's support. It seemed that tears always hovered just below the surface these days.

"The medical team is going to turn off the respirator today," Garrison informed the pastor. "They want to start weaning her. See if she can breathe on her own."

"That's wonderful, Garrison. Sounds like progress to me." Pastor Dill celebrated with them and prayed before departing to complete his hospital visitation rounds.

Later that afternoon, the respirator went still.

The vigil began. At first, all was well.

But through the afternoon hours and into evening, the girl's breathing slowly grew more and more labored. By ten o'clock, Angel began to gasp, her lips turning blue. Liza and Garrison panicked and summoned the nurse on duty.

Within moments, the respirator was back on.

Minutes later, blue gave way to pink lips and Angel breathed evenly, albeit with the help of a machine. Garrison and Liza, chairs pulled up to opposite sides of the bed, each holding a swollen hand, watched the rise and fall of their daughter's chest.

Across the white covers, their gazes connected. Each mirrored the other's sentiment: We got past another crisis. Thank God she breathes.

Fighting despair, both Wakefields retreated to their separate quarters that evening, following a silent, barely touched dinner of leftover pizza. Neither wanted food.

Garrison poured his heart onto the canvas, wondering if his daughter would survive. Angrily, he pushed the thought away, dipping his brush into vibrant, living colors and transporting them to canvas, willing subsistence into the painting…willing Angel back from the darkness entombing her.

But not for long. His hands moved with purpose as the brush stroked and slashed and coaxed life to the creation. Despite air-conditioning, sweat beaded upon his furrowed brow, swelled to bursting, then trickled down his face. He didn't notice.

Music wafting from Angel's dance studio down the hall filled his heart with hope and vision for the future. And he looked up and caught sight of a needlepoint on Angel's wall. From a white background, tiny pink roses and green leaves meandered about large, bold black letters. A gold frame bordered it all. He moved closer to read the message, one from his daughter's heart: "Now faith is the substance of things hoped for and the evidence of things not seen….

His heart gave a leap. His lips curved into a slow certain smile.

You will come back, Angel. You will!

Tonight, after warm-up stretches, Liza's choice of music was unorthodox. But it seemed right. She loved the rich tones of John Barry compositions, especially his movie themes. She found that their deep, mellow sounds somehow drew upon her soul, releasing it into her movements. She inserted her *Somewhere in Time* movie soundtrack CD into the wall theater sound system. Rich melancholy strains filled the chamber and set her sore body into slow, sustained adage movements. And she found herself wondering as she moved, *how will Angel handle not being able to dance again?*

How will I handle it? The thought almost brought her movements to an abrupt halt, but something inside her kept her momentum going, something she couldn't quite wrap her mind around. Something otherworldly, subterranean, and yet to be known.

A peace settled over Liza. She didn't question it. She simply moved in it. Simultaneously, the catharsis of tranquility pushed back darkness just as the movement of dance chased away painful soreness.

Renewal set in.

She switched to another CD, one featuring balletic themes.

Soon, Liza no longer felt pain. Instead, she soared through transition paces to jetés and dizzying pirouettes, grande jetés and more pirouettes, segueing through rotating rhythms and moods.

Mirrors on all sides reflected her grace and brilliance, on and on, into infinity.

But she didn't see that. She saw Angel, rising from her deathbed, beautiful and vibrant.

Alive.

Liza felt tired. But it was a good tired, one that ensured deep rest. She and Garrison passed each other in the hall on their way to their separate beds. Garrison reached out to brush fingers, ever so gently, halting her in her tracks.

Their gazes collided. Confusion gripped her as her body instinctively reacted. Her emotions felt snatched up in a cyclone.

Then, another response rushed to the forefront – offense. Her heart was still too, too wounded.

Tears gathered suddenly and she rushed past her husband, hoping he didn't detect them.

Please…don't let him see my vulnerability.

chapter nine

Angel felt, at times, suspended between being and not be-ing. Somewhere in her mind's sphere, she was aware of sounds. Sporadically, she felt sensations...a needle pricking...metal sticks shoved under her tongue...and that huge thing jammed down her throat that forced air into her.

Pain. Gosh-awful pain. Here. There. Everywhere at times.

Mostly, she floated along a river of nothingness. Wrapped in a black cocoon.

But sometimes, her stubborn brain ticked on. Submerged visual fragments broke loose...a huge rehearsal room? Mama was dancing the ballet *Giselle*. She was so beautiful and grace-ful as she danced away to the far side of the chamber...Mama looked around and saw Angel...the music changed to "Allegro Brillante" as she spun in pirouettes around the room....

She turned and smiled her luminous smile, then beckoned to Angel to follow. "You can do it, darlin'!" Angel began to dance the same steps, exuberant and elated....but suddenly Mama stopped smiling and the room became shadowed.

"Point de toes! Point de toes!" cried Mama in a Russian ac-cent. "It is one movement, not three! One!" Mrs. Vollweiller's features superimposed over Mama's.

Terror struck Angel's heart. And failure. Instantly, Angel's legs grew heavy, then numb…and she toppled again into black nothingness.

Charlcy called Liza that week. Her sister, six years older and eons more worldly-wise, had finally landed back in the States. "I've got a two-hour layover here in Atlanta," she told Liza.

"It's great knowing you're back on home soil." Liza's voice vibrated with emotion.

"Shoot, sis," she said in her travel-weary, husked voice, "you know I'd a' been there the night of the accident, but I was halfway 'round the durned world when you gave me the news. And then you wouldn't let me come!"

"Only because I love you and wanted you to get your money's worth on the cruise." That was so true. It had been a sacrifice to forfeit her sister's presence.

"Anyway, thanks for keeping me updated. I'm gon' catch the next plane out, so keep a light in the window, now, y'hear?"

"God, it's good to know you'll soon be here, sis." Liza could hardly speak past the lump in her throat.

"That is, if you need me. I know you do, but Garrison might not feel that way. Don't wanna intrude if he doesn't, y'know? Folks react to these things differently."

"You gotta be kidding!" Liza's laugh was half sob "Honey, if I ever needed you in my life, it's now. And you know Garrison adores you." Then to lighten up for Charlcy's benefit, she added petulantly, "Probably more than he does me."

She picked Charlcy up at the Spartanburg-Greenville International Airport later that day. Humidity hung hot and sticky in the evening air when she got out to help load the luggage into Charlcy's Land Rover. Her sister had left it in the Wakefields' garage while on her jaunt. "You want to drive?" Liza offered. At Charlcy's refusal, she took the wheel.

"Garrison had to go back to the office for a while." Liza turned on the vehicle's air conditioner full blast. "He sends his love. He'll join us later at the hospital."

Charlcy leaned in, emitting a huff of Passion fragrance, and asked in a lusty voice, "Is he as pretty as ever?"

"Prettier," Liza replied, grinning. "Lots prettier than me."

Charlcy reached into her purse for a phantom Virginia Slims cigarette and already had the lighter on before she caught herself. "I keep forgetting I quit," she muttered with a wicked smile and tossed the lighter out the window. "And, no, I don't have any cigarettes tucked away in there."

"Thanks, Charlcy," Liza said with emotion.

"For what?" She peered at Liza.

"For quitting. I want you to stay around as long as I do. It's no fun being miserable all by myself." Liza's thankfulness knew no bounds in that moment.

They rode in silence for about two minutes. "Heard from Raymond?" Liza asked.

"Nope. And don't want to." Out of the corner of her eye, Liza saw the hand, now trembling, start to reach for a cigarette again and then draw back. "If I never see that no-account, sorry excuse for a human again, it'll be too soon."

Liza rolled her eyes and snorted. "Sorry I brought it up."

"Yeah." Silence stretched out for long moments. "Divorce is a horrible, vile thing. But being married is sometimes worse."

"Doesn't he want to reconcile?"

"Oh yeah." Charlcy clasped her hands in her lap, knuckles white. "Last time we talked – which was too many months back to count – he declared he'd come back in a heartbeat. With me, he had his cake and ate it, too. But I can't forgive him for that 'one night stand,' as he prefers to call it. That broke this old cow's back."

Can't forgive. How glibly those words flowed from the victim's lips. Pain pierced Liza's heart. "Do you think you could ever find it in your heart to forgive, if Raymond truly showed remorse?" Liza asked, desperately hoping the possibility to be there.

"I don't think so, Liza." Charlcy's reply was more sad than angry. "He's probably led a double life, at times, all throughout our marriage. Can't be sure, but I suspect it.

"That's sad," Liza murmured, especially the part about there being no room for mercy when one is violated past a certain point. She recalled how Charlcy had never quite been able to forgive their mother's many abuses, seemingly blinded to the reality that the illness – at intervals – had the power to drive Mama beyond any reasoning. Liza recalled, too, that it had been Charlcy who'd caught the brunt of physical abuse by repeatedly stepping between Liza and their mother. Protecting her little sister.

In Garrison's case of unforgivingness the violation was Liza's role in their daughter's tragedy. And even if Angel survived, her daughter would never again be whole.

If – a big if.

Which was far, far worse – at least in Liza's eyes – than adultery.

Charlcy's breath caught in her throat when she first glimpsed Angel's mangled features and grotesquely intubated, white-shrouded figure lying so still.

"Oh...my...Gawd," she breathed out slowly from the gut. She moved cautiously to the bedside and stared down at a distorted, unfamiliar face.

Liza felt tears gather as her usually stalwart sibling fought to make sense of the disaster lying before her. Charlcy's once pleasingly fluffy, round shape had, since the divorce proceedings, melted down several sizes, remaining at borderline thin. Her once "big" hair now waved in a tamer, yet modern, short style, maintaining its sun-streaked look by daily outdoor running.

Somehow, the new version seemed more vulnerable.

Liza held her breath.

Charlcy suddenly swooped down to Angel's ear. "Hey, baby girl! I know you're in there. Don't play with me, y'hear? You listen up good.

"I'm not gonna mope around and cry over this mess because that's not gonna help you. If anything, I'm gonna kick your butt to remind you to keep on fighting. I'll use my energy to help your mama get through this. Now you do your part and get yourself back here where you belong."

Then she ever so gently kissed the puffy cheek. "I love you, baby girl." Her voice quavered, then broke. "You hang in there, now, y'hear?"

Charlcy straightened, spun on her heel, and bolted from the room.

Liza didn't follow because she knew Charlcy wouldn't want to be seen crying.

Charlcy's return was god-sent.

Liza's sister was not due to resume teaching middle school Special Ed until early September. So she kept Liza company at Angel's bedside now, allowing Garrison more free reign when his business called. Fortunately, Charlcy didn't see what was going on between Garrison and Liza because Angel's bedside was the couple's one consistent together zone. Their one hundred percent truce arena.

Charlcy lived in Greenville, only a twenty-five minute jaunt via I-85 from the Spartanburg Regional Medical Center. On occasion, she would relieve Liza, allowing her to run errands or visit their father in the nursing home.

"Convincing Liza to leave Angel's side takes all my cunning and stealth," Charlcy was fond of saying.

"Ye-es," Liza would respond, raising her palm in supplication.

Liza was no longer at Garrison's mercy.

Oh, he wanted her to be there when he needed her. But she couldn't count on his coming through for her when the dirt was flying. Could she? Not really. She could not yet trust that to be the case.

Penny showed up again a the week after Charlcy's return. "This is so much nicer here at Restorative Care, being able to sit at her bedside," she said to Liza, who'd been writing in her little journal, one she kept tucked into her oversized purse.

"Angel always teased me about this big ol' handbag," Liza said, chuckling. "She called it my luggage bag, appalled at all the stuff I shoved inside it."

This was Charlcy's day to visit their father in the nursing home and Penny's visit was especially welcome. Today, Penny wanted to talk about Angel. Liza soaked up all the warm vignettes.

"She was the best cheerleader on the squad," Penny proudly decreed, smiling at the memories. "There wasn't anything she said 'no' to. She'd volunteer to do the most risky things. Remember her doing the double back flip off Sheila's shoulders?"

Liza nodded, raising an eyebrow. "I'm afraid I do."

"She was so fearless."

They sat for long moments, each lost in thought. "Do you think she'll ever —" Penny's eyes misted over.

"Cheer again?" Liza looked at her with sadness. "Probably not."

Even if she survives....

Reality intruded again. They both looked at Angel, so still, so far away from them. Penny's thoughts erupted on an impatient note. "Will she ever come back?" Then she slumped down in her seat, contrite. "I'm sorry, Mrs. W., I shouldn't say things like —"

"No. It's okay." Liza slowly shook her head. "I don't know, Penny. I want to believe she will. With all my heart, I'm hanging on to that possibility." She sighed heavily. "They keep asking me about organ donations, but I'm not — That's a difficult decision to deal with, you know?"

Suddenly, Penny's eyes widened, as though a light came on. "Do you have Angel's purse? Her billfold?"

Liza frowned. "I think so." She arose and went to the corner locker and opened it. She pushed the jeans, pink pullover, and Reeboks aside. "Here it is." She took the purse and went back to the bedside. Sitting back down, she spread the contents on her lap. She picked up the tan leather billfold and looked at Penny.

"May I?" Penny reached for the billfold and Liza handed it to her, puzzled.

Penny pulled cards from the slots and shifted through them. Then she dug deeper into other crevices. Finally, she stopped and turned one over. As she stared at it, her eyes brimmed with tears. She picked up another and read it, too.

Slowly, she handed them both to Liza. "Here it is."

Puzzled, Liza took the two cards. She unfolded and turned the larger card over. Its logo read "Donate Life South Carolina." It was a family notification card.

Dear Loved One,
I would like to donate life by being an organ and tissue donor. I want you to know my decision because you may be consulted before donation takes place.

Thank you for honoring my wishes and commitment to donate life through organ and tissue donation.

Beneath this was Angel's signature.

Through a blur of tears, Liza read the accompanying blue card, filled out in Angel's neat handwriting and headed, My Commitment to Donate Life, Uniform Donor Card:

I, Angel Wakefield, have spoken with my family about organ and tissue donation. At the time of my death, I wish to donate my organs and tissues.

Donor signature: Angel Wakefield
Date: April 3, 2008

Witness: Garrison Wakefield
Date: April 3, 2008

Witness: Troy Bailey
Date: April 3, 2008

Liza wiped her eyes and took the tissue Penny offered to blow her nose.

"How did you —"

"I just now remembered it. Angel told me awhile back that she and Troy both decided they wanted to be organ donors. It happened after they tried to save the injured dog's life – y'know, Scrounger? And it died, anyway. Remember?"

Liza nodded, overwhelmed.

"So she looked it up on the Internet, got the forms, and they both filled them out. Troy got his parents to sign. Angel said you were gone to visit her Papa Finch that day, and she went to her dad's office to get him to sign. Troy witnessed his signature and signed the other witness slot."

Liza slowly shook her head, perplexed. "Garrison didn't say anything." For some reason, that hurt her. He should have shared something this important with her.

Yet he didn't speak up even when asked about organ donation.

"Angel said her dad was really busy that day and she had to practically demand he take a minute and sign it. She said she doubted he even knew what it was he signed." Penny looked inordinately sad, then apologetic.

"Angel was always saying how she didn't think her dad loved her, y'know?" She rushed to add, "I would tell her that he most certainly did. But that day, she was disappointed that he didn't realize how much this meant to her. You know, how it could give life to somebody else? Angel said that he didn't even comment on it."

Liza's heart was near bursting with pain. "Excuse me, Penny." She didn't want to fall apart on Penny, so she arose and started for the bathroom.

Then she froze. Garrison stood in the doorway, face impenetrable, shoulder pressed to the jamb. She blinked. And in that instant she felt strangely betrayed. "How long have you been standing there?" she asked quietly.

"Long enough," he said sharply. Then he turned on his heel and disappeared down the hall.

"Oh my gosh." Penny arose, clearly stricken. "I'm so sorry, Mrs. W. I didn't mean to say anything that would upset anybody. I just – got carried away talking about Angel. Thinking about her –" She burst into tears and Liza gathered her into her arms. She held her until she snuffled and hiccuped.

"There, there," Liza murmured, sick at heart.

"I'm sorry," the girl whispered.

"You've got nothing to be sorry for. Don't worry, Penny. Nobody's mad at you."

"You won't want me to come back anymore." Her voice broke.

"No no. You come back just like always. I promise you, you won't ever hear anything negative from this." She hugged the girl again and walked her down the hall. At the elevator, she turned her to face her.

"Thanks, Penny." She smiled.

"For what?"

"For letting me know about the life donor card."

A big smile broke out over the young face, lightly tilting the tip of her freckled nose. There was a definite spring to Penny's step when she entered the elevator.

"How was Dad today?" Liza asked Charley later that afternoon when she came by from the nursing home.

"Mean as ever." Charley's laugh was boisterous and contagious. "He's got a girlfriend." Her astute blue eyes gauged Liza's reaction, pleased with the responsive grin. "On his good days, that is. That's when he gives her boxes of chocolates. On his bad ones, he cusses her out for stealing the candy." She shrugged elaborately and spread her hands. "Poor woman doesn't know which end's up. But then, she can't remember what all the fuss is about, anyway."

Liza laughed until her stomach ached. "Oh, Charlcy. You are so irreverent. So bad."

And Liza realized that this was Charlcy's breastplate – irreverence and toughness. It had armed Charlcy, the champion, through the early years' murky battle with an abusive parent.

Charlcy's face grew serious. "Which is better, to laugh or to cry? I figure if you can get some humor out of bad situations, who's to say it's wrong?"

"Yeah." Liza wiped her eyes, still chuckling. "Can't argue with that logic." She sobered up. "Thanks," she whispered.

Charlcy's head turned sharply. "For what?"

"For helping me to see sunlight in all this darkness."

"Shoot! You've practically carried me through this nasty divorce thing. And lots of other things to boot. Like Lindi moving to Atlanta to try her wings and ending up in rehab."

Liza sighed. Charlcy's only child was now in her early thirties. "She's got a happy marriage and a precious little girl. She's a great mother. All's well that ends well. You've weathered things quite nicely, sis."

The wizened blues rolled in derision. "Yeah. Right. Thank God she met Chuck and he put up with her through it all, loved her anyway. He's a candidate for Sainthood." She snorted. "You had a lot to do with keeping me and my baby girl from killing each other at times, Auntie. Seems like ages ago."

"Fifteen years is a long time," Liza sighed and smiled. "Doesn't seem that long."

Then she hiked up her wrist and looked at her watch. "It's bath time." She and Charlcy enjoyed giving Angel her daily sponge bath. It pleased the staff that they assumed this duty and it gave the sisters a sense of contact that only hands on accomplished.

During those daily twenty minutes of cleansing, Liza blossomed.

Dr. Abrams came by on his rounds just as they finished. He checked Angel's vitals, read her chart, and started to leave.

"Wait," Liza said, reaching for her purse. She pulled out the cards. "We found these in Angel's purse."

He looked at the life donor cards. Then he looked at Liza, his eyes searching hers.

"I'm good with it," Liza said. "That's what she wants."

He nodded. "Let's pray it doesn't come down to that."

That evening, Liza drove home alone. Garrison had worked at the office and called to say he would be a little late. At the house, she went to the kitchen to find sandwich chow. Eating alone had never been her favorite thing, but she was adapting quite well. Garrison would be along shortly.

Ham, Swiss cheese, tomato, lettuce, and slices of rye bread swiftly morphed into a relatively nutritious dinner. Just as she sat down in front of the television, she heard Garrison's Jag pull into the garage.

"Got any more of that?" he asked on his way to the kitchen.

"In the fridge," she replied. At one time, she would have laid her food aside, bolted into the kitchen, and prepared his plate. But then, he would have joined her and helped, chatting about his and her day as they worked.

Not any longer.

Plate in hand, he came into the den, each of them seemingly on different planets. They both watched the evening news as though it were announcing the end of time. Liza kept hoping he would broach the subject of today's eavesdropping incident at the hospital.

Finally, she laid her half eaten sandwich aside and came right to the point. "Why didn't you tell me about the life donor card?"

He looked at her for long moments, guarded. "You never asked." His reply was cool and flat.

"That's ridiculous!" she exploded. "The doctors flooded us with questions as to her wishes. I can't believe that you never mentioned something so...so important to Angel. How could you not share it with me?"

He stared off into space for several heartbeats, his features tightly shut down, then shrugged limply.

That fired her up even more. "First, you stood at the hospital door and eavesdropped. You could have let us know of your arrival but chose not to. Then after hearing Penny's account, you simply stood there, making sure Penny and I knew of your presence."

He gazed at the far wall, silence humming.

She huffed, exasperated. "You could have at least quietly left for a minute, pretended you hadn't heard, spared poor Penny the embarrassment. But no, entitled one, you didn't. Then when I needed some explanation, you just walked away."

Liza glared at him, waiting. When he remained as silent as a sealed tomb, she shot to her feet and marched to the kitchen with her plate, dumped the half eaten food down the garbage disposal, and turned it on. She ground her teeth together as the machine whirred and grated.

"Blasted egomaniac," she muttered, washing her plate and glass and slamming them into the dish rack to drain. "Thinks he's above explaining himself to mere mortals."

She let out the dishwater and dashed to get the dust mop in the pantry.

Her feet skidded to a halt. Garrison blocked her way.

"Pardon me," she spat and started to skirt around him. His hand caught her arm.

She looked meaningfully at his grip on her. "Please let me go," she enunciated with crisp hostility.

"Liza, I forgot."

She blinked and looked up into his face. Embarrassment rode his expression. "Forgot what?" she asked, perplexed.

"I forgot to tell you." His gaze flickered and he looked away, releasing his hold on her. He pulled out a bar stool and plopped tiredly onto it.

She pulled out a stool facing him. "To tell me *what* exactly?"

He looked at her then. His features now appeared inordinately weary, wiped of all defenses. Awash with humility. "Angel came to me that day when I was in the middle of the big Sheraton Hotel account deadline." He ran both hands through his hair and threw back his head, eyes closed. "I heard Penny mention Angel today and I stopped, not wanting to interrupt. And when she began telling you about the day –"

He looked at Liza then, his eyes miserable. "I honestly had forgotten about Angel coming to me that day. Angel was right when she told Penny she doubted I even realized what she was talking about." He shook his head, his voice dropping. "I barely remember her and Troy being there at that time.

"It's worse than forgetting," he muttered with shame. "I honestly didn't hear what she was saying. I was so caught up in my infernal deadline of the moment that her excited chatter passed right over my stupid head, got on my nerves. I had this monster headache and every syllable she spoke was like driving a spike into my brain. So I turned off her high-pitched voice, wishing she'd just hurry and leave so I could meet my deadline. All I remember of it was the word 'donor.' At the time, I never connected that word with 'organ.' I thought it was one of her endless cheerleaders' fund-raising things, like you with your charities and causes. I signed the card without knowing exactly what it was, Liza."

The starch went out of Liza. His naked remorse disarmed her. How many times had she herself missed the mark in life? Failed someone? It happened to everyone at some point.

She felt his anguish.

"I'd give anything to go back –" His voice broke and he leaned his head into his hands, elbows on the bar, the picture of contrition.

Liza's heart lurched and she started to go to him. Then, just as suddenly, she backtracked to how reluctant he'd been to forgive her. She froze, unable to reach out.

"I sympathize, Garrison. It's a shock finding that no one is perfect, not even oneself, isn't it?" She gave him a gentle pat on the shoulder on her way out.

As soon as she got to her bedroom, she found that she felt rotten.

Somehow, his comeuppance left her with a bitter aftertaste.

Later that evening, Garrison stood before his easel. He had come to full terms with his father-deficiency. He'd spent time going over all the times he recalled Angel coming to him, the times he'd pushed her away because of his workload or other reasons no longer worth consideration. It all, he now realized, went back to his young days of emotional isolation. He'd learned to retreat into himself, to insulate himself from the outside world, one that inflicted hurt.

God help him – he'd used that denial defense against his own daughter. Then he'd agonized over it until he could no longer bear it. So he'd repented to the Creator, to himself, and, in his heart, to Angel. Until he could do so directly to her, he knew he needed to forgive himself.

All he could do now was to hold on to the reality of her renewal. He no longer thought in terms of recovery. Old things passed away. All things new.

His paintbrush tonight stroked and coaxed as the painting transformed into a gateway to renewal. It floodgated memories of *when*. From down the hall, Liza's favorite music wafted to him, harmonizing with the brush's rhythm of creation, giving birth to new heart insights of things to come.

New things. Better things.

The music swelled, as if hearing his heart. Each stroke of color, of light and revelation, gave dimension. The painting... the dance music...they formed a new song.

"A song of renewal," he murmured.

The brush shaped and highlighted Liza's eyes. He'd worked painstakingly to achieve just the right expression, one of goodness and selflessness and fulfillment. When completed, this painting would freeze the Wakefields' image of the lily pond outing, beneath the Love Tree, with them experiencing the sheer joy of being together.

Liza sprang to life, threatening to leap from the canvas as tears misted his vision. He blissfully swiped the moisture away and continued to add light to the scene...a stroke here... a brush there...until it shimmered gloriously, threatening to pull him in.

He threw back his head and laughed aloud, daring the dark specters that had hovered so long over his family to intrude on this moment's happiness. "Go back to hell, where you came from," he called out, deriding them. "You're outta here!"

His boldness astonished even him. The call to love, nurture, and protect family overwhelmed him, deluging him until he felt he would drown in it.

He looked at the face on canvas again, reverently this time. His gaze finally settled on Liza's eyes. Joy, love, and light spilled from them. And then he saw something else there in the blue, blue depths. Trust. It mule-kicked his solar plexus and his heart tripped into syncopation.

"Garrison, old boy," he husked, fighting powerful, surging emotions, "you're on your way."

chapter ten

Several nights later, Garrison heard music from the studio. It enticed him…like a siren's song. What was Liza doing in her private moments? Curiosity stirred as it had in those college days, when they went to their separate dormitory rooms at night. It pricked and tickled his brain. As his hands propelled the life-giving brush from pallet to canvas, his mind conjured up a scene from the long-ago past. Liza's fluid, graceful movements…her arms and hands flowing artfully, in harmony with her body's interpretive expressions. Perfect coordination. She'd always had it. He ached for her touch.

Heck, just now, he'd settle for her undivided, civil attention. He was so not happy with the shoe being on the other foot and the what-goes-around-comes-around.

But if anybody deserved to eat crow, he did.

The music ended. He stopped his movements, laid down the brush, and managed to slip into the hallway just as she ventured toward the stairwell. He tried not to stare at her sensual shape beneath her silk robe as she moved toward him. She looked a little self-conscious, magenta marking her high cheekbones. But her lips echoed his tentative smile.

In recent days, she'd seemed less resistant to him. Tonight, her eyes still held a measure of wariness, but he noted that she did come to a halt before him, at a much closer range – within reach, actually.

Everything in him wanted to gamble tonight, to take her by the hand, lead her down the hall into Angel's room, and show her the painting, to maybe convince her of his love, despite the chasm still separating them.

He gazed into the blue depths of her eyes, ones swirling with myriad emotions, so mixed he could not isolate or decipher any one of them, except one. Hunger. The insignia was distinct and clear.

He lifted his hand to touch her cheek and, for a moment, she closed her eyes and accepted the touch, seeming to lean into it. In the next instant, her lids lifted and she gazed at him, sorrow and fear etched into her features.

In a heartbeat, she was gone – leaving Garrison with the lingering herbal fragrance of her hair. He closed his eyes and willed the canvas vision to somehow, in that dark cosmos, reach Angel. To reach Liza.

Antiseptic odors tickled Angel's nose, then…nothingness.

Slowly, darkness scattered, like a kaleidoscope shift…a blond-haired teen girl's reflection smiled back at her from the shimmery pond covered with fragrant white and crimson water lilies. The lush aroma of water and vegetation completed the bouquet. Resting on a thick carpet of pine needles covering the forest floor, she saw Mama at a distance, now joined by Daddy. They motioned to her, their lips moving, but…she couldn't hear. She floated toward them but an invisible wall stopped her…something else tried to emerge from a mist. It was shadowy and elusive….Troy.

The look on his face drew her. He was trying to say something to her, but she couldn't wrap her mind around it. She struggled to reach him, knowing him to be an anchor that would somehow tether her to something solid. She couldn't understand what he was trying to tell her. And he wouldn't come nearer. Why? But just as her frantic hands reached out, she began to float...the sunlight dimmed and shadows fell all about her. *Nonono!*

She tried to speak, but felt lifted higher and higher from the voices. From Troy.

Was she on a cloud? No, because the blackness began to wrap around her again, tightening, the cocoon growing firm and comfortable and familiar....

Liza moved uneasily through those following days. Dressing for the hospital that morning, she heard Garrison moving about in the kitchen, making coffee. Within moments, he quietly entered the dressing room, deposited her cup of coffee before her, and left. She felt his gaze upon her but avoided direct eye contact. Too hazardous.

"Thanks," she called after him. Resisting his overtures was becoming less of a struggle. After all, he was a gentleman and he would not force himself upon her. She depended upon that. She had to smile at his darned manners.

She applied lipstick, then blotted it, staring at herself in the dressing room mirror. And yet – was he really as enamored as he seemed? Or was it simply holy lust? She herself fought it daily. Every time she looked at him. He'd not, after all, really talked to her in any depth in recent days. But then, she'd not truly encouraged substance-discussions, had she?

The only common ground they had these days was Angel. Liza's mascara wand paused midair. The reality whammied her. How far apart they'd grown. Outside their parenting bond, all she felt was the sexual awareness. Sex. Her eyes rounded on that note. But that didn't constitute the kind of love they'd once had. The "being there" brand. The "I'll never leave you, no matter what" kind.

Dear God, she'd grown absolutely paranoid. Or were her fears justified? She put away her makeup paraphernalia and went into the bedroom. Immediately her gaze lit on a family photo of them at Angel's tenth birthday party. Liza picked it up and gazed longingly into the three laughing faces beneath silly pointed hats. The images grew misty. How happy they'd been.

Purposefully she set it down. She grabbed her purse and joined Garrison in the foyer. This being Sunday, Garrison's only full day off to spend at Angel's bedside, he snatched his brief-case from the closet and filled it with papers from the office to study later. He added a James Patterson novel for when he finished that task. Liza had noticed him reading more lately. That helped, in her estimation, to ease the strain of silence. Liza also brought along a book, one penned by Francine Rivers, who laced her upbeat, fun stories together with strong moral fiber.

Once at the hospital, she leaned over Angel's bed and took hold of her fingers. "Garrison, look. Her fingernails look bluish to me. And her hands are cold as ice."

He peered at them, his dark eyes troubled. "I'll get the nurse." He darted out the door. He returned with a nurse in tow, who reset the level of the oxygen machine. Soon, her fingernails reverted to a pinkish cast and her hands warmed. Liza and Garrison both drew deep, thankful breaths and gazed at each other in mutual understanding.

How long until the next crisis?

Liza smiled. The overture came spontaneously, and she meant it as encouragement. Garrison looked at her for a long moment, features solemn, unrelenting, and then turned his attention back to his novel's pages.

Liza understood.

After all, a man had his pride. And she knew she'd hurt him badly at times with her arm's length stance. She hadn't meant to. God knew she loved him and didn't want to inflict hurt on anybody, especially not Garrison. But self-preservation would remain high on her agenda for the remainder of Angel's recovery.

Garrison had used the word renewal. Angel must first survive.

Survive. Always with that thought came more qualms. How did she even know that Angel would recover? The long days of sitting and hoping were taking their toll on her. How many times could disappointment beat a person down before she lost the tenacity to pull herself back up?

"Angel won't ever dance again," she said softly, matter-of-factly, knowing it to be so. "But," she looked at her husband, "that's not the important thing, is it?"

He shook his head sadly. "No. No, it's not. Just to have her back awake – that's what I'm praying for."

Liza sighed heavily. "Me too. But it would be nice if she could recognize us."

"Yeah," he murmured, this time his lips echoed her sad smile.

"Y'know, whatever happens with us – this is one place our hearts connect," she said softly.

His eyes flickered to unrest for a long moment. "That's true."

And she knew it would always be.

"I'm going to take a walk," Garrison said, rising from the chair. "My legs need stretching. I have my cell phone, in case you need me."

"Sure," Liza replied, looking up from the book in her hand. He saw the wariness in her face and wished to God it wasn't there. She glanced at the wall clock. 1:45. "Take your time. I'm going to visit Dad in a little while. It's my turn." Even fitting in the nursing home visit, Garrison knew she would still have plenty of time with Angel today. Visiting hours ended at nine each evening and they stayed until the last second, leaving only when the staff chased them out.

Garrison set off down the corridor, relieved to move about. He'd felt unusually restless today. At times, the stress nearly crushed him. He missed Liza, both physically and emotionally.

What a lousy curve life had thrown him. Immediately, he shook his head. He couldn't afford to look at things like that. *That's exactly what I don't need. A pity party.*

Down the corridor, something about the polished mahogany door beckoned to him. He approached it and tried the handle. It opened and he felt an overwhelming sense of welcome upon entering.

The little chapel was quiet, but it was the peaceful kind; the kind that blankets and soothes. At that precise moment, that was exactly what Garrison needed. His gaze traveled to the wooden cross on the white wall, then moved down to the crimson carpet. The stark colors stirred the artist in him. He lowered himself to a velvet-cushioned pew, took a deep calming breath, and soaked up the moment's serenity.

When he returned to join Liza, hoping for some moments of warmth and camaraderie, he found her laid back in the partially reclined chair, asleep. He spotted her small journal, one she carried with her at all times, spread out open across her lap. Dangling, actually. One move and it would clatter to the floor. The pen lay in her relaxed fingers, atop today's entries.

He crossed quietly to shift the notebook to a more secure position, but he stopped when his eye caught the words, "What must I do? Without trust, our marriage cannot survive. How can I entrust my heart to someone who cannot forgive me? Who would abandon me in my darkest hour? I cannot."

Garrison stepped back, stunned. His integrity wouldn't allow him to read more of her private entries. But the claim gave him pause. Did she still detect unforgiveness on his part? Was it still there?

Truthfully? There were moments when he thought he let it go, when they were at Angel's side and he felt that their very souls wrapped around each other. There were other times, when melancholy hit him hardest and the scene of that tragic night replayed over and over, that he still drew apart from her. Especially in the wee hours when the whys were the worst, when his defenses were down.

The best he could hope for now was that their current truce would endure until the crisis passed. For better or worse, it would pass. It would give them both time to regroup and see what remained of their marriage. That invisible atom of doubt pierced his heart. Could he live without Liza?

He didn't want to find out.

The bottom line was that he loved her. At least she'd stopped bolting every time he came near her. But he couldn't argue with her heartrending journal sentiments. She wrote what she believed to be true.

Hands shoved in slacks' pockets, he moved to stare out the window into another hot, humid day. His cell phone's ring broke his reverie, startling Liza awake as well. She caught her toppling journal and tucked it quickly into her nearby oversized purse as he answered his call.

"Yes, Gwen?" He listened for long moments, then said, "I'll be there shortly."

He turned to Liza, who, now awake, eyed him guardedly. "I've got to go to the office for a while."

"On a Sunday?" She frowned, bewildered and still groggy.

"Duty calls," he offered with a long, weary sigh. "Another deadline push."

He started to lean and kiss his wife good-bye, but the look on her face quickly changed his mind. Despite his best intentions and desires, he couldn't put Humpty Dumpty back together. He couldn't unscramble quiche. Something else would have to renew them.

He sucked in a deep breath then blew it out, hoping to release his apprehension with it. He tried to push away the off-kilter feeling, that not-quite-right sensation. He tried to remember that most of what he felt resulted from the tragedy. Tried to remember that Liza was at least pleasant with him. And that was something to build on. Wasn't it?

Still, the unrest refused to budge.

He started toward the door, stopped, and turned to look for a long moment at her, his heart feeling extremely tender.

He said quietly, "I do love you, you know." Then he was gone.

Liza watched him leave. His long stride and confident bearing rang a dissonant note inside her. She watched the nurse's face as she passed Garrison on her way in to check Angel's vitals. Appreciation flashed in the woman's eyes.

Liza was familiar with other females' awareness of her husband's male beauty…his presence. It hadn't ever bothered her before. She'd always marveled that he'd chosen her to be his life's partner. Was proud of that fact.

So why now? She couldn't exactly put her finger on why, but suddenly she was bothered somewhat. She suspected it had to do with her insecurity, her fear of abandonment, and the knowledge that others waited in the wings to take her place.

Somehow, Liza felt she'd hit upon the root of her agitated emotions. Good. Maybe she could put it all to rest now.

After the nurse left, Liza called Charlcy to see if she would come stay with Angel while Liza made the nursing home trek. Charlcy readily agreed. Liza settled down with her book again. She became engrossed and time passed swiftly. The next time she looked at the big wall clock, it was two thirty. A strange sound caught her ear. It came from Angel, and she rushed to her bedside. She realized that Angel's breathing was turning into a rattle. Her lips were bluish.

"Oh God!" She clamored to push the bedside button. "Nurse, please come! Something's wrong!"

With shaking fingers, she punched in Garrison's cell phone number. No answer.

Frantic, Liza hung up. Of all times for Garrison to be gone.

John, the respiratory specialist on duty, rushed into the room and began to attach a pump to drain excess fluid from Angel's breathing passage. "Is she going to be all right?" Liza moaned.

John flashed an encouraging smile. "A few more minutes, she'll be fine. You just relax. Go get yourself a cup of coffee while I finish this procedure."

Instead, Liza retreated to a quiet, more private waiting room down the corridor, one in which doctors held court with caretakers. Once swallowed by an easy chair there, she lowered her head, squeezed her eyes shut, and willed her shaking body to stillness. It was at moments like this that the gravity of Angel's condition became a three-dimensional, glaring reality… hat she realized just how closely death hovered.

Where are you, Garrison?

࿆

Angel saw the light, a fine point that pierced the darkness, a glimmer, really. She swirled toward it, as one in a wind tunnel. After traveling a long way, it grew nearer and brighter… bigger. It glowed like the sun and, at a distance, she saw Troy standing at the tunnel's end. He smiled, but then the smile faded. She called to him. At least she thought she did. He didn't respond, merely looked at her as though in disapproval. Bewildered, she struggled to move on toward him. But her legs wouldn't work, darn it! She tried to twist, turn, and somehow gain momentum to reach him. But she was suddenly tethered tightly to stillness. Then the water came up, up, cold and chilling, sucking her under. Cold! Freezing. Immersed…sinking, sinking…sinking… light getting dimmer.

Stopped sinking…smooth level surface…floating….

Voices…Mama, "Is she going to be all right?"

Man, "You just relax…go get…coffee…."

Pain…throat…pain!

Blackness.

Liza drove from the nursing home. With Garrison gone, Charlcy had relieved her in the late afternoon to allow her to visit her father. Today, her dad had been somewhere else entirely, not recognizing her at all. She supposed she would eventually grow accustomed to it.

Like with Angel? The thought, from left field, stunned her.

Angel would come back. Wouldn't she? The enormity of what-ifs overwhelmed her in that moment, made her think she might need to dip into those tranquilizers again. She instantly vetoed that.

Back at the hospital, Charlcy sat at the bedside, talking quiet nonsense to Angel. "Yeah, that sucker just wouldn't stop his jawing about −" She spotted Liza. "Hi. Sis. How was Pops?"

"Out to lunch. Actually, on vacation." She plopped tiredly into the other chair, kicked off her shoes and flexed her feet in the welcome cool air. "I talked with the doctor. They're going to change his medicine – you know, the cholinesterase inhibitors. They rev up the levels of acetylcholine in his brain. They play a key role in memory and learning. Dr. Bright says he's pretty optimistic about their effectiveness."

"That's great, sis. I'd like to see him be himself again."

"Me too." Liza yawned hugely, closing her weary eyes.

"Hmm. You okay? You seem more tired than usual."

Liza looked at her. "Angel had a breathing problem earlier today. Started rattling and –"

"Why didn't you tell me?" Charlcy demanded, visibly shaken by the news.

"I was still too upset to talk about it. I'm sorry, I just get to the point where I'm on…overload. You know, like tilt?"

"I'll bet you were scared to death." Charlcy's astute blue gaze skewered Liza, concern vibrating in her voice. "Was Garrison still here when it happened?"

"No, he'd already left to go back to the office and then I couldn't reach him. No answer when I called his phone. I have no idea where he was."

"I saw him as I drove into town this afternoon, around three-thirty or so. He was coming out of the Ritz Hotel."

"Oh?"

"Yeah," Charlcy said, "There was a redhead walking out with him. They were talking. Anyway, I thought they were together." She shrugged indifferently. "They might not have been. But I'm pretty sure it was Garrison." She huffed. "That was Raymond, I'd say they were together, but Garrison? Nah."

Then she frowned. "He'd want to know about Angel's breathing problem, y'know?"

"Right. That would have been Gwen, his assistant, with him. A business meeting there, no doubt." Probably was. She just didn't like the little pit-gut feeling she got when she knew they were together. Rotten jealousy. But not the normal kind. Liza knew the relationship was platonic. It was just that Garrison spent more time with Gwen than he did with her.

Charlcy looked at Liza and, despite her attempt at *savoir faire*, her eyes revealed a touch of anguish. "Wish I'd been so lucky in my husband choice. Garrison's nothing like that no-good ex of mine, who's not seen his daughter in months. Breaks Lindi's heart because not only does he ignore her, but he ignores Tootie, too. Once, he doted on his granddaughter." She huffed and shook her head. "Not anymore. Garrison's a real hands-on daddy. A true blessing, you know?"

"I know, he should be here later." Liza said, shaking her head, then changed the subject. "By the way, how are Lindi and Chuck getting along since their move back to South Carolina?"

"Great. Chuck's business is picking up after a slow start and Tootie loves her pre-school. Lindi's job there as a teacher's aide is going well and at the same time, she's close to Tootie."

"That's great, sis." She was glad she'd rerouted Charlcy from her marital discord issues. Again, she felt that urge to dump all her own woes on Charlcy's strong shoulders.

Liza's instincts were suddenly totally at odds with each other. On the one hand, she wanted to throw herself into Charlcy's arms, squall like a newborn, and spill the whole load. At the same time, every sixth sense screamed against Charlcy's knowing that Garrison held Liza accountable for Angel's and Troy's tragedy.

Once Charlcy knew, there was no chance for her to un-know. No way could Liza freely bust up that mutual admiration thing between her sister and husband. A thing that went all the way back and had always, in some mystical way, assuaged some of the guilt Liza had carried, having witnessed her sister's younger years' emotional starvation.

In Garrison, Charlcy had the nearest thing to a doting brother she would ever know, with whom she shared total respect, spontaneity, trust, and unfeigned affection. One into whose capable, nurturing hands, she could finally, in good conscience, place her little sister.

Liza's pulse pounded in her ears, as if a cannon had discharged nearby. *I will not take that tranquilizer that calls out my name.* Liza excused herself, went to the bathroom and splashed her face with cold water, blotted it dry, and took long, soothing breaths. Slowly, her staccato pulse slowed to a peaceful rhythm. Then beneath the running warm water faucet, her icy fingers thawed.

It was settled. Number one, Charlcy thought Garrison could hang the stars and moon. Number two, if that faith were destroyed by Liza's divulgence of Garrison's unforgiveness, Charlcy's dissonant-medley of genes might not render mercy to a Garrison who emotionally abandoned her little sister.

After all, Charlcy had never truly forgiven their mother for being bipolar, something her mom could not help. Could not, in fact, forgive Raymond, the father of her child.

Like Garrison can't forgive me.

Never mind the differences in grievances. Forgiveness is forgiveness. And she'd rather not test the waters between Charlcy and Garrison just now.

No. She definitely could not juggle more guilt.

She thought about Garrison. What a contradiction he was. The man who had loved her so completely was later willing to leave her at her lowest point in life. Could he be two people? How could he, who at one time felt so passionately about her, now refuse to release her from a cruel, unmerciful judgment?

No. She would go this alone, whatever the outcome.

Liza would simply believe for the best.

Liza watched Charlcy leave an hour later, reflecting on how her sister had chosen teaching as her calling.

Her big sister had dressed Liza for recitals and applauded her budding talents. At the same time, by weather-woman reading of their mother's bipolar flip-flops and rear-guarding Liza, Charlcy had perfected the art of sailing perilous waters.

To Liza and their dad, Charlcy had become a force of nature.

Thus, Charlcy's heavy load could only be lightened by yoking with like creatures. She'd decided to teach special ed, a choice only her brilliant, overcharged psyche could rationalize. Liza had wondered at that decision, but then decided that Charlcy, from somewhere deep in her gene mosaic, had drawn on a primitive strain of nobility.

Who was Liza to second-guess her nurturer?

Today, in the quietness of Restorative Care, Liza drank a cold Coke from the bottle, savoring its effervescent, chilly flow to her stomach, relaxed and contemplative – when her mind spun back to another day when she received a call from Charlcy.

Liza had listened to her sister's ever-evolving dialogue through the years and always understood. Unlike Charlcy, she'd not actually taken all the pummeling but had, from the sidelines, like standing on the side of a busy interstate, absorbed the *whooshing* impact of the barreling eighteen-wheeler's violence and velocity.

Liza *felt* Charlcy's heartrending howl for redemption. Experienced by osmosis the need for a raison d'être, a term Charlcy, in her halting French, often used. "Come on, God," she would wail when strain graduated to overkill, "give me a raison d'être, a daggum *reason* for this shipwrecked history!"

Other times the dialogue was poignant and melancholy.

"These kids in special ed with their desolate wishes just a'spilling from their big ol' eyes tug at my heartstrings, you know?"

In the beginning of those first, passionate years, Charlcy poured herself into each student, feeling that her own needy years equipped her with the compassion to help reach the untouchable places and guide them to impossible success.

Liza had watched, year after year, as the hope inside her sister first exploded and lit up the heavens. Later, it flashed and scattered skinny rays helter-skelter. Then it finally sparked and fizzled. So many failures. So many kids from whom the teacher Charlcy failed to excavate and eradicate the torment. So many tears and snotty noses she'd wiped…yet unable to wipe away the bleakness of unattainable goals and unavoidable learning fiascos.

Liza felt her sister's pain and knew Charlcy's desperation came from trying to relive her own pathetic childhood through these children, feeling that somehow, if she could navigate them to stunning success and happiness, all her own losses might pale beneath their brilliance.

One day, after a particularly heartbreaking disappointment, Charlcy had called Liza. She usually stoically dealt with whatever popped up in her classroom world of disorder, peril, and lunacy. That day was somehow different. Charlcy seemed poised on the brink of something gaping and ravenous, lusting to suck her in.

"Remember me telling you about Willie, the one-eyed black boy? He's always been a challenge, but today he –" For an instant, Charlcy's voice choked and Liza's antennae shot up. Charlcy rarely cried. She heard a deep sucking-in breath and release. "Today he was absolutely a terror. When I told him to sit he spun around and pointed his finger in my face, shouting,

'If I want to talk to you, I'll talk to you,' and called me a few choice names."

"Ah, sis," Liza moaned, knowing how Charlcy had tried to help Willie "find himself."

"Oh that was just the beginning, honey. When I took his arm to march him to the principal's office, he swung around and hit me in the face with his fist." She snorted, but to Liza it sounded like a half sob, followed by moments of silence and a lot of throat clearing.

"Were you hurt?" Liza asked gently, her heart breaking because she knew that Charlcy felt that her great, healing love had been thrown back in her face, unrequited, something she had experienced so insolently in days past.

"Hey!" Charlcy's bravado emerged full force. "A black eye is all. Heck, I'm no stranger to those, doncha know?"

"I'm so sorry, Charlcy. I know how much you've prayed for that boy and –"

A harsh, disparaging laugh erupted from the other end of the line. "Pray? I wonder sometimes if there really is a God."

"Charlcy! You don't mean that." Liza was shocked. Through all the turbulence of their lives, she'd never before heard Charlcy sink to this level of despair. Almost, but not quite. Though faith had many times been stalwart Charlcy's last resort, this denouncement undermined all the rock-bottom support that had, in the midnight hours, hurtled her up, over, and beyond ceasefires.

Liza gripped the receiver, eyes closed against gathering tears. "Please don't mean that, Charlcy," she whispered.

"Right at this moment? Honestly?" That ferocious burst of energy, unique to her sister, staccatoed her voice, sizzled over the airwaves and into the phone. "Yeah. I really do mean that. A god that lets women like our mother bring children into the world and create monsters and misfits like I teach every day, whose stupidity and cruelty is passed on from one lunatic generation to the next? I'm sorry, kid, but I'm a little jaded at this precise moment in time."

Liza took a deep, steadying breath and exhaled the shock. "You'll feel better after a night's rest, sis. Just – let it go. Willie's an extremely troubled kid. You've always known that. If you couldn't help him, then no one could. At least not on this level of counseling."

"And how was your day, Tinker Bell?" Charlcy shucked the anger like an October snakeskin. Liza chuckled tightly and chatted for a few more moments, tamping down uneasiness and playing along with her sister's game of "what problem? Who's got a problem?"

Another pathetic episode of the invincible woman-child.

Today, in the hospital, Liza grieved that so much was stolen from her family through the years. Charlcy, the protector, in particular.

Please, God, Liza prayed, *help Charlcy's faith. We need it right now. For Angel.*

Later at home, Liza and Garrison had quick cheese, ham, and tomato sandwiches, neither really eating much. Garrison yawned sleepily and asked, "How did things go at the hospital?"

"Angel had a breathing problem develop. She started rattling and turning blue –"

Garrison's entire body went instantly on alert. "Why didn't you call me?"

"I tried but I couldn't reach you. You weren't at the office."

He frowned. "I was there. My phone must have been –" He stopped, looking a bit bewildered. He shrugged tensely. "I don't know. I didn't hear it." Then his gaze cleared. He snapped his fingers. "Oh, I forgot. I left it in the outer office after making some business calls. I even had a business meeting at the Ritz. I found it later. I'm sorry, Liza." He shook his head, clearly troubled. "What did they do to correct Angel's breathing?"

"John, the respiratory specialist, came in when she had the attack." Liza went on to explain the treatment process to him in detail and he seemed to relax.

He ate quietly as she sipped coffee and pondered the day's events.

"In the future," he said as he arose, "I'll be more careful with my phone. I need to be accessible."

"That would be wise." She realized that her earlier sense of panic had ebbed. For the moment, she would enjoy the peace.

chapter eleven

Penny watched as Cindy, the nurse, worked with Angel's arms and hands, flexing each joint. She bent the hand back at the wrist and then forward. She flexed the elbows and lifted the arms at the shoulder joints, rotating them.

"Does that really help?" Penny asked.

"Oh, yes." The nurse shook her head emphatically. "It helps with their range of motion. Keeps them flexible."

Penny's eyes lit up and she grinned across the bed at Liza, who sat facing her. "That means that when she wakes up, she'll be good to go."

"You bet." *Thank you, dear Penny.* Liza's heart lifted at the optimism of those words. At least for the moment she could entertain a ray of sunshine.

Nurse Cindy moved to clean Angel's eyes and apply eye-drops. "This keeps her eyes moist." She addressed Penny, who now stood on the opposite side of the bed, hanging over and watching the procedure at close range.

The nurse then took a stick with a padded end, dipped it in antiseptic – a mint-scented solution – and proceeded to swab out Angel's mouth, with close attention to her tongue, gums, teeth, inside cheeks, and the roof of her mouth. "That thing looks like what you polish shoes with," Penny remarked, "except the stick is longer."

"This is strictly for sanitation upkeep." Nurse Cindy winked at her and tossed the swab into a trash can. "You want the spec to bathe her?" she asked Liza.

Liza chose to bathe Angel herself, with Penny's assistance.

Thirty minutes later, Angel's face appeared less wan, with freshly scrubbed skin. Liza leaned over her and whispered encouragement into her ear. "Everything's gonna be okay, darlin'. Keep on fighting, y'hear?"

Penny gasped. "Her fingers moved. Look, they curled up into a fist!"

Liza excitedly called in the on-duty nurse to see.

"Just reflex," said the nurse, smiling sympathetically after examining the fingers.

After she left, Liza straightened the sheets over Angel, hiding her disappointment from Penny. "False alarm. But it will happen."

"Got that right." Penny grinned and shot her a thumbs-up.

"I wish we could powder and perfume her," Penny murmured regretfully. "But I know the rules. It would mess with her breathing."

Two orderlies came in to turn Angel to her side, being careful about repositioning her casted legs. This process took place every two hours, night and day, to help with circulation and prevent blood clots.

Penny took her bedside seat and grinned at Liza across the sheets. "She always smelled so good." Reminiscing, her voice dropped to a reverential hush. "I'd ask her what scent she was wearing and she'd tell me something different every time. Did she really change perfume that often?"

"Oh, yeah." Liza laughed. "Some girls turn into clothes horses? Well, Angel's passion has always been fragrances. Her dresser top is full. Her taste is great, mind you. It's just that she gets bored easily with the same old thing."

"Yeah," Penny nodded, enthusiasm building. "She was always the one who came up with new ideas for the cheering squad. Coach always gave her space to at least experiment with fresh moves. Most of her ideas worked." Her face grew sad. "Coach really, really misses her input." Her shoulders gave a limp shrug. "Everybody misses her."

They sat quietly for long moments, and then Penny unexpectedly giggled. "I remember one time when she —"

Garrison's sudden appearance stifled Penny's exultant flow. "Hi, Penny," he said warmly. "Don't let me interrupt you."

"We were just reminiscing about Angel," Liza said, smiling encouragingly at Penny. She knew by the look on Penny's face that she was replaying how Garrison had acted when he'd eavesdropped on Penny's divulgences. He'd embarrassed the teen by walking away after letting her know he'd overheard her uncomplimentary comments about him. She wondered now at Penny's ability to get over it.

She needn't have worried. Big-hearted Penny quickly read Garrison's intent.

He slid the girl a big, open smile and pulled up a chair. "Please...go on."

Penny grinned. "I was just talking about the time Angel..." The afternoon passed swiftly as they sat about the bed sharing Angel vignettes, ranging from hilarious to serious to touching.

"She always loved animals," Penny said, visibly moved. "She even complained that frogs were killed to use in Biology dissections. Did you know that?"

"Uh-huh. She said as much to me." Garrison nodded. "That girl couldn't resist anything hurt." He stretched out his long legs and crossed his ankles, hands resting across his lean midriff. "She adopted out more strays through the Humane

Society shelter than you could shake a stick at," he said softly, proudly, a tender smile warming his face. "She'd have kept every one if we'd allowed it."

"Yeah." Penny's face was pensive beneath the shock of dark spiked hair. "She told me that Troy wanted to be a vet. They were so perfect –" She choked up. "I-I'm sorry, I don't want to upset ya'll by talking about Troy and –"

"Shh." Garrison's eyes were soft and compassionate. "S'okay."

Liza looked at him. Was it really okay? How about with her, Liza?

As though discerning, Garrison drew his gaze to hers. He must have read the question in her eyes, because he looked away, suddenly quiet. Within moments, he glanced at his watch and murmured, "I've gotta run back to the office for a while."

"Bye, Mr. W.," Penny called to his retreating back.

"Bye, Penny."

Liza stared after him. Her sunshine drifted behind a cloud. He hadn't even said good-bye to her. And she knew. It wasn't okay.

Garrison uncovered the canvas that evening, recalling the afternoon at the hospital. His abrupt departure had hurt Liza. He'd seen the disappointment in her eyes, in her very posture. He hated to see that beautiful dancer attitude flatten and wilt.

But what did he do with the agony-kick he experienced when faced with the violence of Troy's death and Angel's life-or-death trauma? It refused to go away. The kick had bulk and weight – enough to squash Garrison down deep inside himself when he glimpsed that replay of Liza sending the teens into harm's way.

God. What must he do? He had not yet dug himself out. Didn't yet know how.

They ate dinner, a quiet affair of deli rotisserie chicken and salad, before the television. He recognized it as Liza's ploy to deflect the tension and silence that marked their evening time together. To a degree, it did help.

Both were obviously relieved to retreat upstairs to their individual nocturnal pursuits. Tonight, Garrison gazed intently at the black-and-white family photo from which he worked, the one he'd taken years back while pursuing artsy photography for portrait subjects. In the painting, Liza already lounged in their secluded wooded oasis. He pondered which figure to add next. At the same time, he was suddenly certain that he'd not completely captured Liza.

He looked at the subjects in the photo awaiting transition to canvas. They now narrowed to Garrison and the completion of Angel's evolution. He'd begun sketches of her. Without the distraction of color, it suddenly became much easier to identify the light, middle, and dark values. Sometimes myriad colors in a photo distracted him from distinguishing values clearly.

Adding Liza's figure to the landscape scene had forced him to work through the process of placing her in the strong sunlight reflecting off the lily pond. He knew that the figures would command attention wherever he placed them in the painting and he knew just where he wanted them.

Concentrating on technique soon relaxed and focused Garrison and, as he readied pencils and paints, his mind wandered back to his golden heyday of youthful success and the promise of things to come.

"Garrison Wakefield's talent," wrote one *Greenville News* art critic, "is to accomplish a fine balance between the subjects and the landscape." After the recall, confidence buoyed his vision and approach.

Rather than being monochromatic, this painting's land-scape scene was colorful and lively, with sunlight reflecting over the pond, whose rippled multi-blue surface sprouted white and crimson water lilies with green, green pads. Liza's rosy, sunlit face came forward in space where the dark, abstract reflection of trees in the water cut behind it, leaving a sharp outlined edge.

"The Three-Dimensional Artist," noted artist and art critic Laurel Hart had called Garrison. "Garrison Wakefield's expertise in using diffused, abstract background shapes contrasts nicely with the sharp, in-focus figures, making the subject the eye's main attraction." That was one of the highest compliments of his life.

He'd been blessed with the opportunity to study with Hart one summer, learning her techniques and applying them to his own. Slowly, intently, he reviewed all he'd learned and applied it to what lay before him.

Something deep, deep inside him told him that this was the single most important project of his lifetime.

He squinted at the canvas, absorbing the overall blend of detail. Then it hit him – this painting's subject was light, particularly the way it illuminated Liza's figure, revealing fluid form and enhancing warm flesh tones. He stood back and gazed in awe, remembering an artist's proverb. *Light gives life to everything it touches and makes whatever it falls on more beautiful. It is, in itself, a master artist and is the force that guides my brush.*

Light. Life.

That force would propel him. It would give Liza life. He willed it to fill her with life. When light framed and consumed his world once again, only then would he be whole.

In that moment, he lived it. The force moved him, guiding his brush and his vision. He added depth to Liza's eye color, recalling Henry Theodore Tuckerman's words, "The eye speaks with an eloquence and truthfulness surpassing speech. It is the window out of which the winged thoughts often fly unwittingly. It is the tiny magic mirror on whose crystal surface the moods of feeling fitfully play, like the sunlight and shadow on a quiet stream."

Ahhh. Garrison agreed. The eye is the mirror of the soul. That's why the artist in him must get it right.

Now he proceeded with all the passion of an artist's heart, exaggerating the color of Liza's flesh tones in sunlight, gaining momentum as his brush stroked, teased, and coaxed, while his heart took wing and he soared above all the darkness of recent days.

Light gives life.

He flew like an eagle, up, up into the light.

Temperatures had not fallen below ninety-four degrees for the past five or six days and the world seemed sun-bleached to a blinding paleness. So the thunderstorm that rumbled in today was welcome, even though it did not break the heat but rather exhaled a smothery wetness into it. Through the hospital window Liza watched the angry clouds' slow surrender to the savage sun.

"Where's Angel?" Coming in the door, Charlcy looked around the hospital room. "Her bed's gone."

Liza blinked back fatigue and shifted in her chair. She'd almost buzzed off before her sister's appearance. "Ummm. She's having hyperbaric oxygen therapy." She squinted bleary-eyed at her watch. "Should be back soon."

"Oh." Charlcy plopped down in a chair. "How do you know if that helps a comatose person? I mean – she's been having HBOT all along, hasn't she?"

Liza nodded her head. "She has, from the first week. Unfortunately, improvement isn't always immediate. Comes more gradually. I only know that it's pretty customary treatment in these comatose cases."

Charlcy opened a Snickers bar and bit off a big hunk. "Missed lunch," she said, chewing with relish. "They put Angel in that chamber thing to do HBOT, don't they?"

"Yeah. Way I understand it is the pure oxygen administered during therapy ups the concentration of oxygen in the bloodstream – six times over what a person normally gets breathing. It's supposed to carry healing to all parts of the body, even to bones and tissue the red blood cells can't reach. It improves the white blood cell function, too. It's even used with burn victims, I understand. You get the picture."

Liza stood and stretched her stiff legs. "This hospital sitting is not for sissies," she grumped and took a bathroom break. When she returned, she asked, "Got another one of those things?"

Charlcy cut her eyes balefully and fished out another Snickers bar. "I didn't know you ate such crap, Miss Ballerina."

Liza snatched the bar from her. "Thou shalt not hoard goodies. No, I don't usually eat stuff like this. But what the heck?" She shrugged, ripped off the wrapper, and commenced tackling the chocolate-nougat-nut comfort. She leaned back in the chair and munched contentedly, enjoying the incomparable succor it doled out. "How was Dad?"

"He was there. Two hundred percent there." She burst into bawdy laughter and flipped a used disposable wipe into a small trash can. "You'll never guess what he was doing."

Liza laughed at the gleam in her sister's mischievous eyes. "No. Tell me."

Charlcy scooted to perch on the edge of her seat. "They were sitting on the front porch at the nursing home. I came in the side entrance and went to Dad's room, which overlooks the porch, y'know? Well, I saw them through the window. Like on a dad-blamed movie screen. There they sat on the bench, right in front of the window, he and this gray-haired lady patient – you know the one I said he was sweet on when he's here, right?"

Liza nodded, gurgling with anticipation. Charlcy continued. "He had his arm draped around her shoulder and then he leaned over and blew on her neck. Can you believe that? Pulled out her collar, at the nape, and blew on her neck."

"No!"

"And then he leaned and kissed her neck. Nuzzled it. The lady loved it! Looked at him all smiles. And I thought, whoa, where is this going? Then he reached over and they kissed, sis! A lock-lips, suck-face kind, as Lindi would put it."

Liza's hands covered her mouth to stem the laughter. "Heavens…to…Murgatroyd."

Charlcy leaned in, arms on denimed knees. "Hey!" She spread her hands and shrugged eloquently. "They don't have to worry about what anybody thinks anymore, don'tcha know?"

"No." Liza wiped her eyes of mirth tears, ones that felt good. "They don't."

They settled into a comfortable silence. Lulled by unrivaled sisterly camaraderie, Liza reached way inside herself for other good recollections to sustain the pleasure, so seldom there these days. "Remember when Mama took us to the circus that year when I was in second grade?"

At Charlcy's distressed grunt, Liza inwardly groaned and attempted to veer into a safer direction. "Daddy was determined that we go, remember? Wanted us to experience –"

"Something good in our lives," Charlcy flatly injected, October blue eyes now wounded. "But he sent us off with that crazy woman, knowing good and well that –"

"She wasn't crazy, Charlcy," Liza softly but firmly objected.

"Y'know, you sure could've fooled me, when she started cursing and challenging one particular clown to a duel to the death, *for Chrissake?*" With visible effort, Charlcy reined in her temper. Liza knew it was for her benefit that Charlcy did so.

"She was sick. There's a difference." Liza heard the desperation in her voice but didn't care. How many times had they gone round and round this stupid hill with the same results? Like a dog's tail-chasing – always coming up short, yet always idiotically and enthusiastically pursued. How she wanted her sister to remember their mama with love, not bitterness. Or at least allow Liza to entertain some healthy memories.

Charlcy, whose face was now flooded with the flush of suppressed fury – which Liza had learned to dread all during those early years – curled her hands into fists, a sign that she battled demons of recall.

Her voice was low and controlled, edged with steel. Implacable. "Liza, sick or evil, it all adds up to the same thing. A cobra, whether treated kindly or not, when it strikes, it's venom is just as deadly. That was our mother. I'm proud that you want to see the best in her, but it's just not in me. I can't betray the veracity of my existence by romanticizing our mother's tragic, ravaging, earthly jaunt. Too much carnage left behind, y'know?" Vented, she sagged back in her chair, eyes haunted, features slack and tired, looking suddenly older than her forty-five years.

"I'm sorry, Charlcy," Liza whispered, tears pushing against the back of her eyes, stinging her nose. "I shouldn't have brought it up." She should have known that Charlcy, a capital R Realist, could not deal, close-up, with the harsh replays of yesterdays – except when she sat at the controls.

Charlcy snorted and shifted herself upright, recovering as quickly as she'd lapsed, "Shoot. You can't know what'll set off your nutty sister, honey. Even I don't always know." She shrugged elaborately and smiled that big old

Charlcy-with-the-world-by-the-tail smile. "Hey! Maybe I have a strain of the same crazy-bug as Mama Mia."

"No." Liza blinked back tears and murmured, "you had it so much worse than me. You always protected me and all." She shook her head. "I don't know how you endured it."

Fully recovered and distanced from the angst of moments earlier, Charlcy lifted her shoulders. "I've learned to live beyond myself, honey. Simple as that. And I've grown quite adept at denial, doncha know?"

Liza felt herself relaxing, descending slowly to her comfort zone. She'd weathered those chaotic years of balancing her emotions, which depended upon the moment's happenings, and to some degree, had maintained a modicum of reasoning. Charlcy's plight had been more severe and now, looking back, she was passionately grateful for the hedge of safety Charlcy had built around her little sister.

"You helped Dad stay sane, too, you know?" Liza sighed and looked at her. "Many a day I watched you coax him back from the very end of himself. You really did. And that helped me, too, to have him to, you know – keep it all together. The family, I mean."

"Mmm," Charlcy agreed.

"Ironic, isn't it?" Liza sighed sadly. "Just when he was able to have peace of mind, his mind started leaving."

"Yeah." Charlcy looked at her and melted back in her chair, her face going solemn. "He comes back when you least expect it."

Liza's features, too, settled into somber lines. "I pray that will be the case with Angel."

Liza shared the incident of Angel's fingers curling and her disappointment at the nurse's reaction.

"Huh. What does she know?" Charlcy grunted with characteristic cynicism. "Sis, she's gonna make it. Y'hear me?" she said in her brook-no-nonsense way.

"Yeah," Liza's lips curved into a wobbly, grateful smile. "I hear you."

Charlcy blinked back moistness, cutting her gaze to the door. "Hi, Dr. Abrams."

The doctor halted just inside the room, obviously on the run. "Angel will be brought back to the room shortly. I want to encourage you to be patient. This HBOT is the most up-to-date treatment used in cases such as Angel's. Even so, these things take time. Research has shown evidence that brain neurons may dwell in an idling state for years. With restored oxygen levels, the idle – or sleepy – brain cells can become normal once again and regain electrical activity. There's a reported fifty percent success rate in the treatment of a long term coma."

He smiled and disappeared.

"That's supposed to be encouraging?" Liza looked at Charlcy, whose eyes reflected her own qualms. "Years? Did I hear him say years? And long-term?" Liza muttered hoarsely. "God!" She rolled her eyes heavenward and whispered, "Please?"

Charlcy, looking uncommonly shaken, took a deep breath, blew it out, and then squared her shoulders. "She's gonna come back, sis."

Liza nodded, her eyes closed for long moments, absorbing the impact of possibilities. Would she see her glass half full or half empty?

Suddenly it was a major decision. A choice. Yes, by George, it was a choice.

Liza opened her eyes and smiled tremulously at Charlcy. "You betcha."

She had no form...was a weightless untethered thing. Her world was one of darkness and shadows broken only by interludes of disconnected light and images and sound...they floated about her like cosmic entities from sci-fi realms. The current she felt sporadically lasted for but a short span...the awareness in bits and snatches...being lifted and moved...warm swabbing on her face and limbs...a young, vibrant voice floated in and out...Penny's voice.

WHOOSH!

The cheerleaders' formation was daringly tiered... "Come on, Angel!" they chorused...seven girls and two guys, in vibrant colors...navy blue and gray. They gestured, beckoning to her, pointing to her flygirl spot at the top, the apex. Peggy's grin and challenge pulled at her to a forward-hand-flip to the group but when Angel took a deep breath to flex and push off on her toes, her breath cut off...her body turned to concrete...she could not move...she struggled to breathe past the painful thing jammed in her throat...pain...nooo!..life!..Shadows.

Another voice...Aunt Charlcy's.... "Come on, baby girl. You're gonna do this thing or I'll kick your skinny butt. Y'hear me?"...What thing? Somebody please help me!

Mama's voice.... "I love you, Angel. Everything's gonna be okay, y'hear? Keep fighting."...Fight!... *Help! Please help me! Blasted nothingness!*

But she knew, somehow she knew. No one could help her. She was on her own...that's what Aunt Charlcy meant... shadows began to close in....

Angel's hands curled into fists...fight..."keep fighting!"... blackness.

"I remember when you were tiny, Liza." Charlcy had come home with Liza that night for a while and she was in a rare reminiscent mood. "Your feet, even then, danced to the music inside you. You leaped and twirled like a fairy, soared like a great bird, face as serious as could be. You used to put on cute performances for the family."

Liza snorted softly, enjoying every drop of it. "For everybody who'd watch me. I was a little ham. And you were my greatest fan.

"Guilty." Charlcy rolled her eyes and shrugged.

Liza sighed contentedly. "Then there was Dad." She smiled. "And Mama, too. That is, sometimes." Her smile faded when she saw Charlcy's expression flatten. "She did love us, you know, Charlcy." Her declaration fell just a hair short of a reprimand. Gentle but firm.

Charlcy's features relaxed a bit, but the robin's-egg blue eyes still sparked. "I know, I know. Wish I had your grace and forgiveness, sis." She shrugged elaborately. "But I don't." Liza's chest felt tight from the frustration this always heaped upon her. "I don't get it," she said. "You were always my savior, Charlcy. You brought light and safety to me when I could have gone under and drowned." She frowned and spread her hands in dismay. "But you yourself haven't brought the light with you. You're still walking in that darkness. I can't seem —"

"I wish I could leave it behind, honey." Charlcy had gone limp, plastered to the easy chair like a half-alive sea creature out of its habitat. "I've tried. Lordy, how I've tried. And I kept a lot of her stuff from you. And Dad." Her smile was bitter and her gaze tormented, faraway. "Her little sexual escapades? Too many to count. I got rid of the string of brainless idiots as quickly and brutally as I could manage. Needless to say, I couldn't always stop her from screwing up everything Pops, *we* – treasured."

She stopped for a moment, clamping her teeth shut and blinking back tears. Conviction blazed in her eyes. "Our mother reverenced nothing, Liza. At least I saw little of it. It was a day-to-day, sometimes hour-to-hour battlefield of her mind raging before my eyes. I learned to live a life of vigilance, tried to ward off the worst of the onslaught – tried to help you and Pops have just a little peace."

"Aah, Charlcy," Liza groaned. "You didn't have much of a childhood, did you?"

Charlcy snorted and shifted her body into what Liza recognized as her I'm-A-OK stance. "Heck, I probably fared as well as Pops. The adultery was the least of his worries. He had his work cut out keeping the checkbook and credit cards stashed away from her. I think that – like me – the poor guy was thrilled when she collapsed into bed during her depressive states. It gave him a few moments' reprieve."

"I know." Liza slid Charlcy an understanding look. "I hate to admit that I sometimes enjoyed the time she was actually there. Yet, her suicidal talk always upset me. And Daddy went into overdrive at those times, hiding razors –"

"Not always in time," Charlcy huffed stingingly. "How many times did I have to clean up blood in the bathroom or kitchen? The *kitchen* for gosh sake – where we ate! Huh? Six? Eight? Hell, it coulda been a dozen.

"Pop's knee-jerk labors to get her help in time. All those nights when she couldn't sleep, talking, talking, *talking* nonstop, paranoia eating her alive, waking me up to accuse me of gosh-awful outlandish things like putting poison in her tea, or – or stealing one of her gross spike-heeled shoes that I wouldn't have been caught in a casket wearing. She would've shot me had she found a gun. Or Pops, if he got in the way. Gawd!" She sprang to her feet and strode to the window and glared out into the dusky evening. "Why don't you remember anything bad?" She sounded truly mystified. "Though I'm glad you don't."

Liza sighed, then shrugged limply. "Because one chooses to remember or not to remember. I think I was young enough to refuse to have a memory. There's something to that adage about the resilience of children."

Charlcy snorted. "Sure didn't come my way."

"I prayed a lot, Charlcy."

"Y'know, honey? So did I. But God must've been real busy elsewhere during those years."

"C'mon," Liza said gently, her mind reeling anew at her sister's revelations. "Sit down, Charlcy. It's all over. Don't you see?" Charlcy continued to stare outside, memories fairly parading before her. Liza knew because she saw the familiar body language that came with the nightmares. The squared shoulders, clenched fists, ramrod straight back, tight lips, brittle, searing eyes.

"No, sis," Charlcy muttered hoarsely. "I'm still furious that she allowed herself to go crazy over and over by not taking her medicine. She was allowed to check into lunacyville almost at will, while I was required to remain sane and in control. I got to where I hated her for that fact. She controlled it all, to my way of thinking. It was always her script – I just learned the lines." She ran out of breath for a moment, then began shaking her head. "No, it's not all over, Liza. Never will be."

"But it will. I pray and believe it will," Liza insisted desperately, knowing that Charlcy's faith had gone south a while back. Would it ever return? Liza hoped with everything within her that it would.

"No." The statement was flat. Implacable. "No, it won't." Charlcy turned slowly and gazed unwaveringly into Liza's eyes. "Because she was totally selfish. She knew what would happen if she didn't take the blasted medicine. She knew, Liza."

"She was sick, Charlcy," Liza tried again, knowing the futility.

"She enjoyed the *high*, sweetheart." Charlcy plopped back in the chair, sprawled and in piss-mode again, causing the band in Liza's chest to tighten, building pressure until it was near to imploding.

"That's why she refused to take the medicine. Period. That was the depth of our sweet mama. I'm sorry I can't paint a more pleasant picture for you."

The realist in Charlcy was Liza's nemesis. Again, it sunk its teeth into her and gnawed mercilessly. "I know. Let's let it rest for now," Liza said, sucking in and exhaling a deep, cleansing breath.

"Right." Charlcy's flat, over-bright eyes slid into civility again as Liza watched her pull her heavy denial-cloak tightly about her. Liza knew how difficult it was for Charlcy to stomp down those memories deep inside her, where dark things hibernate. Wished like crazy she didn't have to, that she could work them out of her mind and soul, totally rid herself of them.

"I'm sorry, honey," Liza said. "I shouldn't talk about her. But sometimes, I just need to –"

"You don't need to apologize – nor explain," Charlcy, the champion, the danged Nyoka of the Jungle now spoke. "She was your mama. Remember, I have kids in my special ed classes who need an ear from time to time? And I listen to them and encourage them." She shrugged. "I just feel like leftover potty because I can't do the same for you, my little sister."

"Hey!" Liza threw up her hands, palms out. "I'm not so little. I'm good. You take care of yourself now. It's time for you to retire. You've sacrificed enough for two lifetimes."

Then she rushed to Charlcy, pulled her to her feet, and embraced her soundly, rocking back and forth. "I love you, sis," Liza whispered.

Charlcy could not speak but Liza saw her blinking back moisture. Knew she would not cry. That would be totally at odds with the safety-net paragon, Charlcy.

Liza gently released her and they spent the next hour laughing and ruminating on Liza's early ballet and dance exploits and Charlcy's boyfriends.

"Raymond was so cute. And sexy." Liza couldn't help but include him, regretting it the moment the words were out of her mouth, seeing the tightening of Charlcy's expression.

Then quite unexpectedly, Charlcy guffawed. "God, child! Look at you. Am I that transparent?"

At Liza's solid nod, Charlcy's face gentled. "It's okay, honey. I still love Raymond. I hate him, too. The – the *plague*." The words were halfhearted. "It's really hard to talk about him right now. Give me some time. It might help." She skewered Liza with a sharp gaze. "Then again, it might not."

Liza burst out laughing. She couldn't help it. Charlcy's survival, as well as her own, had ridden upon her big sister's ability to stand up and fight battles. It depended upon her grit. She had to respect that combative strain.

Charlcy left shortly thereafter for home. Garrison was upstairs, painting. Liza remained on the sofa, letting the memories slide through her mind and warm her anew. She lingered in days gone by, childhood times when she couldn't distinguish where she ended and dance began.

Angel probably felt the same way. The thought triggered a ravaging hunger to see her daughter dance again. It might somehow assuage this gnawing craving for the continuity that no longer was.

Liza bounded to her feet and plundered through the entertainment cabinet for Angel's ballet videos. She and Garrison had recorded them all through the years, from the time Angel was five. She found them and plopped one in the player.

Returning to the sofa with the remote, she flicked on the video. The first was *The Nutcracker*, in which Angel was one of a flock of tiny birds. Liza watched, transfixed by the innocent, somewhat fierce expressions on the cherubic faces of budding ballerinas who flitted about in a splendid riot of regalia.

Liza laughed and cried through the series of performances. Angel graduated to *Nutcracker* role levels where, at nine, she wore a stunning red feathery costume of a larger bird, the steps becoming a bit more intricate.

A couple of hours later, Liza remained transfixed, growing more solemn by the moment. Somewhere along the way, in Mama's camera sight, Angel's demeanor had begun to morph. At first, it was subtle. Later, the camera captured facial expressions and body language that startled Liza. She'd attributed Angel's reticence to join in Liza's excitement to preshow jitters. But now she got an entirely different reading.

From the screen, Liza's pride in her daughter came through as loud as a cannon discharge, while Angel appeared more and more miserable as her body shrank to near emaciation.

Angel hated ballet. The truth sunk in to Liza – a branding iron searing her very soul.

It was obvious that Liza had blinded herself to Angel's true feelings all through the years. And hounded her about her weight. She'd tried not to but, looking back, she shamefully acknowledged her police tactics. Tears gathered behind her eyes and a knot of pain pulled together in her chest.

Dear God. What had she done to her baby girl? She'd forced Angel to live Liza's life. *I've been living through Angel. How sick.*

Liza had always hated pushy, backstage mothers. Now, she faced the ugly truth.

She was one of those detestable women.

Angel hated to dance but loved to see her mama dance. Therefore, Liza would now dance for Angel.

And for myself as well.

On one level it didn't take a mastermind to figure it out, but in Liza's case, she hadn't truly known, until this tragedy, how very many of her hopes she'd invested in Angel.

The videos had opened her mind to what she'd been doing all along. It stunned her. It buzzed and sizzled like a crazed hornet swarm. She had so much to make up for and she prayed she'd have a chance to do so. To survive, she had to believe it would happen.

The next night, she went to the studio refreshed, focused. Donning a black leotard and pink tights, she felt transported back in time. This time, it was her, Liza, seeking her own destiny. She recalled how, by age twelve, after experiencing grueling years of training, pain and monotony became ingrained. Now, she realized that dance had offered her a providential escape from the pathos of her childhood and young adult years. That escape had preserved her sanity and allowed her to be, to some degree, a child, a luxury that bypassed Charlcy.

She still marveled that she'd never despaired or become bored. Never did she lose sight of her goal to become a great ballerina. Music filled the chamber and Liza acknowledged anew the miracle of dance. It wasn't simply memorizing choreography, miming teachers, or being robotic in the execution of steps. It was the phenomenon of the voice of her body harmonizing in a dramatic way with the music, doing it in a way uniquely hers.

Tonight, with music strains of variations from *Don Quixote*, Liza's performance was explosive, her interpretation dramatic. Her hands were dramatically telling, right down to the tips of her fingers. Her body became an expressive instrument, the notes bursting with Spanish flair.

At times, she became Angel…this time a good thing. She discerned a strange light descending over and about her. The glow swallowed her as she danced. It limned her like a halo, moving with her through stunning pirouettes. In the mirrors, she glimpsed her iridescent flight.

She changed the music to "Scherzo Fantastique" and she twirled through the steps, feeling like a graceful spinning top. Somewhere during the past eighteen years, she'd forgotten why she'd chosen to be a ballerina. Now she remembered. Dance was both an act of will and a means of expression. Ballet was the link she'd made between thought and action. It was her body's silent voice.

Now, luminosity converged with it all. She tasted and smelled the clean radiance of the light, like a pure, fragrant mist that permeated her pores and lifted her as though she were a feather.

It converged with her as she danced for Angel She would be Angel's legs and feet. She would carry Angel with her into this cloud of light.

Through her, Angel would dance.

Liza's language was dance. It was, to her, life and light. Through this light, Angel would live.

Through this light, Liza had found herself. It transported her from where she'd buried herself in her daughter's life − to renewal.

Tonight, she celebrated. She danced with a new fervor. She was the magnificent plumed creature of her sister's description, set free at last.

Garrison faced a decision. He stood before the canvas about to introduce Angel into the landscape scene next to Liza. At what stage of life would he portray his daughter? The black-and-white family photo showed a small girl. Certainly, that child was part of the composite of Angel burrowed deeply in his heart. But so was the sixteen-year-old girl. Suddenly he felt strongly that Angel should appear as she was today, only whole and well. Happy.

Excitement gripped him as he began to sketch from a more current photo of Angel with the cheerleading squad. His natural artist tendencies rushed to the forefront as he worked for proportion, ensuring that Angel's image was correctly in scale with Liza's. He considered the four basic components to his work of art: sight, shape, shade, and accuracy. At intervals, he turned the canvas to the mirror, giving himself a fresh view of his work, thrilled each time it validated his accuracy.

As his pencil sketched, his mind first filtered out all but Angel's barest shapes. Then he concentrated on subtle forms that emerged from the school photo. Shading came next, requiring careful attention but bringing reality to the features and contours. Swiftly the pencil moved, pausing only for Garrison's tortillon, actually rolled paper tips, to blend and smudge tiny areas. Again, the mirror rewarded him with reflections of accuracy. He worked late into the night.

Finally, his brush began to stroke life into Angel's features. At times, tears blurred his vision of her sweet face, but he swiped them away and kept adding life-giving flesh tones and vibrant blue eye color. The brush moved defiantly, as if battling the demons of death.

Somewhere deep inside, Garrison knew that, on some level, this was exactly what transpired. The insight staggered his mind and propelled him on into the wee hours.

Weary but elated, he recognized that this endeavor was the most important of his life. It would bring back to him what he had lost. Again, as in painting Liza, strong sunlight enhanced Angel's rosy complexion and described the form of her features.

Light. Life.

Unlike Liza's darker background, a white cloud reflection on the pond framed Angel's wheat-streaked hair, making her appear to pop out in space by contrast. Garrison stood back and squinted. Diffused, abstract background shapes contrasted pleasantly with the sharp, in-focus figures. Liza and Angel were the main attraction to the eye.

His eyes relaxed and a rush of emotions invaded him. Relief. Fulfillment.

Contentment. Garrison lay down his brush and discovered his fingers nearly cramped from the long hours' exertion. He flexed them and solemnly surveyed tonight's efforts. Light shimmered from the scene, telling him in some mystical way that somehow, some way, he would get past the darkness.

They would get past the darkness. With divine help, he would help rescue them all from the darkness.

chapter twelve

Angel came to Liza during the night. She sat on the side of the bed with a big old grin on her face and said, "I was just joking, Mama!" She burst into laughter. "Look. I'm okay!" It was so real that Liza reached out to gather her into her arms...and awoke to the shock of reality. She swallowed back tears before wrapping fresh courage about her to face the day.

Liza dressed listlessly, sensing some portent hanging in the air. She didn't know quite what it meant. Perhaps it was simply an offshoot of all of the stress of recent days. "I'm trying to keep a positive outlook," she told Charlcy that afternoon after returning from the nursing home to relieve her sister from her bedside vigil. "But I feel like I'm running out of steam. It's like this dark cloud follows me around, you know?"

Charlcy cut her a *duh!* look. "Honey chile', I wrote the book on dark clouds – one of which – the *cumulus* is my ex. It looks nice and fluffy and is associated with hail and tornadoes. But we won't get started on that. Don't want to pull you down any lower."

Liza looked at her, eyes narrowed. "Charlcy, don't you think you could be a little more charitable to Raymond? I mean, after all, he *is* Lindi's father."

Charlcy seemed to give it deep thought for a moment, then shook her head. "Nah. I don't think so."

Irritation and impatience spurred Liza beyond her usual tolerance for her sister's feistiness. "Charlcy, this has to be uncomfortable for Lindi; her parents not even being civil to each other. Think how that must make her feel."

Charlcy squared her shoulders. "You're behind on the news bulletins, precious one. Raymond didn't even remember her birthday back in April. And she hasn't heard from him since. So I'm actually trying to get her to keep it in her head that he really does love her, y'know?"

Then Charlcy did an entirely uncharacteristic thing. She puckered up and began to weep.

"Aah, sis." Liza rose and went to her on the opposite side of Angel's bed. "I'm sorry. I know this is tough for you." She put her arms around her sister and held her until the stormy weeping subsided and Charlcy pulled away to blow her nose and snuffle. Liza returned to her chair and allowed her space to regroup. Charlcy detested signs of weakness.

She gazed at Liza with red, swollen eyes. "I still love him, you know," she declared hoarsely. "I fight this battle daily, loving and hating him at the same time." She shrugged and twisted her mouth in a self-deprecating way.

"Wouldn't it be easier to simply forgive him?" Liza asked quietly, heart in throat. Oh God. If only Garrison could forgive her. If she'd just once look at Garrison and not feel guilt at the blame lurking in those condemning dark eyes. She believed he was at least trying to forgive her.

But she still, in his unguarded moments, glimpsed the darkness in his eyes.

"I don't know," Charlcy said, sighing deeply. "Sometimes I think I have, but then something reminds me and –" She shook her head and looked Liza in the eye. "Forgiving is not simple.

Don't ever think it is. But then you've never had major issues in your life that require forgiveness. Marriage-wise, that is."

Liza refused to touch that. She changed the subject.

"Anyway, I feel this thing hanging over me, more and more, every day."

Liza felt suddenly chilled. She shuddered.

"You cold?" Charlcy asked.

She shook her head. "No. I'm good," she lied. She hesitated. "But I am exhausted. Do you think you could –" She raised her brows in appeal.

"Stay awhile longer with Angel?"

"Yeah. Could you?"

"Be glad to. And, sis? Get some rest."

Liza slept even more fitfully the next night. She tossed and turned, wrestling demons of insecurity and guilt. She went to the kitchen for a glass of water, moving in a pall of guilt so thick and consuming that she could barely stand under its burden.

She tried talking sense to her brain but it persisted in telling her there was no hope for her marriage and that she was responsible for the tragic accident. It told her that her daughter most likely would not survive. That she'd failed both Garrison and her daughter. And Troy. Dreadfully. She crawled back into bed to stare into the darkness. In the murky predawn hours, she plunged to her lowest point ever.

Then something her dad had said after their mother's death years ago swooped in like a beacon of light. She sat up in bed, allowing it to wash over and soak into her. "Always maintain a sense of normalcy. Keep on doing it, and soon it will feel right again."

He'd been right before. Liza hoped it would work again for her. She slipped from her bed and quietly climbed the staircase to the guest room. She found Garrison flat on his back, arms thrown out like wings, his breath that deep, even kind of complete slumber.

Can I endure all this guilt...along with the life-or-death vigil at Angel's bedside? She truly didn't know. But she had no other option. Right now, she simply needed to see her husband.

She was tempted to fling herself across him and cling like a June bug.

Garrison is my heart.

The realization exploded inside her...profound...reverberating to infinity. She silently returned to her own bed, staring helplessly into the darkness.

God, how she loved him.

The crisis came suddenly, without warning. Liza was alone when Dr. Abrams delivered the bad news. "She's losing ground," he said without preamble. "She's not responding to treatment as I'd hoped." Then he propped against the bed, arms crossed over green scrubs. "Angel's bones are very fragile. Borderline osteoporosis, as evidenced by the X-rays and the bone breaks. Osteoporosis is abnormal for someone her age." He looked at Liza gravely. "Did she – I want to put this delicately. Did Angel ever show signs of having an eating disorder? She is, after all, painfully thin, even with the nutritional IV. With all the other complications arising...makes me wonder."

"No," Liza replied quickly. "Oh, she watched her weight like a good ballerina. It goes with the turf. But no, she didn't have an eating disorder."

The doctor looked at Liza for long moments, clearly skeptical. "Well, think about it. The condition of her bones suggests otherwise. Another thing – her kidneys show strain, possibly the beginning of failure. I don't like it."

Liza felt bile rising as terror spliced through her. Had she missed something? Those videos had shown just how thin Angel had grown. But she'd shown none of the classic signs. No. Liza would have known. "Is she –" Liza couldn't get the words out. She tried again. "What will happen – with the kidneys, I mean?"

He took a deep breath, blew it out slowly, and looked her in the eye. "I can't tell you that, Mrs. Wakefield. I wish I could. The kidneys could be only the beginning. The one thing Angel has going for her is her youth. But that's not a guarantee. We're administering drugs for the kidney infection, hoping to stem it before they go into failure. She also has ARDS, acute respiratory distress syndrome."

He shifted his weight and continued. "It often results in multiple organ failure and it is very serious. We'll carefully monitor her urinary output. Also, the ventilator now requires higher settings, which is a bad sign – her breathing is growing more labored. Organ failure is our major concern now. Her lungs are inflamed because they were bruised in the accident. Her long-term illness – as well as prolonged use of the ventilator – probably triggered ARDS."

Liza's head reeled. Her voice was wispy. "What can be done for her?"

"We're going to do a tracheotomy – insert a smaller tube directly into the trachea. This will make her more comfortable. We'll do cultures to determine which appropriate antibiotics to use for ARDS. We'll also use moderate doses of corticosteroids for the inflammation."

"Oh Lord. I need something to give me hope," she whispered. Liza felt so drained…. Numb. "Can you give me some idea of whether – if she survives this and wakes up – whether she'll know us?" *Oh God, please – give me something.*

Dr. Abrams shook his head, his weathered face grave. "It's all in His hands." He pointed upward, pushing away from the bed. "I should warn you to prepare for the worst, and pray for the best." He shrugged tightly.

As soon as he left the room, Liza dialed Garrison's number, fingers trembling violently. He'd earlier told her he wouldn't be by the hospital until later. She ignored the buzzing in her extremities now. She also refused to take a darned tranquilizer. She didn't need to be a zombie on top of all this. Good deep gulps of air would have to suffice.

Angel needed her more than ever. "Garrison?" she croaked into the cell phone.

"Yes? Liza, is everything all right?" Alarm rang in his voice.

She filled him in on Dr. Abrams's bleak prognosis. "Garrison, he's not at all encouraging. He also said the longer she's in the coma, the less chance she has of surviving." Her voice broke. "He's rather fatalistic."

Silence. Then Garrison said with male logic, "He can't afford to give us false hope, Liza, is all. Else, if things don't go well, he figures we'd take him to task. And we would."

"Yeah." She sniffled.

"Anyway, we want her back, no matter what. And even with the worst case scenario – if she doesn't recognize us – *we* know *her*.

His declaration was so passionate that Liza felt more tears gather. For this instant in time, no matter what happened, they were solid.

Together.

Another thing filled her – the golden certainty that Garrison loved their daughter with everything in him. His love for their creation was such that Garrison would lay down his life for her. In that instant, she forgave his lapses of the past, knowing in her deep, deep soul of souls that if he had the chance, he'd make it all up to their daughter.

"Absolutely," she replied huskily, her whole heart humming…singing it.

"We've gotta believe this is going to happen, Liza. With everything that's in us, we must believe," he murmured hoarsely, with a fervency she'd not heard from him in a while.

"I agree," she whispered and swiped at a runaway tear. For that heartbeat, she would bask in his strength. Draw from it. She closed her eyes and flowed with it.

"Liza – I have an important business meeting this evening to close one of the biggest deals of our life. It will help us through these medical expenses. I'll cancel it if I have to. Tell me what to do. Do you need me there right now?"

Of course I need you; like oxygen. "I'm good. Go ahead to the meeting. It's okay. Really. I'll call if there's a change."

She shut off the phone. She didn't want to need him so desperately.

But her heart didn't know that.

Liza drove straight home, heart pounding with dread. She began a search of Angel's room. She looked in her nightstand, and then rummaged through the chest of drawers. She rifled through Angel's footlocker, her daughter's secret squirrel-away place.

Dropping to her knees, she sorted through secret things a girl hides away. Old photos of boys she'd had crushes on. A T-shirt given to her by her coach in appreciation of exemplary cheering squad teamwork. Souvenirs from everywhere meaningful; Troy's and her favorite pizza parlor, movie stubs, ballet programs with Angel's name way down in the credits. One old program, yellowed and crinkled, featured Liza's picture on it. She was the principle ballerina that year in *The Nutcracker*. Angel had saved it.

The tears came from nowhere and everywhere. Liza lovingly replaced the treasures as she wept, and then resumed her search. On a hunch, she lifted the mattress and felt under it. Nothing. She went around to the other side and lifted that corner. Still nothing. Further probing closer to the center was fruitless.

Liza wondered where she herself would hide something she didn't want found. She thought for a moment and then got on her knees and looked under the bed. There, taped to the bottom of the box spring, was a large plastic Ziploc bag. She stretched to pluck it loose and sat atop the bed to dump its contents over the pink bedspread. Among the cache were packets and bottles of laxatives along with Ipecac to induce vomiting. Other containers held over-the-counter appetite suppressants.

"Oh, Angel." Remorse oozed through Liza like hot molten rock.

But she couldn't buckle under that right now. Some day, she owed herself a good old-fashioned nervous breakdown. She gathered the items up and then dumped them all into a small garbage bag stored in Angel's bathroom cabinet. Her heart thumped loudly as she wondered how long her girl had been torturing her body with these substances.

How many times can a heart break?

How could I not have known? Memories swarmed in on a kaleidoscopic swirl. She regretted every time she'd cautioned Angel about overeating. Other things zoomed in...Angel's immediate after-meal bathroom trips...pre-recital appetite loss...picking at food. Desperate pleas for help when she relayed her ballet instructor's rude comments following any healthy weight gain. *How stupid can I be?*

Liza would deliver these medications to Dr. Abrams and confirm his suspicions. That way, if – no, *when* Angel awoke from the coma, he would know what to work with in her recovery. Liza had to believe there would be a recovery. A renewal.

She recalled Garrison's words. "We've gotta believe…with everything that's in us, we must believe." *Garrison, how I love you.*

Urgency gripped her. She must confirm for the doctor what he already suspected.

Liza's discovery of Angel's grim paraphernalia further stretched her tenuous hold on self-control. She'd given over Angel's arsenal to an unsurprised Dr. Abrams. He informed her that he'd scheduled Angel's tracheotomy and new medications for early the next morning.

Now, after leaving Restorative Care at ten o'clock, Liza drove across town, her mind like a sped-up old-time movie flickering horrific images of Angel starving and dying, of Troy's funeral. Guilt churned it all until its black, vile froth rose to unbearable putrid heights.

Liza pulled into the garage at home and shut off the motor. There, she laid her head on folded arms at the wheel. For long moments, she sat there, head spinning and nerves vibrating like an old washing machine agitator she remembered in her maternal Gramma's country cottage, where freshly baked bread fragranced the air.

What she'd give to be back there, in the haven of Gramma's arms, away from the wreckage at home, when it was just her and her Gramma, who unconditionally loved Mama just as Liza did, who whispered in her ear, "Shh, everything's gonna be okay, honey." With none of these cataclysmic events rocking her very existence.

But then, she wouldn't have Angel and Garrison, would she? *You can't go back.* She took several deep breaths like she'd always done before ballet performances. Slowly, the swirling in her head settled to a mild pulsing.

Inside the house, familiarity wrapped her in a modicum of succor. She dropped her bag on the way to the den and stepped out of her shoes before plunging into the sofa's softness. There, the dam broke. The weeping was torrential, as violent as guilt and remorse and self-hatred can detonate. Liza cried until she hiccuped and snuffled, until she was boneless and Novocain numb. Until exhaustion toppled her into deep sleep.

∾

"Liza?" Garrison hovered above her, his face worried. It swam. "You okay?"

She blinked, feeling the heaviness of her swollen lids and the dampness still clinging around her eyes and in the creases of her face.

"What's wrong, honey?" Garrison slid onto the cushion, facing her prone, limp shape. His finger gently wiped the wetness beneath one eye. "You've been crying." His deep voice vibrated concern.

"Mmm," she rolled onto her back, inhaling a deep waking breath. "You just get in?"

"Yes." He looked long and deep into her eyes. Then he swooped to kiss her lips. A soft, bird's wing brush, one filled with longing and care. Liza felt it to her toes. Then, ever so gently, he reached to help her sit up. "Tell me about it."

Liza didn't need him to clarify. "I've been so confused in recent weeks, Garrison."

She decided to gamble then. Either she could trust him with her heart or not. This would tell. She went on to explain how her mind had worked in recent weeks and how alone she'd felt beneath his emotional exile. And how abandoned she'd felt when he was about to leave her, bringing back loud echoes of childhood desertion. The words, now coming of their own accord, tumbled out and over one another. On their summit rode pain. When the flow ebbed, much of the pain was gone. Where, she didn't know. She just knew it had subsided.

Finally, she looked him in the eye and said, "There's more. I feel responsible for Angel's current crisis. I didn't mean to nag her about her weight, but I did. Not consciously. But I did. Her eating disorder complicates her recovery. I've asked God to forgive me. I had to forgive myself. Now," she gazed into his eyes, "I ask you to forgive me. Not just for that – but for everything. Because if you can't, Garrison, I don't know how we can go on."

There. I can breathe deeply again.

He reached for her hand and laced his long artist's fingers through hers, squeezing gently. "I may be many things, Liza, but I'm not crazy. I've never wanted to leave you." He moved closer, drawing her into his arms. He looked at her, heart in eyes. "Ever. I only wanted to give you space during this hard time. I wanted to protect you. From me. Can you understand that?"

Liza gazed into his pleading eyes. And in that heartbeat, she got it. She nodded.

"Furthermore," he murmured, his lips brushing hers again, "I'll never leave you."

"Promise?" Her lips reached out for his.

He leaned back and gazed into her eyes, touching her soul. "Promise."

"Another thing," he murmured, solemn. "I've had no right to hold you accountable for the tragedy when I've made such a mess of fathering Angel in recent years. I've had to pray for forgiveness. Now, I ask you for your forgiveness. I don't deserve it but —"

"You're forgiven, darling," she said softly. "And now we can get on with life, huh?"

"Oh!" Her eyes white-rimmed. Can we toast tonight's deal?"

"I'll just say this." His smile slid wide and white. "This is the beginning of great things for all of us." Then he sobered. "As soon as Angel comes back."

They embraced for long moments before Liza reluctantly moved from the warmth of his arms. "I'm going to the studio for a while," she murmured, her fingers trailing down his arm and squeezing his hand once more.

"I'm going upstairs, too," Garrison stood and helped her to her feet.

Together, arm in arm, they climbed the stairs, reluctantly parting ways on the landing. And for the first time in ages, Liza felt a complete oneness.

～

He watched her go and his heart followed. It warmed him, the realization. It inspired him as he went into Angel's room and began to work on the painting. His heart soared as his brush stroked life and energy onto canvas. Moments later, Spanish flavored music wafted from Liza's direction.

He laid aside his brush. The music swept him down the hall to the studio, where he quietly pushed open the door. Then, he saw her. Kitri, from his wedding-gift portrait. Not in costume this time, rather in tights and leotard, but she was there in spirit. In dance. Just at that moment, as the music swelled, Kitri leaped – an awesome jump, a kick-jeté in which she soared so high and arched her back so far that her head touched her back leg. A beautiful explosion in air. It captured the joyous elevation of Kitri's spirit.

Garrison's heart nearly stopped at the sight of her. The majesty of her movements took his breath.

She's back. My Liza is back!

Garrison watched her from the doorway as the music ebbed and she gracefully moved to the barre for a towel to drape over her elegant shoulders and use to blot her brow. She spotted him and froze for a moment. Then she smiled at him, a luminous one that shot through him like a taser.

In that moment, he decided to make a wager of his own. He reached for her hand. "Come." She did so and allowed him to lead her down the hall and into Angel's room. "I've got something to show you. It's not finished, but I want you to see what I'm working on."

He placed her nearby and he crossed to the painting, lifting the covering.

From the canvas, the lily pond glistened with sunlight and the Love Tree, their trysting place of early married days, stood tall, kissing the azure sky. Bold letters, artistically engraved into the bark, spelled "G Loves L." Along with this was a notch denoting each of their years together. The notches formed a flower – with each current year's mark forming its stem. An arrow pointed downward to "Loves Angel." A perfect heart enjoined the entire eternally joined threesome. Other tiny round notches, the beginning of a rose, commemorated their daughter's visits to the lily pond.

Beneath the tree lay a golden pine carpet, where Liza lounged. "It's one third of the way to renewal," he said gently as he showed Liza the photo from which he worked, the one from long ago days that he'd found in the attic. In it, Liza, Angel, and Garrison bubbled over with laughter and love.

In the painting, happiness radiated from Liza's very pores. Garrison's attention to detail hummed from the minutest flecks in her eyes.

"Oh God – Garrison," Liza gasped, gazing poignantly at the painting. Then she burst into tears.

Garrison had not expected this reaction. "Aah, Liza," he murmured gently. "I didn't intend to upset you. I just thought it might give you hope, darling. I'm doing more sketches of Angel now, trying to get just the right expression. I've already done some preliminary, practice images of her on canvas. Now, I'll add her to this scene. Just as this portrait isn't finished, neither is our destiny."

"I – I know," she snuffled. "It's just so – so beautiful."

A smile slid across his face, mere inches from hers. "Just wait till it's finished."

He kissed her, long and hard. She whimpered in protest when their lips parted. He smiled her a slow, lazy promise before releasing her. "First order of business is to move back to your bed."

That accomplished, they spent the next few hours doing what they enjoyed most. "I've always said that any time spent out of bed with you is wasted time," Garrison murmured in her ear and against her soft neck. "So we've got lots of making up to do."

"You always were marvelous at making up," Liza purred hours later as they languished in bed. She sighed contentment, reminding Garrison that in the midst of calamity came this love oasis. A miracle.

"You're so easy to ravish," he groaned and swooped in again for a kiss.

"Garrison!" she squealed with delight. "We've got to get some sleep."

"Speak for yourself," he growled and claimed her lips once more.

chapter thirteen

They sat at Angel's bedside, truly together and with a new anticipation. Their profound coming together, in Garrison's estimation, had to offset something in their daughter's precarious situation. Something so…explosive could not go ignored by the forces that be.

Everything of faith in him hummed this morning. And he saw it in Liza as well. The helplessness and despair was no longer in her blue, blue depths. They now radiated something beyond mere hope.

Expectancy. It was a certainty that something was imminent.

It bloated and simmered in them as they took opposite sides of Angel's bed, facing each other. After a while, they slipped quietly from the room. Down the hall, they knelt at the tiny altar.

"Please, Angel," Liza prayed, clasping Garrison's hand. "Come back to us."

Blackness cocooned Angel. A sound? Voices? "Please, Angel, come back to us."

Mama? Suddenly the blackness scattered and Angel was dancing across a vast expanse of wood parquet floor in Mama's wake…"Angel!" One voice, masculine and persistent, froze her into stillness while Mama pirouetted away, oblivious. Angel pivoted and danced in the opposite direction, spinning like a top, backward…backward in time, toward the one beckoning her.

Her bare feet sank into the pine needle carpet surrounding the lily pond, now sparkling beneath a warm morning sun. The blossoms were brilliantly white today. Rustic silvery gray wood benches sprouted from the forest floor, ones Daddy built long ago for this forest oasis of theirs.

"Angel!" Troy's voice. "Come help me with the dog. He's hit bad."

Troy Bailey hovered over a heap covered with a red, plaid, woolen blanket, shaded by the roof of their picnic shelter, a square, weathered wooden pavilion with a storage room. "I saw the car hit him." Anger flared Troy's nostrils. "It just kept going." His dark eyes pinned Angel. "Can you imagine being that cruel? Just to leave him lying there in the road, bleeding?"

With hands so very gentle, he pulled the blanket up a bit.

"By the time I pulled over and ran back to check on him, he'd disappeared. I followed the trail of blood down here, where he'd dragged himself. I'm sorry, but I had to force the storage door open for a blanket to wrap him in to subdue and cover him. I'll pay for the lock."

"It's okay," Angel murmured. She peered over her neighbor's shoulder and gasped. She gazed at the ugly, mangy mongrel that'd pestered the entire countryside for years now. All he was good for was foraging in trash cans, digging up flowers, treeing cats, and in general making a nuisance and creating messes.

"Yeah. It's him," Troy muttered. "Everybody and his grandpa have shot at him at one time or another but he's wily and seems to have ten lives."

"Not today," Angel whispered, squatting down to reach out and gently touch the straggly brow.

"Don't," Troy cautioned. Angel jerked her hand back. She'd never been particularly attracted to the dark-haired, muscular Troy, who lived on the dairy farm bordering their land. He'd always tended farm animals. *Goes with the territory*, she figured.

But today, armed with a near hypnotic intensity as his dark eyes surveyed the canine patient, he seemed more – provocative. From the black tangle of mangy hair heaped on the concrete floor, equally obsidian, glazed eyes seemed to plead in some way. In pain, the animal looked vulnerable. Terrified.

"He's already gnawed my arms to smithereens after I loosened the blanket," muttered Troy. "Just instinct."

Angel gasped at the multiple bite wounds scattered over Troy's sun-bronzed hands and arms. "He probably won't bite you. He's too weak now to lash out," he added sympathetically.

Angel dashed for the first aid kit in the storage room and cared for Troy's wounds, disinfecting and wrapping them with a gauze dressing. But he grew anxious to get back to tending the animal. Something in the way his hands moved over the dog to check injuries, gentle...kind...twanged a chord inside Angel, one that bonded them in mutual love for helpless creatures.

She looked more closely at the dog. "That's the mutt who scrounges in our garbage," she said softly, almost reverently, because suddenly, the dog was something besides a pest. He seemed, in his dying condition, to have a soul behind those pitiful dark eyes. Pain rendered him somehow – dignified.

In the next breath, the dog rolled over and struggled to pull his useless legs behind him toward the lily pond. "He's thirsty," they said in unison. Angel rushed to get a bowl from the storage room and dashed to fill it with clear, cool water. She set it before the animal and murmured, "Here, Scrounger. Here's some water, boy."

Troy chuckled and cocked his eyebrow. "Scrounger?"

She grinned. "Yeah. It suits him, don't you think?"

Troy's head rolled back in laughter. "Yeah. It does."

Later, Mama and Daddy came down to view the injured, failing Scrounger. Mama was sympathetic, but her distaste was evident. "He can't come to the house," she said apologetically. Angel couldn't blame Mama, because Scrounger did smell to high heaven.

So the two teens kept watch there beside the lily pond. Scrounger made two more attempts to pull himself to the pond while the two of them rooted him on, praying for him to rally. Angel's breath would heave as he struggled, his courage astounding her. But exhaustion and pain aborted his feeble, valiant attempts and they brought the water bowl to his mouth and lifted his head for him to lap the liquid.

The last time, he refused to drink.

Angel and Troy combined efforts to make the dog comfortable and be there in his final moments. In the wee hours, lying on each side of Scrounger's blanket, the teens dozed. Angel was the first to awaken as dawn scattered the night. "He's gone," she whispered. Together, they mourned the dog that never had anything going for him. That nobody wanted. Yet – they'd both seen something redeemable behind those brave eyes and their hearts broke that, in life, he didn't ever get a helping hand.

"I've always wanted to be a veterinarian," Troy said in a choked voice. "I want to help animals like Scrounger."

"Please, Troy," she said, touching his arm, "carve 'Scrounger' on the Love Tree...so his courage will be remembered." Then shyly she added, "You can add your name, too, if you like."

A mist dropped over the scene. Darkness encroached as Angel reached out and they embraced in mutual grief.

Blackness swallowed her again. She floated and swirled through what felt like a tunnel.

The cocoon was no longer welcome and she willed the movement to continue…she didn't want to connect with the cocoon.

Darkness scattered and daylight filtered through a window…in Troy's den, she saw a ceramic figure in a pet catalogue. "It's Scrounger!" she said to Troy. "Only prettier. I want it." she sighed wistfully. "To remember him by. I don't ever want to forget Scrounger. I want to remember his courage."

Grayness…another night flashed past…in the car, on the way to the concert…Troy held Angel's hand as they drove through the evening rain.

"I've got you a present," he announced proudly.

She squealed. "Where is it?"

"No, no," he said. "You'll get it in a day or two. Patience, my darlin'."

Darkness swallowed Angel again…then she began to float…sunlight glimmered through for a moment before it dimmed and shadows began to fall all about her.

Nonono. She tried to speak but felt herself lifted higher and higher from being. Blackness began to wrap around her again, tightening, the cocoon growing firm and familiar….

The decision was a difficult one.

Charlcy was the first to remember, when she saw the date on her cell phone screen. "Oh my gawd, today's Pops' birthday."

She, Liza, Garrison, and faithful Penny held vigil at Angel's bedside on that beautiful August day. The sun outside was mercilessly cheerful in the face of the invisible, encroaching darkness that hovered, at times so closely that Liza felt she would suffocate.

Angel's condition hung in peril. Dr. Abrams, by now on quite familiar terms with the Wakefields, knew that they felt torn about leaving their daughter during daylight. Especially now in this time of critical wait and see.

"This is a special occasion for you folks. It will mean a lot to your father to have you there. And it won't hurt for you to be away for a couple of hours. Angel is closely monitored around the clock, so she's in good hands." Dr. Abrams smiled, a rare thing. "Please? It will refresh you for the hours to come. Doctor's orders."

"Go ahead," Penny urged them. "I'm already here, and if anything changes in the next couple of hours, I'll call you. I promise. Scout's honor." She raised a militant hand, cracking everybody up, albeit it tight laughter, expunging a bit of the understandable strain. "You need some time to chill out, folks."

"Yeah," Charlcy agreed with Penny and the doctor. "We're no help to Angel like this, tied up in knots like a lassoed steer."

So, feeling ganged up on, Liza and Garrison consented.

On the drive over, Charlcy asked, "Can you tell a difference in Pops lately?"

Liza replied, "I've seen a marked improvement in him since Dr. Jones switched him from Razadyne to Aricept."

"How long will it be effective?" Charlcy asked from the backseat. "I've not had a chance to speak with the good doctor."

"Well, I asked Dr. Jones about the best case scenario. He said that it postpones the worsening of symptoms in about half the cases for perhaps a year."

"I'm knocking on wood that Pops is among that fifty percent."

"We need to attach some prayers to the wood-banging," Liza added.

"So he's responded well so far?" Garrison asked, slamming on his brakes to avoid a too-close-for-comfort cut-in motorcyclist. "Road hog," he muttered. "His coffin's already been made. He's not even wearing a danged helmet."

Liza ignored the Hells Angels wannabe. She was loathe to desecrate this time by fretting or fuming over trivia. It was a sacrifice leaving Angel, but she knew in her heart it was the right thing to do in this instance. "So far, so good. The staff members say he's had fewer wild-blue-yonder episodes. Says he's more often – you know – the old Charlie."

"Good for Pops," Garrison murmured huskily.

They stopped off at a Publix bakery and got lucky. A double-sheet birthday cake sat in the glass case unclaimed. An ocean of white buttercream frosting swathed and oozed from it. "Can we buy that?" Liza asked hopefully.

"Sure can. The lady who ordered it called before I finished decorating and said an emergency came up and to sell it if we needed to. What do you want added?"

From two tubes, the baker quickly squeezed perfectly round blue and yellow icing balloons across each fluffy white corner. Then he meticulously added streamers and, in the very center, bold red letters proclaiming "Happy Birthday Pops!"

"We need seventy-five candles." Charlcy took off to the appropriate shelf and grabbed several boxes. "*Holy Toledo*, we're gonna cause a bonfire when these are lit." She grinned like a mad scientist. "That'll be the day's highlight, won't it?"

She tossed them in the shopping cart then paused, fingers pressed to her lips. "Let's see – we need something to torch these with." She jogged back and grabbed a box of matches and added it to the cart.

They all congratulated the baker on his superb, swift artistic adornment, paid at the register, loaded it all into the Jag's trunk and headed for Concord Place Assisted Living Facility.

There, Charlcy sneaked the cake into the kitchen staff's care with instructions for later festivities to which all residents were invited.

Liza intercepted a newer staff member and looked at her name tag. "We'd like to see Charlie. He's probably at recreation right now. Would you bring him out to the sunroom, please?"

"Sure thing."

Liza, Garrison, and Charlcy breathed a collective sigh of relief that they'd accomplished setting a special event in place to honor Pops. In less than an hour. And Liza was amazed that she'd not had the time to dwell on Angel's precarious hold on life for that span.

One minute at a time. She reminded herself that this sentiment had gotten her through hell and back.

They waited on the near-deserted, parquet-floored sun-porch, a beautiful window-enclosed wing with wall-to-wall rocking chairs. In each corner, live, riotous-colored basketed flowers draped from the ceiling. Central air conditioning hummed and spread the entire sunlit area with comfortable coolness.

Awed by the gorgeous, unexpected burst of nature, Liza left her chair and moved to one trailing bloom, reaching out to touch a dewy petal.

"*Ah ah!*" piped a strident, piercing voice.

Startled by the sharp, reverberating reprimand, Liza spun around to see a dried up female-gnome, sans false teeth, perched militantly on the edge of her frozen rocker in a far corner.

Attack mode. Liza could almost hear battle trumpets blaring.

Deep-set black, accusing eyes blazed at her as the woman's entire persona drew up into a knot of righteous indignation. "Don't touch 'em. You do not touch the flowers again! Ever."

All three of them stared unbelievingly at the dried-apple, rage-contorted features. A white knitted cap stretched over a small skull and a mismatched shawl tightly trussed humped, emaciated shoulders. Stick legs poked from beneath wrinkled, nondescript clothing, disappearing into fuzzy pink mules. Liza, Garrison, and Charlcy gazed at each other with raised brows then, as one, shrugged.

"Sure thing, sweetie." Charlcy smiled placatingly until the ancient sentinel folded back into herself and commenced rocking again.

Liza let out a breath of respite and sank into the nearest cushioned seat. Liza noted that the trio's earlier levity at the Publix bakery had taken flight, extinguished by the patient's bizarre departure from conventional behavior. It was a grim reminder of reality. One that jolted and jarred loose fears tucked and hidden away.

And unevoked, Angel's presence hung in the air like a cathedral bell's toll. It mingled with the uncertainty of what Liza would find here today. She forced her mind in more positive directions. *Dad is alive.* That was something to be thankful for.

Liza lolled her head back against the chair's padded headrest. She inhaled deeply, thankful for the cleanness of the facility. No cloying chemical fumes to cover urine/fecal odors assailed visitors here. The setting was in a quiet country atmosphere. They even let her dad use his own furniture.

"We need to change Pops' dried flower arrangement in his room," Charlcy said, as though reading Liza's thoughts. "It's been there since the *Mayflower.*"

"Yes," Liza replied. "I'm glad they allow us to furnish his room. It lets Dad be surrounded by the familiar."

"That's important to a man," Garrison agreed, folding and laying the *Spartanburg Herald* aside. Clasping hands across his abdomen, he began to rock serenely.

"To everybody, actually," Liza added. "It's essential to hang on to a bit of one's self in these situations. Dad always loved his flowers and these beautifully landscaped grounds would have to be a gift to him on his good days."

Their dad's facility unit housed residents more dependent upon assistance, who could not do certain things for themselves, such as bathing, dressing, toilet, and even feeding in many cases. Strategic entries and exits remained locked for patients' safety.

So far, Charlie could tend to himself on most critical levels, but there were times when his lapses to *otherness* sabotaged his autonomy. He'd only recently been demoted to the current unit, where freedom of behavior shrank.

"I'd rather look at this change as good," Charlcy now opined in glass-half-full mode. "Good that he will have his needs met. At least we won't have to worry about neglect."

Liza agreed. The care at Concord Place was exemplary, not the case in many such settings. And she and Charlcy should know. They had thoroughly checked out dozens of other assisted living institutions.

Oh, how she wished for the funds to afford one of the loftier, elegant choices, but neither she nor Charlcy, with their limited finances, could carry such a financial burden.

Their father's savings had long ago been bankrupted by their mother's extensive medical expenses. The daughters had been forced to sign over the bulk of his forthcoming retirement and estate to Concord Place. Of course, some of their father's services were covered by insurance or Medicare. The only thing left that was truly his was his room's furniture, and even that was subject to question.

Concord Place did not supply all the luxuries, but it did provide comfortable at-home-ness and excellent care. The package was conveniently unbundled so that Charlie's expenses were customized to his needs.

"In all," Liza said, "we made a good choice, Charlcy."

"Yup." Charlcy yawned hugely, stretched, and then growled, "What's taking them so long?"

"He was doing his recreation thing," Liza, too, stretched, growing groggy in the warm sunlight spilling through the tall, floor-to-ceiling windows. "He's probably walking today. She has to locate him." The supervised walking was one of the things here that she appreciated. Dad needed his exercise. It could perhaps improve the quality of and even prolong his life.

She rose and strolled out to the next-door deserted lounging area where a big-screen television played Oprah's interview with John Travolta. Charlcy sauntered in moments later. The lounge sported plush earth-toned easy chairs and sofas in comfortable conversational arrangements.

Well stocked library shelves lined an entire wall in the lounge. Liza had learned that the books, all genres one could imagine, were donated. She was also delighted to learn that many of the residents still enjoyed reading during lucid periods.

"Penny's a real sweetie pie to stick by Angel's side like she does," Charlcy said over Liza's shoulder as they fingered through the book collection. "It's good to know that she'll call us if she sees any changes."

Penny was always happy to do hospital duty in emergencies. This celebration wasn't exactly in that category, but things being unpredictable, Liza took nothing in life for granted. Somehow, she needed her father more now than ever before. She was certain Dr. Abrams had sensed that very thing. She prayed fervently that her dad would be lucid today. Even if he wasn't, just being near him was life affirming.

"I'm glad Garrison chose to come with us," she told Charlcy. "I wasn't sure he'd agree to pry loose from the hospital, but I'm glad he did. He and Dad were close all through the years."

"Pops has always been like a father to me," he'd told Liza earlier when she suggested he come along. "Sometimes even more than my own dad. Yeah, I'll go with you. I'd like to see him. It's been a while. Charlie was always sharing words of wisdom along the way, just when I needed 'em. I really miss that."

"Yeah," Charlcy said, dragging Liza's attention back to the moment at hand. "Dad was always easy to love. Always a generous spirit."

Liza and Charlcy shared a smile, one of unique sisterly affinity.

"Where did everybody go?" Garrison appeared in the lounge, impatiently scratching his head. "Where did she have to go to get Pops? China?" They all laughed and went back to settle into rockers again. It seemed as though each of them now flowed in peaceful acceptance of what the day would bring.

Eventually Pops appeared, still dressed in white Reebok walking shoes with rumpled, mismatched conventional clothes. "How are you today, Dad?"

He lowered his long length into the cushioned seat of one of the rocking chairs. "Aah," he closed his eyes and sighed. "This cool feels good. It's hot as Hades outside."

Simultaneously, Liza and Charlcy heaved sighs of relief at Charlie's lucidity. Liza knew that Charlcy, like herself, would relish the moments, however brief. However tenuous.

"Where's your girlfriend, Pops?" Charlcy said, venturing onto dubious ground.

He frowned for a long moment, during which Liza noted his fresh, closely cropped haircut. One of the services at Concord Place was an on-site barber and beauty shop, which was a god-sent convenience. Suddenly, Pops' bushy white brows lifted in enlightenment. "Oh, you're talking about Sally." He slowly shook his head, entertaining some mysterious musing. "She's playing bingo, I suppose," he finally said, crossing his long, spindly legs. Liza's heart gave a lurch at seeing the bony appendages poking out from beneath loose, flappy brown slacks legs, remembering how compact he used to be. Not heavy. Just solid. Healthy.

Young.

Vital.

As she took a seat near him, Liza also noticed that his socks did not match. One was athletic white, the other dress black. At that moment, it didn't matter. At least his rumpled burgundy shirt was clean and buttoned right. Almost. His gray hair had wet comb tracks.

Liza swallowed back a lump and smiled. "Happy Birthday, Dad."

His blue-gray eyes focused more keenly on her. "What day is it?"

"August twentieth."

A tiny cloud passed over his features, then lifted. "By George, it is my birthday, isn't it?" He smiled then. A warm, *there* smile.

"Dad." Liza rushed to capture the *there*-ness. "Tell me about Sally." Why did she say that? Because it was the first thing that popped into her mind. She needed that Daddy-connection like oxygen. She longed to hear her daddy talk – about anything on the universe as long as she could hear his sweet, rumbling voice.

"Well," he leaned back, one crossed-over leg swinging slowly, chin raised in contemplation, "she's nice. Most of the time." He chuckled mildly. "Pretty, too, when she takes time to primp. Sometimes, however, she's not so nice. Steals things, you know?" His brow scrunched. "Not always. Just sometimes. I have to hide everything here. More sticky fingers around this place than you can imagine."

They all watched him, thankful that for that moment, his mind latched on to the here and now. "Y'know," he said suddenly, softly. "I'm a very lucky man to have my two daughters and a wonderful son-in-law here with me on my birthday."

Liza's breath caught in her throat at the vivid coherence of his words.

"Say Pops." Charlcy stirred restlessly, obviously antsy to detour him from maudlin directions. "You never finished telling us about Sally. What's happening with you two?"

He skewered her with a piercing look and lifted an imposing finger. "That is none of your danged business," he snapped. Then he smiled smugly, crossed his arms stubbornly across his concave torso, and rocked vigorously.

"*Whooee,*" Liza chortled. "I guess he told you!"

"I reckon he did." Charlcy shifted in the rocker with mock indignation, and then burst into a contagious grin.

Chuckling, Garrison pulled his chair over and started chatting with Pops for a spell of light man-banter, ignoring the times his father-in-law failed to recall certain instances, filling in and guiding him to safer topics, bringing tears to Liza's eyes with his gentle sensitivity and respect.

"Where's Angel?" Pops suddenly asked. "Did she come with you?"

Garrison shot Liza an inquiring look. She shook her head, frowning.

"Angel couldn't come, Pops. But she sends her love." Garrison smiled tightly, obviously uncomfortable with dishonesty.

"Sweet girl, Angel," Pops murmured, rocking more sedately and lazily swinging his leg in rhythm.

"Look at those squirrels, playing on the little red birdhouse," Liza squealed, pointing out the window at a beautiful berm of flowers and shrubs encroaching on the mulched foundation of the pristine white pole supporting the critters' playhouse.

"See the one hanging upside down from the birdhouse?" Pops asked. "He's my buddy. Name's Squiggy."

Squiggy was indeed, dangling upside down from the tiny red birdhouse, tail twitching happily.

Pops continued his pleasant rhetoric. "I was a'comin' out and feeding 'em all for a while. I'd save my breakfast bread to feed 'em each morning." The warmth faded from his creased features. "Then they found out and took it away from me."

"Who, Dad?" Liza felt dread settle in her chest. Indignation rose up from the cement heaviness. How *dare* they forbid him to feed the critters bread crumbs.

"Everybody," he grouched. "They saw me feeding them and then they started bringing bread crumbs and – -" He shrugged morosely. "I just let 'em have it. Such hateful people."

"The others didn't know how much it meant to you, Pops." Charlcy said, attempting to smooth over a simmering situation. Paranoia was raising its ugly head.

"Oh, they did." One stern finger shot up like a flag. "They're just mean is what they are."

Liza felt another piercing longing for her daddy. *Oh God. Why?*

She looked at Charlcy and saw the same emotions mirrored in her. Liza determined again that she would get through this. She would continue to take it one minute at a time. Savoring each peaceful, rational one.

Moments later, they moved to the dining room, where frothy white cake frosting rippled and glowed beneath the fire-light of seventy-five candles. "Make a wish and blow 'em out, Pops." Charlcy led him over and helped him huff enough air to extinguish them.

"What did you wish, Dad?" asked Liza.

Without hesitation he said, "Oh, I wished I could see my lovely wife again."

Startled, yet curiously warmed, Liza gauged Charlcy's re-action. Her sister's face remained unreadable. Untouched. But for once, Liza didn't care. Her dad was reliving a happy mo-ment. He *so* deserved his happy memories.

Under Charlcy's direction, the motley gang broke out into a totally dissonant rendering of "Happy Birthday," one in several keys and with a number of staggered endings.

Music drifted over the intercom as they ate. Pop tunes, including Broadway numbers. "I Could Have Danced All Night" and "Do Re Mi," among others.

"Dance with me, Dad?" Liza heard herself saying, surprised. At the same time she was glad she'd acted spontaneously, because her father unhesitatingly stood and held out his hand.

The song was Robert Goulet's "If Ever I Should Leave You," the melody and lyrics so poignant Liza felt as if she would drown in emotion. It swirled and pummeled her insides for long moments, threatening to take her under. But when she looked up into her father's lined, once-handsome face, one now smiling and content with his little girl in his arms, she felt a peace settle upon her like she'd not felt since early childhood, before Mama's emotional state was shot to wads.

It took her back to a carefree time when just a touch from those calloused, gentle hands could calm all her fears. She laid her head over on the skinny shoulder, and for just that moment, let her peaceful heart connect with his.

She knew that this moment was a gift from above. One she'd never forget.

"Move over, you hog," Charlcy said, nudging her. "Let me show Pops how to really dance."

Liza stepped away as the old fifties tune "Dance with Me Henry" struck up. Liza noted that all the tunes were rather smooth and easy-paced. Noninvasive. Important in that setting. Several other residents were attempting to shake a slow leg as Charlcy and Pops did a fair version of a stammering jitterbug. Liza and Garrison then jumped in the pitiful fray to level out their musical sensibilities. They fit smooth shag steps to the old ditty, enjoying every moment of it.

Festivity reigned, as much as it possibly could considering both the physical and mental limitations of the partygoers. Cake and ice cream loaded plates served to lighten spirits, even of those with the most dire challenges.

Liza's curiosity piqued when she heard, "There's Sally." She turned to watch a petite, white-haired, rather well-dressed lady who'd arrived late.

"Bet she was a knockout twenty years ago," Garrison muttered out the side of his mouth.

Liza had to agree. Charlcy leaned to whisper in her ear, "Sally's having a good day. Last time I was here, she hadn't combed her hair for at least two days, nor changed her clothes. That time she was shrieking at Pops. Called him Frankenstein, she did."

The corners of her mouth twitched upward before she cleared her throat, sobering. "Sad. Today is a real improvement."

Remarkably attractive for her circumstances, Sally rushed to plant a big smooch on Pops' flushed cheek. "Happy Birthday, Charlie," she gushed, and was rewarded with a lopsided, silly smile.

Liza and Charlcy's gazes collided and they both burst out laughing, a sound swallowed by all the commotion the kiss drew from the group. Everybody was pointing and muttering and snickering. Some of the more mentally challenged remained passive as staffers spoon-fed them cake and ice cream.

"Y'all are disgraceful," sputtered one plump, gray-haired woman from a nearby table. She glared at Sally, pulled herself up self-righteously, and stuck her nose in the air.

"You're just jealous," singsonged Sally, still rooted near Charlie's chair.

"Yeah, Gertrude," yelled another dark-haired female resident from across the room, this one standing and waving a fist. "You just want 'im for yourself."

"So-rry," sang Sally, grinning at the protestor like the Cheshire puss. "Can't have 'im!"

Gertrude sprang to her feet, tossed her head back, and stomped from the dining room, muttering obscenities.

"Would you listen?" Liza leaned over to whisper to Garrison, seated next to her at one of the white-clothed, six-seater tables with multicolored silk flower arrangements sprouting from their centers. Guest of honor, Charlie, sat at its head with two other residents flanking him. "Women are fighting over him."

"That's a problem?" Garrison quipped, chocolate-brown eyes glimmering with laughter.

"Not for him," Charlcy leaned from Liza's other side to mutter. "He couldn't care less, doncha know? Look at 'im."

Sure enough, when Liza gauged her father's reaction, she saw him sitting placidly, face straight ahead, expression bland.

Sally dragged a chair up to him, nudged another resident over to squeeze her seat in, and plopped down beside the birthday guy.

"How old are you, Charlie?" she asked coyly.

Pops thought for a moment. "I'm…fifty."

"Dad," Charlcy reminded him, "You're seventy-five today."

"Nope," he insisted, rather huffily. "I am *not* seventy-five. I'm…sixty or sixty-five." He gave a *so what* shrug of his thin shoulders, eyes straight ahead, features set stubbornly.

"Dad." Dread slid through Liza. "You're *seventy-five*." She forced the desperation from her voice. *Lighten up.* "It's okay, Dad. You're just on the wrong channel today."

Her father looked at her, frowning. Then smiled. "Wrong channel." He grinned widely, nodding in approval. "I like that. I'll just switch channels."

Liza relaxed, thankful that Pops' brain conduit had switched to clarity again.

Then he looked at Charlcy, focusing intently for long moments. "Where is Raymond? Isn't he with you?"

Charlcy stiffened, glancing at Liza. "N-no, Pops. Raymond couldn't make it this time." She picked up her water, and Liza saw her hand tremble when she turned it up for a gulp.

"Why not?" His voice turned testy, his lined face stormy. "Raymond hasn't been to see me for a long, long time. Why doesn't he come to see me anymore? As far as that goes, why don't *you* come anymore? I haven't seen you in ages, girl. That's not showing respect for your father."

"Pops." Charlcy visibly fought to hold it together. "I come three or four times a week. Every week. Liza comes the other three or our days. We rotate."

"Nobody comes anymore," he intoned, gazing off into middle distance, his countenance inordinately grieved.

"Dad." Liza reached to take his hand. "We come –"

He snatched his hand back as if stung by her touch. Then he stared at her in a way that chilled Liza. It was that blank yet hostile set of his features that sparked dread. The unknowing eyes that snatched away her cloak of daddy-security. The hairs on her neck and arms sprang to life.

"Who are you, anyway?" His voice rose on an exasperated pitch. He peered around as if trapped in a horror chamber. "Get these people out of here," he commanded. "I don't want them here. Why are you all staring at me? Huh?"

An aide appeared at his shoulder. "Come on, Charlie. We'll go to your room."

"I don't want to go," he sputtered, resisting the tugs on his arm. "Please don't touch me."

Liza felt Garrison gently grip her arm and nudge her to leave.

"Dad —" Tears stung the backs of her eyes at the pitiful desperation in her father's voice, this man who was once so indomitable, even in the face of her mother's barrage of indignities against him. He'd remained, even then, a protector, good and honorable…loving unconditionally.

Now he was reduced to pleading. *Please be kind to him.* She heard herself exhale on a sob.

"Shh." Garrison nodded to the door. "Let's leave him in peace."

With tears flowing, Liza allowed Garrison to steer her from the room. Her father's shouts trailed them.

"Get away from me, you crazy woman." His wrath toward Sally rattled the airwaves and Liza recoiled at the vehement display, one so unlike the father of her upbringing.

Liza turned in time to see the aide and another staffer pry Sally from her Dad's side and propel her from the room. She was in tears, confused and distraught.

"Why is he shouting at me?" Sally wailed pitifully, unfortunately lucid.

Liza wanted to cover her ears, squeeze her eyes shut, and delete the entire scene as, outside in an early dusk, Garrison jogged to the parking lot for the car. She and Charlcy huddled on the curb waiting for him.

Silent. Stunned. Despite her earlier resolutions to soar above the clouds, Liza felt it all caving in on her.

Angel.

Daddy.

But just then, she felt Charlcy's arm slip around her.

"It's okay, baby," her sister whispered. "It's okay."

And she knew that it was.

chapter fourteen

Garrison refused to let his spirits dampen when Angel didn't immediately return to them. He and Liza agreed on that point. They would not let despair creep back in to sully their belief. In truth, they agreed on most everything these days.

"I'm glad to have you back in my bed," Liza said, stretching sinuously against her husband. He loved it.

"Mmm, glad to be back." He rolled half over on her, twining his leg with hers, his lips exploring her neck. "You've got the softest, most beautiful neck and shoulders." He snuggled closer. "You feel so good," he groaned. "All that dancing is making you into a streamlined form of yourself."

She pouted her lips. "You didn't like the old me?"

"I loved the original…but baby, just look at you now." He gazed into her eyes. "I don't ever want to leave your side again."

She captured his face with both hands and whispered, "You'd better not."

He grinned then. "If you ever leave me, I'll just tag along."

"I'm counting on it."

Yep, they agreed on most everything lately.

"Garrison?" She gazed deeply into his eyes.

"Hmm?"

"I don't see it anymore."

"What?"

"The condemnation."

"I'm sorry, Liza," he whispered. "That should never have been. I'll spend the rest of my life making it up to you."

Her eyes darkened. "Making up...mmm...sounds delicious."

His lips curled into a slow, lazy smile. "My specialty."

And in those moments in time, they were able to put aside the dark crisis that raged at Restorative Care. It shatterproofed and recharged them for the battle they faced.

They packed up the unfinished painting and Liza's portable stereo with some of her choice music discs. "It can't hurt, having these there in the room. Y'know?" she said.

"I agree," Garrison said, carefully placing them in the car trunk.

At the hospital, they set up the easel and painting in the room's far corner, facing the bed. Liza began softly playing selections of her music.

They resumed their vigil on either side of the bed. Across the white shrouded figure, their gazes now reflected hope.

Two days later, Liza, purse in hand, joined Garrison downstairs, where he'd gone to the foyer closet to retrieve his briefcase and double check his agenda. They'd both dressed in casual jeans for the Saturday Restorative Care bedside vigil.

"I should be fairly free for a few days." Garrison's appreciative eyes scanned Liza from head to toe while hers swept his lean frame, assessing the finely chiseled features and softly waved, slightly wayward salt-and-pepper hair. And it was as though this was that first flush of intimacy all over again. The excitement of discovery, of exclusivity. Awareness shot through her in the most cherished, timeless way. In a way that felt scrumptious and right.

Liza couldn't believe the blast of chemistry between the two of them since the night of their renewal. With its upsurge came the power to face all other adversities.

"The Vanhauser account put us over the top." Garrison opened the closet door. "I just want to take stock of the list Gwen has compiled of pending accounts in different time slots. I'm pretty certain none are coming up for several days."

He tugged the briefcase from the top shelf. It snagged a package that toppled out, barely missing his head and bouncing off his shoulder. It thudded onto a colorful Persian runner and landed at his feet.

Liza picked up the package "What's this?" She turned it over and read the mailing label. Her heart leaped. "This is from Troy. To Angel." She looked at Garrison, who gazed back, eyes mirroring her own powerful emotions.

"I'd forgotten it was there," he muttered.

With trembling fingers, she tore open the box. Slowly, she lifted out a tissue-wrapped figurine. Her fingers trembled. It was an idealized version of Scrounger, the mutt Angel and Troy had so sadly mourned. But the resemblance was uncanny. She pulled the accompanying note from the box.

She read it and handed it to Garrison.

Stunned, they gazed at each other. Liza started to put the figurine back on the closet shelf. Then a gut feeling kicked in. She tucked it and the note in her large purse. "This belongs at her bedside."

Dr. Abrams' prognosis remained grim. "We did the cultures to determine the appropriate antibiotic and the proper dosage to use for ARDS. Along with that, we've also used moderate doses of corticosteroids for inflammation. Now, we just wait and see. I wish I could promise that she'll recover. But at this point – honestly – the bottom line depends upon her will to live."

Garrison repositioned the easel and painting near the window, where sunlight blended with the light spilling from the portrait.

It would either happen or not. Liza carefully placed the ceramic figurine and stood the note on Angel's bedside table, facing their daughter. Then she and Garrison pulled chairs up to either side of the bed and held the girl's hands. Charley and Penny sat unobtrusively in the background, keeping silent vigil as well. Liza's music wafted softly from her portable stereo. Today's selections were from *Don Quixote*, along with John Barry's *Dances with Wolves* and *Out of Africa* movie themes.

Garrison's and Liza's eyes met across the bed. Liza said softly, gathering courage about her, "It's up to her now."

Garrison nodded, his eyes dark with purpose. They closed their eyes and focused on the portrait with the lily pond and the Love Tree. On family love....the mystical healing of unconditional love and forgiveness. On renewal.

Heads bowed, having done all they could do, they once more took up their vigil.

Blackness clung and cloyed as Angel struggled toward the glimmer of light.

She groaned soundlessly and broke free into the misty light spilling over the dance floor where her feet connected with parquet. She recoiled slightly...wanting to be somewhere else. A sideboard in the distance, laden with gooey frosted cakes and goodies beckoned to her...tantalizing her...her finger dipped furtively into frothy icing, but guilt stopped her from indulging.

From the barre, Mama, face worried, silently called to her, holding out bread to her. Angel couldn't understand what she was trying to tell her. On the far side of the studio, Daddy wiped his paintbrush on a cloth and smiled at her. Love pulled so strongly at her that she nearly flew through the air to them, but – something held her back. Angel spun away from them both…away, away, away…floating toward him…she knew he was there somewhere near the lily pond. But where?

"Troy?" she called. Or did she? She no longer knew in this state of nothingness.

There! She saw him! He stood beneath the Love Tree where the sun rays, tossed over the lily pond, were so bright, the water sparkled like diamonds.

The Love Tree stood out in three-dimensional clarity. Troy leaned indolently against it, foot crossed at the ankle, arms folded across chest. Yet – something in his eyes, sober and disquieting, drew her. She tried to get to him, but each time she thought she was getting near he faded into a haze.

Everything grew misty…she could barely see him as he pushed from the tree and began to move silently away…she tried to open her eyes to see better…tried to run…wouldn't move. Frantic, struggling…*can't…reach…him!* "Troy!" she screamed. At her urgency, Troy turned and moved a little closer…a slow smile of encouragement broke across his face.

And she saw Scrounger beside Troy. No longer sick but grinning, his tongue lolling.

"I've got to go now." The words floated from Troy, unspoken.

"But –" She lifted a hand in supplication.

He hesitated, then said, "I want to show you something." A mist wrapped and floated around them. When it parted, she felt like she sat upon it, like a cloud pillow, her feet dangling like a little girl's. Troy sat beside her and held her hand now. She curled her fingers into its warmth.

He pointed below them, to the medical team who dispensed extreme measures to the same patient she'd seen before. She looked at Troy questioningly. He nodded toward the activity below. "Watch." The female doctor this time pushed her way through the thick doctors' throng to the patient's side, pushing aside other groping hands in an authoritative way that scattered them like startled birds. Angel felt a fierce, mystical connection to the doctor. Spellbound, she watched the woman lean over and put her ear to the still chest. Then she straightened and pounded on the at-rest bosom…she began a deep massage… she spoke to the inert form. Angel leaned in, keen to hear but only telepathic waves filtered to hear…. I can do this…I will do this! By God, I will do this!"

Angel looked at Troy, puzzled. "What does she mean?" Her silent question vibrated between them. Troy again nodded toward the medical clan below, who shook their heads in wonder at the now-breathing patient. The female doctor exited the room silently. No one even seemed to notice her.

Angel's mist-cloud seat followed her. The doctor slowly removed her mask and cap…blond hair cascaded free and blue eyes shimmered with incandescent purpose and courage.

Angel gasped. "It's me, Troy."

He laughed, a pealing, joyful sound. "It's *you*. Go back, Angel." The silent words were gentle but firm as he loosed his hand from hers. His eyes darkened with sadness, then just as quickly, it evaporated and his smile returned. "Soon, you'll know why. Go back."

From somewhere drifted rich, wonderful music.

His smile broadened as the haze deepened and mist moved in to swallow him.

"Remember!" he called, "I love you. And don't forget your present!"

WHOOSH!

Blinding bright light bounced against her slitted eyes. Soft music…everything blurred as Angel squinted. Slowly, ever so slowly, the two hovering blobs morphed into Mama's and Daddy's smiling, tearful features.

"Wh–" her lips moved but no sound erupted. The thing in her throat – it stopped the sound. She cast her sluggish gaze about. White everywhere. Weird machines and sounds. Numbness in parts of her body. Pain in others.

She cut her eyes sharply to the right. Bedside table…the black ceramic figurine zoomed in. Then she saw the note. Squinting, she made out the letters "Remember I love you. All my love, Troy." Suddenly, she smiled as tears rushed to her eyes.

She knew.

chapter fifteen

"So you've decided to come back to us, huh, brat?" Charlcy gruffly addressed Angel, and Liza knew it was to hide deeper emotions. Angel was back.

Barely. But thank God, back.

She still had problems speaking. The doctors had removed the respirator two days ago. But her throat remained sore as it healed from the lengthy intrusion of the ghastly, life saving tube, and later, the tracheotomy. Her voice was terribly hoarse. Dr. Abrams had said it would take time.

Just as it would take time to see how thoroughly Angel's back and legs would heal. Angel's most clearly enunciated words were "I will walk again." They were not mere declaration. They were a vow.

Liza felt the vow in her bones. She prayed with everything in her that it would be so. But in the meantime, more pressing health issues faced them in the hour by hour, day by day seemingly endless crisis. Pain was her most vicious adversary. Next to that was the numbness below her waist and learning ways to cope and compensate. So far, so good because Angel rose to each in typical daredevil mode.

The doctor's prognosis for her future was more grim. "Don't get your hopes too high" became a familiar mantra. But Angel's stubbornness, her patience and grit, astounded Liza. Angel's stoical acceptance of her limitations bolstered Liza's own spirit. Garrison, too, benefited from Angel's pluck and optimism. He told Liza repeatedly how their gutsy daughter had kept him going.

"You gonna let her talk to you like that, Angel?" Penny piped in, winking at Charley. "Unless o' course you deserve to be called 'brat'."

Angel nodded, a big old lopsided grin stretching across her face. Liza watched her interact with her aunt and still couldn't believe Angel was actually there and, miracle of miracles, recognized everyone. Her speech, though slow and halting, was not too affected, nor was her memory, except for the moment of the tragic impact. Of that, Angel had no recall, which was normal according to Dr. Abrams.

It was a miracle. Of that, Liza would never be dissuaded.

Penny stepped up to the bed. "We're not gonna have any of that head nodding," she scolded good-naturedly. "Come on, let's hear it. Mute is so not you."

"Yes," rasped Angel, and grinned like a doofus at the chorus of cheers.

Charley sat sprawled in one of the hospital's ultrafirm leather chairs. "These chairs weren't made for wimps, brat," she grumbled to Angel, shifting herself in an unsuccessful bid for comfort.

Angel's eyes lifted a bit. "Wanna...change...places?" she rasped unsteadily, grinning lopsidedly.

"Smart aleck," Charley muttered blandly, winking at her niece.

"Ummm." Liza stretched bonelessly and slid her feet into comfy Cole Haan slippers. Garrison had gone to the office for a while, whistling as he exited and with a distinct jauntiness to his step that she'd missed for longer than she cared to think about. Today's sunshine spilled into and over the room, it's heat causing the air conditioner to hum incessantly. But Angel wanted the curtains thrown open and Liza was determined she'd have them open.

It seemed that was everyone's sentiment, to celebrate to the hilt Angel's return, from the cheering squad's pizza party last night to Charlcy slipping her Snicker bars when nobody was looking. Liza saw but would have stood before a firing squad before denying her resurrected daughter anything her heart desired. Especially food. She'd learned her lesson in the most heartbreaking way.

A nurse came in and administered Angel's pain medication and left.

Sitting with her back to the door, Liza didn't at first detect the footsteps. It was the narrowing of Charlcy's eyes, fastened furiously on the door, that raised her antennae. That look on her sister's face usually forecast ill-omened events.

"Uncle Raymond!" Angel rasped, weak eyes struggling to focus.

Liza spun around in her chair, nearly gasping in shock.

Six feet three inches of raw, craggy masculinity towered uncertainly in the doorway. He nodded at his sister-in-law, clearly uncomfortable. "Liza," he rumbled, then cleared his throat.

"Hi, Raymond." Liza's voice was whispery, surprised. Warm, she hoped, because she'd truly missed this man in her life.

Then his attention swung to Angel and his stony features softened a tiny whit. "Hey, little bit. Heard you've been away." His deep voice, so familiar and so resoundingly family, drew tears to Liza's eyes. Then abruptly, her gaze swung to gauge her sister's reception of this Texas-proportioned cowboy who had, according to Charlcy, done a splendid, bang-up job of doing her in.

His rodeo days were long past, but as Charlcy loved parroting, "You can take the man out of the rodeo but you can't take the rodeo out of the man." Corny cliché that it was, it fit Raymond like Saran Wrap. A back injury had taken him from the rodeo circuit but he had, at least before he'd lost contact with family, continued to work with training horses.

Beneath the white Stetson, hawk-focused eyes, as fierce as ever, gazed gently at his niece. The strong, firm bridge of his nose sported a small fracture-bump, a souvenir of his tough rodeo years. It took nothing from the dangerous, rugged good looks that had snagged Charlcy on that long ago visit to a Texas rodeo while on vacation.

Charlcy's exuberant, immediate phone relay to Liza had been, "Gawd, he's the most gorgeous hunk of man I've ever laid eyes on. I could eat him alive! Wait till you see 'im."

And indeed, he'd lived up to every descriptive adjective in Charlcy's worldly-wise repertoire.

As an afterthought, Raymond snatched off his Stetson and ran quick fingers through his auburn-cast, over-the-collar hair. Liza saw threads of silver in his sideburns, which only added to his primitive beauty. He dropped the hat on a close-by chair, terse and awkward in his movements.

Charlcy's white face hung slack, like she'd been slammed in the midriff by a hulking, maniacal quarterback and had just been peeled from the ground. *Is she breathing?* Liza wondered, watching her skin turn a chalky gray. Charlcy licked her dry lips. A quick, furtive gesture. Her glazed eyes remained fixed on Raymond Benton's face.

"Why?" Charlcy's lifeless lips quivered around the word.

Raymond looked steadily at her. "Why what, Charlcy?" he drawled.

Despite Charlcy's mounting bravado, hurt pooled heavily in her eyes. "Why did you come? What can you possibly want after – after *pulverizing* me last year, then skipping out? Huh? You could become a billionaire by giving seminars on 'Ten Easy, Quick Steps to Ruining Lives,' Raymond. Well, playing the martyr is so not my style. Am I supposed to fall at your feet now and thank you for coming back? Is that your script?"

"Maybe this time, it's not all about you, Charlc." He nodded toward Angel's bed. "Other things figured into my coming."

Charlcy lifted her chin in pitiful insolence and crossed her arms, clearly trying to hide how affected she was. "W-who told you about Angel?" Her voice sounded like a weak clarinet.

"Lindi." Raymond gracelessly shifted his lanky frame and shoved big hands into loose jeans pockets as Charlcy's gaze swept his long length, over-bright eyes lingering on the muscular chest beneath his western shirt and the uncharacteristically thin waist cinched by a silver buckled belt with turquoise inlays. Her perusal, one which struck Liza as insolence-aimed, stopped at the leather cowboy boots only to return quickly to the ultra-slim midriff.

Liza noted that Raymond's former Super John Wayne frame had diminished considerably since she'd last seen him. She knew that Charlcy had taken note as well by the shimmer of concern that bled through her narrowed gaze.

"When did you and Lindi talk?" Charlcy's eyes narrowed even more.

"Last week."

"Sit down, Raymond. Please," Liza insisted, gesturing to a chair near Charlcy.

Raymond nodded politely and folded himself into the leather chair, elbows too long to sit on the armrest. They ended up resting on his hips, large calloused fingers clasped across his lap.

"Lindi didn't say anything to me," Charlcy said, relentlessly returning to the tabled subject.

Raymond's gaze lowered to the floor. "Raymond?" Charlcy's voice slid to a strident – then tentative – note. "Something's wrong. What is it?"

Raymond's head snapped up. "Nothing's wrong." His gaze wavered, fingers grew restless.

Charlcy's eyes narrowed to slits. "Spit it out, Raymond. If there's one thing I can smell, it's trouble." She snorted. "I've got this built-in radar, doncha know? Course you do. Didn't ask for it, but the forces that be decided to bestow me with this gift of sniffing out *caca*." She rolled her eyes balefully. "*What a crock.* So what is it this time? Why are you in town?"

Liza felt herself tensing and was about to attempt to defuse the situation when Raymond spoke.

"First and foremost, I'm here to see Angel." His hurt gaze rested on Charlcy. "I didn't know about Angel till Lindi told me – she had my phone number all along. Why didn't you call me, Charlcy? You know how I feel about –"

"Call you?" Charlcy peered testily at him, as though he'd grown buffalo horns. "Case you don't recall, you sorta dropped off the planet in the past year. Where have you been, Raymond? I'm surprised Lindi will even talk to you. You broke her heart when you failed to call her on her birthday – or for that matter, Christmas."

"I called her at Christmas."

"But you missed her birthday. Unconscionable."

She sat back, crossed her arms and legs, and peered at him intently, as though deciphering an ancient text for the first time, as though he were testifying at a murder trial. Raymond shifted uneasily, rolling his neck and shoulders. "Don't. Don't look at me like I'm under a microscope, Charlc. In view of all your stated grievances, all justified, it was very difficult for me to come here."

Charlcy reached out, palm up, and pumped her fingers impatiently for more. "And?"

"Hell, Charlcy," Raymond muttered and swiped a big hand across his face and closed his eyes for a moment, clearly fighting to hold on to his composure.

"Charlcy." Liza could stand it no longer. She felt like a voyeur. "Should I leave?' She began to rise, cutting a concerned glance toward Angel's bed,

"She's asleep," Charlcy said softly, picking up on Liza's need to protect Angel from upsetting scenes such as this. "If anyone leaves, it will be Raymond and me. I'm sorry, honey. I wasn't thinking clearly. But I did see that she was asleep."

Raymond rose quickly to his feet and snatched up his Stetson. "I'm sorry, too, Liza. I truly wanted to come and see Angel – all of you, in fact. I've missed you. I'm glad Angel's rallied. Lots to be thankful for."

"We've missed you, too, Raymond," Liza said. "And yes, we are grateful beyond words that our girl has come back." She hugged her brother-in-law warmly. At least he would be family for a little while longer.

Charlcy stood then. "You never did tell me what's going on, Raymond."

He looked at her like he wanted to hit her. Gazed at the ceiling, fidgeting with his hat brim. Then he visibly caved in. That was the only way Liza could later describe it to Garrison. He sort of wilted. "Okay, Charlc. I've been in Atlanta for the past few months. Near Emory."

The fury in Charlcy's blue eyes slid into wariness. Her mouth dropped open. "Emory? What –" Then realization visibly hit her like a Seaboard Coastline freight train.

"The big C, honey," he said softly. "I didn't want you to see me —" He took a deep, dragging breath and bucked up, eyes moist as they met her stricken ones. "That's why. I've got to tell Lindi. Will you help me?"

That did it. Liza, heart in throat, watched Charlcy's last arsenal walls crumble, topple into dust. Saw terror seize her — something that looked so alien in Charlcy that it altered her entire persona. How vulnerable she looked. It splintered Liza's heart.

Raymond fidgeted, craggy face uncertain, consoling as he watched Charlcy's disintegration. "Aah, honey," he groaned, threw the Stetson aside, and held out his arms to her.

After about five seconds of virtual hand-wringing resistance, Charlcy sailed into his fierce embrace, where she gulped back tidal sobs, grasping in her white fingers the back of Raymond's shirt until Liza listened for it to rip. She herself stood frozen, hands to mouth, tears spilling over.

Moments later, they excused themselves to journey down the hall, into the little chapel for a private talk. Liza watched them leave, emotions flailing inside her. Sadness, fear, happiness — they bounced against one another, none willing to concede.

Who would have thought the world could turn on a pinhead so swiftly? So unexpectedly. The ramifications of Raymond's and Charlcy's situation stunned her. The emotions agitated inside her, churned until a profound thing that had all but vanished from Charlcy's odyssey separated itself from the conflux and rose to the top like golden, sweet butter.

Hope.

How Liza had prayed for her sister to grasp on to something solid, something that would pull her up from that pit of disillusionment. Something to renew her. Who'd have believed it might turn out to be Raymond?

Charlcy had been so implacable in her unforgiveness toward him. But things were subject to change with love thrown into the chaos, weren't they?

Liza smiled and walked over to Angel's bedside and peered down into the young sleeping face. As though sensing a profound occurrence, the long eyelashes fluttered, then opened.

"Mom?" Angel said, blinking against sedation and gazing blearily about. "Where's…uncle Raymond? Why did you…let me sleep? I wanna talk to 'im."

"He'll be back." Liza's laugh slid from her, loose and rich. It felt good. "Honey, my bet is that you'll have plenty of opportunities to talk to Uncle Raymond."

Yes, it felt good.

Garrison's paintbrush flew over the canvas and he felt a sense of being set free and soaring with life's goodness. Late, late that night, he stood back and smiled at the results. From the canvas, his own features regarded him with a celebration of life and joy.

Of fulfillment.

Henry David Thoreau once said, "Most men lead lives of quiet desperation and go to the grave with the song still in them." Garrison smiled at having escaped that fate, knowing that his journey to find his heart's song had delivered him to this very moment in time. No money in the world could buy the feeling of waking up each day and doing a job he loved, that used his talents in a challenging way.

Garrison had found his song.

His heart now sang with it.

"That was tough." Raymond's big hands clenched the steering wheel. He and Charlcy had left their daughter, Lindi's Atlanta home over two hours ago and were exiting I-85 into Spartanburg. "But she took it like the trooper she is."

"She is that," Charlcy agreed, her voice thick with emotion. She was quiet for long moments. "But then, she's had lots of practice in recent days." The words were weary rather than accusatory, and Raymond seemed to understand because he didn't react. Not outwardly, at least.

Charlcy knew he was hurt by her directness. At the same time, she was aware that he also knew she was put together and wired for unqualified candor. That's why it had always worked for them. They understood each other. At least

until –

"Hey!" Raymond said suddenly, swiveling his head to gaze at a landmark. "Let's stop by Hank's Place."

Charlcy perked up. Spontaneity was one of the things she'd always loved about Raymond. "I would love one of their frosty root beers. It's been ages, hasn't it?"

"As the crow flies, about a million years, sugarbabe." Raymond swung his red Toyota pickup into the graveled parking lot. He jogged around and opened her door, causing her eyebrows to lift. This new Raymond was no slouch when it came to being attentive. Of course, he'd always been considerate, but this was a brand new level for him, coming around to assist her from the vehicle. Made her feel real special.

Outside, they passed smokers loitering about, grumbling about the new no-smoking policy inside and calling out good-natured insults and insincere flattery to one another.

Garth Brooks' jukebox song spoke of friends in low places as they swung through the door. Raymond's Western garb fit right in with the Levis and Wranglers, boots, and a spattering of Stetsons. They singled out a corner booth, away from the dance floor and bar, where the music appeased rather than thrashed.

Charlcy felt his hand surreptitiously cup her denimed bottom as she walked ahead of him. When she cut him a sharp look, he winked at her and she grinned in spite of herself.

Raymond slid into the seat opposite Charlcy, his eyes doing a slow, thorough search of her face, as though he'd lost something and could find it there amongst her features. This was the Raymond who'd literally knocked her off her feet in a Gilley's-type bar all those years back.

She and her teacher-girlfriend had been enjoying the echoes of *Urban Cowboy* in the highly publicized Texas Café/Bar when she'd trekked to the bathroom. On her way back, a cowboy slammed into her as he exited the mechanical bull. Next thing she knew, he was picking her up from the floor and setting her on her feet as though she were no heavier than a toy Chihuahua.

For full-figured Charlcy, that was no mean feat.

Gazing into her eyes with genuine concern was a Sam Elliott double, mustache, low, drawling voice, and all.

Gawd. He was gorgeous.

She had immediately recognized him from the rodeo earlier that day. What a figure he'd cut on that broncing horse. *My-mymy*, the energy bursting from him created an aura of power that nearly blew her away. "Don't you get enough punishment without doing that bionic-bull thing?" she'd wisecracked, drawing an eruption of pure appreciative masculine laughter.

"Sure thing, sugarbabe," he'd quipped right back in his lazy Texan drawl. "But then I wouldn't be standing here flirtin' with you right now, now would I?"

Those eyes had never left her face on that long ago night. Just as they adored her at this precise moment.

Charlcy felt the heat-flush start at her neck and crawl slowly upward. "Where's that waitress?" she snapped to cover her feelings. Still, those hawkish eyes never wavered. Charlcy took a deep breath, glared back at him, and said, "What?"

He gave a lazy shrug and lolled back against the seat. "I just wanna look at you, Charlc. You're still the most beautiful girl I've ever seen." Belying his laid back demeanor, the words husked, thick with emotion.

Which only amplified Charlcy's discomfort, stirring up and bidding unpleasant memories of betrayal. "Why? Have you been looking?" Immediately, she regretted flapping her tongue so indiscriminately.

His eyes flickered for only a moment, then settled back into their intense surveillance. "Nope."

The Western-garbed waitress's arrival scattered the hovering dark nuances of deceit. They ordered two root beers and all-the-way hot dogs.

"What?" Charlcy sniped, though the corners of her mouth tugged upward. "No real beer?"

"No more alcohol," he growled, deadly serious. "Cost me too much."

When they were alone again, Raymond unexpectedly reached across the table and grasped Charlcy's hand. "C'mon, let's dance," he murmured, tugging her to her feet and steering her to the peanut-shelled dance floor, causing Charlcy's heart to do a little flippity-do.

God, the guy was so…*manly* in his confidence. In that moment, a double-edged sword pierced her with both love and hate – love for this sensitive, caring man – hate for the one who'd shredded and barbecued her, then left her in a smoldering heap not so long ago.

But when he pulled her into his arms for Anne Murray's "The Rest of Your Life," she melted against him and inhaled his own special smell of aftershave, leather, and soap.

All man.

He caught her in his long, strong arms and swung her around in a whirling, perfect countrified waltz. And she felt utterly content. Then she wondered crazily how one woman could feel so many emotions so at odds with one another?

Lordy, she didn't know. All she knew was that right then, at that precise moment, she felt complete while they moved as one over the crowded dance floor. Her cheek pressed to his, she smiled. For a broncing cowboy, he was sure light and graceful on his feet. As for rhythm, she didn't even want to go *there*.

Anne Murray's song ended and they returned to the booth, where they dug into their hot dogs and cooled off with the frosty mugs of icy root beer, relaxed and living in the moment.

The moment began to ebb when memories elbowed their way into Charlcy's fragile psyche. She resisted them for as long as she could before her up front, in-your-face side stepped up to bat.

Charlcy's finger drew circles on her mug. "Raymond, why did you cut us off? Lindi and me? Why didn't you let us help you? I was angry at you, sure. But if you'd just told me you were sick, I'd have been there for you."

He shifted, his eyes going grave as they focused on his big hands clasped before him on the table. "Because – I didn't feel free to tell you. I didn't think you'd be able to forgive me for –"

He shrugged tersely, cleared his throat and began again. "With prostate cancer, I didn't know how things would turn out. With surgery, sometimes a man can't always…."

"Raymond." Charlcy leaned forward, reaching to cover his hands with her own. "It wouldn't have mattered to me." She knew in that heartbeat that she meant it with everything in her.

"But it did to me. You're too much woman to settle for –" He shifted, frowning. "Heck, I know there are ways to please each other without – well, anyway, I decided not to go the surgery route. It was a gamble – a sort of damned if I do and damned if I don't, y'know? I chose another course of action, brachytherapy."

He shifted his lanky frame forward, elbows on table. "And as for Lindi, we talked several times. I didn't tell her about being sick. So she didn't understand why I stayed away. I knew she was angry and hurt."

Charlcy frowned, perplexed. "I don't understand why Lindi didn't share that you two were in touch."

He leaned back, brow furrowed. "She knew you were angry with me. An' you had every right to be. She didn't want you to be mad at her for seeming to take my side. She simply didn't want to rock the boat." He flexed his long fingers, then reconnected and studied them on the table. "It's hard to explain. As long as I didn't tell you two, it didn't seem as real. The Big C's like a death sentence when you dwell on it. So I didn't. Any more than I had to. But I wanted to see if this brachytherapy thing would work. My doctor agreed to try it."

"What is it? Charlcy asked.

"Well, brachytherapy is where they use a needle to plant these little radioactive seeds – about the size of a rice grain – directly into the cancerous tumors. They went through the skin of my scrotum to put 'em into my prostate gland – I'm not freaking you out, am I?" He peered anxiously at Charlcy, who'd felt the blood leaving her head moments earlier. She blinked against the dizziness, swallowed, and shook her head.

His expression was dubious, but he continued. "I was put to sleep for that procedure, by the way. Brachytherapy has been real effective in knocking out prostate tumors without surgery. Less risk of losing sexual function than with surgery."

He slanted her a searching look. "Even if that happened, there's always Viagra."

She shrugged that away. "What happens to the seeds ?"

"Still in there. In the prostate. There's no problem leavin' 'em there. Least that's what the doc says. I'm not aware of 'em anymore. Actually, they used the strongest radiation seeds – Palladium, I think they call 'em."

He shrugged and sighed, obviously exhausted and wanting to leave the subject. "The radiation has slowly decayed – can you believe that's the term they use? Decayed?" He gave a dry laugh. "Anyway, I'm not contagious at this stage."

"Is it all over? The treatment?"

He smiled tightly. "Yep. Now, it's a game of wait and see."

Charlcy's heart was thumping so hard she felt it would leap from her chest. "Is it working, Raymond?" *Oh God. Please say yes.*

"So far, so good." His smile grew more relaxed. "Doc says the tumor's shrinking right on schedule. I go in every three months for checkup. If it shrinks too fast, not good. Too slow, not good, either. So the danged varmint is dwindling just right."

"That's great, Raymond," Charlcy whispered, so relieved she felt that she was melting into a puddle right there on that hard seat. "Are there any side effects?"

"Well – there are. The worst being the piss complications. That's 'cause the prostate swells from being tinkered with and puts pressure on the bladder."

They had not discussed, in depth, his treatment until now. He'd backed away from it, saying he didn't want to play on her sympathy, which to her was pure crap. Even if she couldn't forgive him for his infidelity, he was the father of her daughter. And one of the best friends she'd ever had. She couldn't turn her back on him now, could she?

Deep, deep down, on a very primitive level, Charlcy knew her own arguments against reconciliation were also pure crap.

But on another level, she could not let go of the violations. Not at this point. So she pushed them aside – tabled them for the time being.

"Another thing." Raymond cleared his throat. "I've been going to AA for the past seven months. I don't want to bring up that thing that hurt you so –"

"Then don't." Charlcy took another slug of root beer, frowning against its growing tepidness. She was hoping against hope that he'd drop this particular subject because it was like banging her head against a cement wall to relive even one second of it.

"I have to, honey," Raymond murmured and took her hand, forcing her to look at him. "I'm not excusing myself, but had I not been a drunken sot that night, I wouldn't have done what I did. As simple as that."

"Simple?" Charlcy glared at him, pulling her hand loose, astonished that her rage was so *there*, near the surface. Ready to explode. But she couldn't stop her tongue "How dare you put it in so easy a term. Your *simple* little indiscretion cost me dearly. As well as Lindi and –"

"It cost me more," he rumbled softly.

Somehow that almost inaudible little declaration pierced the hostile screen she'd thrown up to ward off the blows. It knocked her off balance for long moments. Then, from long years of self-defense and survival experiences, the tiny rupture plugged itself up and storm clouds regrouped stronger than ever. "Ah, so now we're in a pissing contest as to who's the most pulverized?" She tossed her head back, rolling her eyes. "Spare me."

"I'd win hands down." He gazed at her, a gaunt portrait of misery. "Because I'm the one who blew it. I have to live with that, darlin'. I threw it all away."

Charlcy stared at him, the anger fizzling as she suddenly glimpsed his wretchedness. She blinked and looked away. She didn't like what she felt. She didn't want to feel anything. She'd lived her life for others, deflecting pain from them, taking it upon herself to be a freakin' protector.

And – God help her – the one person in her life she'd counted upon to protect *her* had let her down, defiling the sacredness of that trust. How could she just…let it go?

Raymond was watching her, his expression all soft and caring. When she met his gaze, he whispered, "it's okay, Charlc. I don't blame you. I don't deserve forgiveness." His smile didn't reach his sad eyes as he picked up the ticket and sauntered to the cash register. She retrieved her purse and followed.

Raymond had given her a pass. He didn't expect forgiveness. That should make her feel better.

But it did not.

chapter sixteen

Angel sat in her wheelchair, situated near the hospital window. Her newly assigned room rendered a more colorful view, overlooking raised berms of artistically arranged, crimson-blossomed crepe myrtle trees, sculpted shrubbery, and riotous summer flowers – all burgeoning with life, reaching inside her to dredge up an affirming response.

The thing was, though, she felt once-removed from almost everything these days.

"Survival mode" was how Dr. Abrams described it. "You're simply working through survival. All these other feelings and reactions will come eventually."

Angel wondered at that. It seemed lately that something else stirred deeply inside her, something she could not quite label. She'd begun to have unsettling dreams and little flashbacks of dark, dark times. Just snippets, but they were growing increasingly disturbing in nature. Maybe Dr. Abrams was right, though. Maybe it was normal in a case such as hers to feel this way.

Penny sat next to her, chair pulled close in case Angel grew faint from low blood pressure after her extended stagnancy.

Eyes closed, Angel sat in a pool of sunlight whose marvelous warmth penetrated her down to her waist. Below that, she felt nothing. The nothingness still blitzed her at times – not quite shock but some muted clone of it. Earlier that day, lower body spasms, in her paralyzed regions, had tugged at her upper tendons, while milder upper body spasms made her uncomfortable. Range of motion therapy was helping her upper body twitches.

Seeming to read her mind, Penny asked, "Have the spasms eased?"

Angel nodded, in that moment too weary to speak. Every willful act taxed her beyond measure. But Penny always seemed to understand and she loved her anyway.

Meds like Valium, Baclofen, and Dantrium gave her relief. Dr. Abrams explained that the spasms had a positive side, in that they improved the circulation in her extremities during this cycle of paraplegia. She refused to consider this a permanent thing.

No way.

For the moment, she would enjoy the beauty of life outside her sick chamber. In the next instant, though, a gush of anger welled up. "B-be glad when…I'm outta here," she grumbled feebly.

"You'll be out of here in no time flat," Penny decreed and reached out to squeeze Angel's hand. Penny was always upbeat, but not so much as to lope ahead of Angel. Penny's compassion penetrated Angel's apathy fog, releasing *hope* to advance in minuscule increments. "In the meantime, you've got to go to therapy. Which is it this afternoon?"

"Recreational T," Angel said. "*Yuck.*"

"But with Internet sessions, you get to check your e-mail, don't you?" Penny's genuine interest smote Angel on some wispy, subterranean level. Shock still subdued her senses and emotions, but she was slowly coming back.

She felt Penny's fingers gently squeeze her hand before loosing it, and gratitude emerged in semi-translucence. *There* but ghostlike. Angel felt, at times, like she was a voyeur of someone else's drama. Even Troy's death seemed surreal and distant. Dr. Abrams said that was normal after being comatose. He said it took time. She figured it was like landing on Earth again after a long stay in outer space, going through the process of getting back one's Earth legs.

Only now, she didn't have legs. Even that thought failed to shock her senses. It was like listening to a foreign language with no interpreter.

Total balance would take a while, wouldn't it? At least she thought it would. Counted on it.

Anger had more impetus, more kick – such as it was in her addled state.

"Yeah, check...e-mail. Hardyhar-har. Dense games...too much to handle at once. My head – still loopy." Angel's speech still stumbled but was improving daily.

Penny giggled, a bit self-consciously. "Hang in there. You'll be good as new soon."

"Darn right." Angel gazed out the window, demeanor glazed and faraway. Then she looked at Penny again, eyes suddenly over-bright. "Thanks."

Penny's expression grew puzzled. "For what?"

"E-everything. Being here. Like this. Staying for...the long haul."

At that moment an all-white clad, tall, jock-looking guy with a butch haircut burst into the room. "Ready to rock, Angel?"

"Yeah, Mark. Let's rock 'n' roll." Angel rolled her eyes at Penny and then set her features in resignation.

Penny trailed the chair to the elevator, where they said good-by.

Angel watched her friend wave until the elevator doors slid shut and she felt herself hoisted to fourth floor. She now knew what "best friend" was all about. Solid. Unwavering. Unconditional. *Penny.*

Therapy. Tears gathered suddenly. Where had they come from? She'd not felt them in so long they felt bizarre. But they were there. At least for that heartbeat in time.

The words of her psychiatrist, Dr. Carlsbad, flashed through her mind, haunting her. "Don't get your hopes up, Angel. Most likely, you'll not walk again." A parade of specialists agreed. "Accept it. Prepare for what's ahead. You'll be much better off if you adjust quickly."

I will not let negative people determine my self-worth.
Nor my hope.

She would not cry. No matter what they said. Because if she did, that would mean she'd given up. That would not happen. That's what she prayed for – to not give up.

She closed her eyes and curled her hands into fists.
I will not give up.

"Aren't you going to stop today and eat?" Liza called to Garrison, who perched on a ladder in the big upstairs studio, shooting nails into bookshelves. They would hold Angel's books, CD and DVD collections, and whatever else her heart desired.

He looked down at Liza and wiped his brow with his forearm, damp even in the air-conditioned coolness of the upper chamber. "What time is it?"

She smiled and sent his heart into a tailspin. He'd never again in his life take her for granted. "After two. Lunch has been ready for the past couple of hours. C'mon, let's rest a few minutes and chill out." He felt her warm gaze on him as he descended the ladder.

"Please, madam, let's ride down in style." He bowed eloquently and swept his hand toward the newly installed elevator. Liza's peal of delight at the picture he made in his baggy coveralls and courtly demeanor pleased him immensely. He'd decided to tune into her world of humor, hook up and fly with it. Chortling like kids on holiday, they boarded and descended smoothly to their destination, stealing kisses along the way. This was the second project Garrison had determined to complete before Angel's homecoming, an avenue of transportation.

The first had been the outside ramps, now in place.

"She will not be limited here," he'd emotionally vowed after she'd first regained consciousness. "Her life will be as rich and free as possible." It was now his mission to transform the dwelling into a sanctuary in which she had full mobility and access to as many of life's joys as he could make happen.

He had a lot to make up for.

Liza had joined in to reroute passageways and open up avenues of light and space, comfort, and accessibility. She'd designed the bathroom renovations, from the Italian tiles to the crisp white, double-crown molding. An oversized Spanish archway – cornered with snowy pillars – replaced the original French doors, to open up the dressing area, lending the flair of a backstage Broadway dressing room.

One fit for this season's headliner, in this case, Angel Wakefield.

Liza had gone to great lengths – looking for bargains in the process to have surfaces nonslip-treated to ensure Angel's safe mobility. The tub was the latest in accessible-paraplegic designs, raised up on a pedestal with a sliding door as in a van, where entering and exiting was like getting in and out of bed.

Since it was designed to fit into Angel's existing five-foot tub, it could later be removed if and when her condition changed.

Liza and Angel had discussed this, and she and Garrison were determined to honor Angel's faith and hope, regardless of the dismal prognosis of the medical team. In the meantime, nothing was too exorbitant when it came to Angel's comfort – on this she and Garrison agreed. Liza had to laugh again, as she'd done throughout the reorganization.

"What?" Garrison asked.

"Us. *Me*. For one who hates pushy, backstage moms, I feel downright hypocritical. Just look at the dramatic setting we've created. It just – fits. Am I terrible or what?"

"Horrible." He dipped his head for another solid kiss then murmured, "But then, so am I. In our eyes, she is and always will be a star."

Downstairs, the aroma of fried chicken whacked him and immediately his mouth watered. Even cool, it was crispy and succulent at once. After they ate, they adjourned to the den and propped their feet on the coffee table. Garrison sat sprawled on the sofa with Liza's head rested on his shoulder.

"We've got to be at the hospital by four," she reminded him.

"Hmm. Right. I want to get there in time to practice our loading and unloading." He chuckled suddenly. "That still sounds gross when I speak of transferring my beautiful daughter from bed to chair and back again. I need a better term to use. Something like 'butterfly lift.'" He sighed, at a loss for a fitting idiom

Liza reached up and tugged his face down to hers. "Seeing you lifting her so gently, placing her so carefully…stirs the loveliest feeling inside me." Her eyes moistened as she softly kissed him. "Thank you."

He kissed her back, getting into it. "For what?" he murmured.

"For being you."

Most of the time, Angel felt that gloom and doom were the order of the day. Why couldn't the medical staff have the same positive hopes as she did? She'd learned quickly this was not the case.

Paramount to them – in her estimation – was to shield her from hope. Hope was portrayed to her as some slimy cretin-imposter stalking like some Shrek-like ogre, ready to pounce and eat her alive, leaving only the smoldering dregs of paraplegia and hopelessness.

Today, Penny listened good-naturedly to her grouching. "I told Dr. Head-Shrinker this morning that I'd dreamed that same dream last night. You know – about God and faith? You'd think I slapped him." She didn't tell Penny about the other dream she'd had the night before, the distressing one. She'd tucked it away in her denial knapsack.

Angel's audacious mimicking face as she described the psychologist's reaction caused Penny to giggle. "You told him, huh, Angel?"

Angel humphed. "Yup. Told him I...didn't want to hear neg...negative stuff."

"What did he say?"

She grinned mischievously. "He jus' stomped out. Hates for me to hope." Her smile dissolved and sadness slid over her features as she looked out the window. "Why?"

Penny reached over and took her hand. "He's a knuckle-head. That's why."

Angel laughed suddenly and Penny joined in. "What do they know?"

"Yeah." Angel grew solemn. "What do they know?"

"Don't get a…a hernia, Daddy!" Angel croaked, laughing as Garrison lifted her and shifted to get a better balance before turning to the raised bed.

He looked down at her, only slightly winded. "Real men don't get hernias from lifting beautiful little Angels. You're light as a dove."

"Aunt Charlcy keeps feeding me…Snickers…I won't be."

"Oh, I don't think we have to worry about that in the near future. Enjoy life, punkin'. Every moment of it."

Liza watched Garrison tenderly place their daughter on the bed, moist-eyed as usual when she witnessed this little daily interaction. She'd never tire of seeing that father-daughter spiritual connection.

"Here." Angel gently pushed his hands away. "Let me." She struggled to use her arms to lift and turn her body, a long, arduous task at times, surrendering to her father's help only when her strength ebbed. This too was a daily battle for Liza and Garrison. To help Angel recognize her limitations without stripping her of her sense of worth.

Or hope.

To let her be herself – be the new Angel she'd claimed somewhere along her dark journey back.

Twice-a-day physical therapy brought Angel more to life than any other hospital routine. At least she was *doing*. Not just being. Range of motion exercises had already brought her back in touch with her upper body.

Occupational therapy was slowly moving her toward the self-reliance she craved. Right now it was very basic, such as the small gestures of using her arms and hands to compensate

for her lower body paralysis. She'd mastered operating the motorized chair and looked forward to going home and using the
brand-new, high tech vehicle her parents had ordered.

The spasms were, with drugs and exercise, diminishing. She
felt strength returning to her upper torso and extremities. Using
her arms to shift her weight was becoming easier. Angel worked
diligently with small weights now to increase muscular strength
and agility in her arms, shoulders, and hands, often sweating
with exertion and concentration.

Sometimes now in the wee hours she thought she felt a
slight tingling in her legs. It came and went. "Phantom sensations," was the consensus of the specialists.

Of the medical staff, Dr. Abrams alone seemed to really
listen to her. "Time will tell, Angel," he always responded in
his kind, fatherly way. He did not – as others did – caution her
against hope. She watched his reactions carefully, and many
times when she vowed to walk again, she thought she saw a
glow behind those thick lenses and a softening of austere features. Was it admiration or pity? She didn't know but she trusted him.

Somewhere along this extraordinary expedition Dr.
Abrams had stepped into a nurturing role, beyond the medical. At times, when they were alone, he'd pull a chair up to
her wheelchair or bed and talk at length, asking her questions,
encouraging her to share her aspirations, understanding when
she did not delve deeply into fears. He seemed to know that she
held them at bay, not allowing them to overshadow her hope.

During those times, the once-reserved physician disclosed
his own journey from an impoverished childhood, through
long, difficult, struggling years of college and medical school,
to proudly hanging out his own shingle and becoming a "bona
fide medical doctor." He allowed her to see his pride and then

his humility at what he called a "providentially led" road to accomplishment.

Angel shared with him Troy's unfinished veterinarian dreams and her own aspirations of going into medicine to help others. But when she opened her mouth to tell him about the bad dreams, something always stopped her.

It was like when she was cheering. Like running to get her momentum to do a triple somersault, and when she prepared to push off, stopping on a dime, freezing to the floor with fear.

It was a new thing to her, fear. And she didn't quite know how to handle it. Didn't even know how to own up to it. Her mouth simply would not spit it out.

Several times, during descriptions of her comatose visions and awakening to her loss, she saw Dr. Abrams' eyes moisten when he removed his glasses to clean them.

"Do you think about him much?" Dr. Abrams softly inquired one day.

"It's strange," she replied. "Sometimes it all seems like a dream. It's beginning to change, though. Sometimes now it hurts like…really bad homesickness. Y'know?"

He nodded. "You're still protected by the shock, to a small degree. The feeling – homesickness – means that your emotions are beginning to reemerge. You're handling it all remarkably well, Angel. I commend you. If you ever need to talk about it, don't hesitate to summon me. Okay?"

"Okay," she replied, feeling ridiculously cared for. It was a good feeling, though. Not like the cosseted feeling under which she was beginning to smother and squirm, like when she was forced to submit to others doing things for her that she'd always done before. Intimate, personal things.

That was tough to deal with. With Dr. Abrams she felt safe.

chapter seventeen

The psychological visits always forced Angel to stretch for emotional equilibrium. Today was no exception.

"Are you not angry?" asked Dr. Carlsbad, trying not to furrow his brow. Angel knew it took great effort for him to maintain a passive mien when she so obviously did not receive his prognosis nor, indeed, his counsel.

"A little," she said quite honestly, casting a glance at his attractive brunette female colleague, Dr. Blair, who seemed to be studying her handheld chart quite studiously. "But not about my current condition."

"Current," he mumbled and wrote something on his chart. He looked at her then, eyebrows raised above dubious eyes. "Then what *are* you angry about?"

She took a deep breath and exhaled, determined to slow down, take her time, and not stammer as much in her speech. She looked him square in the eye. "I refuse to have you feed me neg...negative crap any longer."

At his pursed lips, her indignation swelled. *Slow down.* "I have...the right to hope. And *believe*! And nobody should take that from me. But if you try – I...I'll still not give up." Her fingers curled into tight fists.

Instantly, tears stung her eyes and nose, surprising her as much as they did Dr. Carlsbad. *He should be pleased to see anything emotional*, she thought hatefully, since he seemed bound and determined to make her cry. But his face quickly softened and he patted her shoulder as he averted his gaze from her stricken, over-bright eyes.

"I'm sorry, Angel. I didn't mean to upset you. We'll talk another time, huh?"

Dr. Blair, the silent female, looked at her for long moments before she followed her associate from the room, something at once sad and speculative in her gaze, as though she felt torn about something. Angel watched her go, fighting anger and, worse, desperation.

Mama and Daddy came in a few minutes later, scattering the smog of desolation with their affectionate, upbeat banter. Daddy dress-rehearsed her home-going by doing the dove flight, his final choice of words to label the chair-to-bed-and-back transport.

"We're going to go grab a bite of dinner in the hospital cafeteria," Mama said, winking. "I need a break from kitchen-duty. We've been busy in the upstairs —" At Daddy's loud throat clearing, she stopped and waved a hand. "Never mind."

"Mama!" Angel whined. "What aren't you telling me? You know I ...h-hate surprises."

Liza reached out her finger to tap Angel's nose. "Little snoop. You hate *not knowing* what the surprises are. Too bad, kiddo." Then she dropped a kiss on Angel's wheat-streaked crown. "We'll be back in a few minutes. Need anything?"

Angel shook her head and watched them go, feeling their warmth leave with them. She despised that hateful little dark cloud that hovered overhead, stalking, just waiting for an opportunity to pounce and swallow her up.

She looked out the window for a while, letting the peace of white frothy clouds and infinite blue soak into her. Still – it wasn't enough. Uneasiness oozed through her, puzzling and alarming her.

"Angel?" She was surprised to see Dr. Blair, the pretty psychologist who'd earlier assisted Dr. Carlsbad, appear suddenly inside her door

"Nobody is to know I'm talking to you," the doctor said quietly. Then, rather furtively, she looked outside the door both ways before approaching Angel's chair and pulling up and taking a seat to face her.

Resolutely, she began speaking. "Three years ago, I had a stroke. I lay exactly where you are and was told by the 'specialists' that I would never walk, much less practice medicine again."

Her smile was quick and rueful. "I listened to Dr. Carlsbad earlier – tamping down your hope. He means well and thinks he's doing the right thing. That's what we're taught about dealing with cases such as yours. I know all the lectures against offering false hope."

She took Angel's hand in hers. "But I've been on the side you're on and I know how devastating it is for you to hear that you must accept never getting better." She huffed and shook her head. "Imagine. One has not a clue unless they sit where you sit. Because I've been there, I understand your anger and frustration. I just want you to take a good look at me and know that *there is hope*. It took a lot of determination and guts to stare down and defy the naysayers hovering about me when I lay so helpless and desperate. But I did it."

Angel felt tears pushing behind her eyes and her throat tightening. Excitement, so alien to her in recent days, trickled through her as the words and their implications connected. "You mean – ?" Angel's gaze probed the kind features, feeling herself wondrously tethered to support and empathy. From someone who'd actually overcome all odds to reclaim all she'd lost.

A medical person, no less.

Hot dog!

Dr. Blair's lovely full lips slid into a smile and her hazel, compassion-pooled eyes glowed. "I mean you can do it, too. At least give it all you've got. You told Dr. Carlsbad you feel a tingling at times? Then go with it. Where there's life, there's hope. That's not just a cliché."

She stood. "And Angel – there *are* miracles."

Her hand reached to take Angel's cold fingers, gently squeezing them. "Remember, we never had this conversation."

Angel nodded and swiped away a tear.

With that, Dr. Blair turned and walked purposely away. Angel watched her dark cloud of curly, bobbed hair above a white lab coat vanish through the doorway. In her wake sizzled a brand-spanking-new *expectancy.*

Angel gazed out the window into the clear blue sky, whose frothy clouds reached out and reminded her of something. She closed her eyes, her mind reaching back in time…for something profound. Then, in a heartbeat, the scene from her coma-vision swooped in. From above, she looked upon the operating room – sawAngel lying there, not breathing. Then she saw the medical mask removed from the provocative, involved staff member – who turned out to be Angel.

There was a profound Presence with her, giving her strength. That same Presence gave Angel the power to revive herself. *She did it.*

And Troy –

The tears welled again. *Dear God, Troy's gone.*

That gutting emptiness flooded her again, relentless, ripping and tearing at her.

Angel wept turbulently, off and on for hours after Mama and Daddy left but she did not fight it, knowing this grief must come before healing. She would survive her loss and heal – in time. She breathed a prayer of thanks.

And she knew. From all the heartache and pain would emerge the real Angel.

chapter eighteen

Angel dreamed of sitting on top of the snowy mist, legs dangling…it was a brilliant morning and she rode a cloud that reacted to her head's slightest tilt, taking her in any direction she wanted to go. It was a panoramic, eagle's-eye tour of her home and the forest oasis. Familiar places. She was absolutely intoxicated with the joy of being.

But then uneasiness began to intrude upon the euphoria, diluting…scattering…. Below, in the meadow leading into the green forest, stood Daddy smiling up at her with Mama by his side, wearing a long flowing skirt of blue chiffon. They watched her with intense pride radiating from their faces, one that smote her in a strange, perplexing way.

She inclined her head in another direction. The cloud veered to move placidly above the Bailey Dairy Farm, where Rocky Bailey sat astride his John Deere tractor, wiping sweat from his brow with his arm, overseeing grazing cows. When he looked up and saw Angel, he frowned for a long moment before sadness settled over his rugged features. Then June Bailey joined him. When he pointed, his wife spotted Angel and began to weep, turning her head away and pressing her face into her husband's overalled chest.

Quickly, Angel navigated the tour-cloud toward the forest, rocking back and forth to expedite the movement…getting few results. Slowly, impatiently she approached the clearing above the lily pond. There the cloud upon which she sat stopped, hovering above the Love Tree with its etched names limned so clearly she could read every letter. A far shore, way beyond the lily pond yet clearly visible, caught Angel's attention. It rose up into the sky, like the ocean from a distance, and the rise of it was laid with wildflowers of every color and description. The beauty and fragrance was like nothing she'd ever experienced and it pulled at her.

Then she saw him.

Troy.

Angel could hardly hold back a shriek of sheer joy. But somehow she knew that to do so would shatter the moment. In spite of that, she rocked and lurched to thrust the cloud forward…to Troy. She moved closer.

He stood tall and straight, wearing jeans and a hunter green Adidas knit pullover, his features more mature than she remembered. He stooped suddenly to ruffle Scrounger's fur and was rewarded by a sound licking over his entire face.

A laugh of sheer ebullience spilled from Angel and she felt tears flood her eyes.

She renewed her efforts to thrust her cloud forward – "I'm coming, Troy!" – but all her lurching wouldn't budge it this time.

"No, Angel!" He straightened to full height as his thoughts floated to her, soundless. "Stop. You don't belong here."

"Yes, Troy! I want to come!"

"You cannot come here." The reprimand was soft. Kind. "It's not meant to be. Don't you see?"

"I've *got to* come, Troy. Don't you understand? I *have to. It's not fair!*" Her heart was thumping like a bass drum and her cottony tongue stuck to the roof of her mouth.

"Go back, Angel, and think about what you just said."

Then the cloud began to disintegrate and the gray cocoon that had trussed her all those recent weeks began to move in and wrap around her, only now it was icy and wet and suffocating.

Angel began to struggle and flail and gasp for air.

She woke up fighting for her next breath, her face wet with tears. She sucked in a deep gulp of air and raised up on her elbows in bed, peering around the hospital room, now dark at her request. Still not proficient with changing positions, she lay back down and took deep breaths until her hammering pulse began to even out and her trembling body stilled.

Her eyes slowly acclimated to the darkness and she began to see the first silvery light of dawn filtering around the edging of her drapes. Still several hours before sunrise. Those were the hardest to deal with.

Go back, Angel and think about what you just said."

What?

What had she said just before that?

She closed her eyes and tried to remember. The harder her effort, the more jumbled her thoughts grew. Try as she may, she could not relax back into slumber after the dream.

She tried to think of something good. Positive.

She thought of Penny. Her friend.

Angel had once enjoyed Penny's company. But now, her desire to be alone superseded that. *Is that not totally catawampus?* She huffed in exasperation. From a gal who was supposed to love people. At least that's what her parents had always called her: a real *people person.*

Not now. She could spend the rest of her life alone. A genuine *Aye vant to be ah-lone* character. And no, it was so not funny.

Then suddenly, like a lighting flash, it came to her.

"I've got to come, Troy. Don't you understand? I have to. It's not fair!"

"It's not fair!"

When she realized what she'd said, she turned icy cold. The import of those words shook her to the bone.

She had a death wish.

Angel did not talk about it, figuring her folks had enough to contend with these days. And the psychologists would think she was going off her rocker for sure if she really opened up to them.

She could not put it into words. It was too horrific.

Penny was the first to notice the change in Angel.

"Why are you so quiet?" she asked one day. "You seem so… distant."

Angel cut her a so-what-else-is-new look?

"I mean, more than usual, Angel. You're so *down*. Especially on yourself. I can't believe you're beatin' yourself up this way – like not thinking you're making enough progress."

When Angel did not respond, she went on. "And it's so not like you to stay in bed."

"I'm tired," Angel mumbled.

Angel had asked to be put back in bed today, saying she was worn-out. Which was absolutely true. She didn't have the strength to breathe, much less to do agonizing exercises that were getting her absolutely nowhere.

Besides, she didn't care anymore. She didn't care about anything.

Outside her window, angry clouds wept while thunder growled and roared, a definite negative on this particular day. Storms had lately set loose some wild thing inside her, one that jerked her around in some inexplicable way. The rain itself pushed some vile button inside her.

But it went beyond weather, this distraught feeling tugging and knotting her insides. Ravaging her mind. She couldn't even joke that the lower half of her was spared the discomfort. Humor was playing hide-and-seek with her.

No. It was not exactly a physical thing. It *was* physical in that sound sleep had begun to evade her. More and more. And loss of appetite. But it encompassed more than flesh and blood and nerves and tendons and food and *blah blah blah*.

"You okay?" Penny persisted, sparking through Angel tiny fissures of annoyance at the intrusiveness.

"I'm good," she muttered to Penny, then closed her eyes. "I really don't need you to stay."

A long moment of silence stretched. "You don't want me here?" Penny sounded hurt.

"It's not that," Angel murmured listlessly – flat, like she felt. "I'm just not great to be a-around…right now." How she hated her halting, pathetic speech. "Don't really feel…like talking. Y'know? Sorta…need to be alone."

How her emotions shrieked and screamed for solitude.

Penny stood abruptly. "I'll leave," she said rather sharply, snatching up her purse.

"Please don't…be mad." Angel spoke to Penny's stiff, retreating back, yet she knew her words carried no conviction. No remorse for offending her.

Penny swiveled to face her, eyes over-bright, wounded. "No problem," her voice quavered, broke. "Just call me when you need me." With that she turned and fled.

Angel covered her face for long moments, hating herself, wishing she could cry, wishing she could feel *something* but for some reason, the flatness in her lay like cement, drying and

soaking up any kind of emotional release from the wretchedness that was *her*.

Yep, she was wretched.

Why?

For the life of her, Angel did not know. The nightmares
had spawned this new worthlessness inside her. It was alien, the
draining sensation she had at times, like someone had pulled
the main plug inside her and everything within her continually
surged downward. She could actually feel it slushing as it spilled
through her pores, like some earthen magnet beneath her was
sucking out her very substance. Each subsequent nightmare
she'd had caused the thing to grow, like slimy green mold on a
wet forest floor. Or spread like mildew in the corners of damp,
sealed chambers.

She struggled to lift her weight up on one elbow and use the
other arm to propel her body over and away from the window
view. She didn't want to see the rainy day outside and would ask
the nurse to close the drapes when she came in again. The turning over task exhausted her and she lay for long minutes getting
her breath back and willing her mind to turn loose of dark
thoughts prickling and probing at the periphery of her mind.

This is not living.

The thought blared out like from a huge brass tuba and
emblazoned itself on the wall Angel now faced. She squeezed
her eyes shut, but the words were etched on her eyelids. *This
is not living...this is not living...this is not living.* Her eyes popped
open and her breath caught in her throat as a terror she'd never
known spliced through her. And another thought leaped to life.

I can't go on.

But how to escape? *How?*

Her breath now came in gasps as she stared wildly at the
wall, her mind groping for a way out, clawing at her for a solution. Horrible visions swirled and collided against each other

in her cerebral slideshow, each modus operandi more horrific than the last.

She groaned and closed her eyes for long moments, demanding a time-out.

Suddenly, as crystal clear as Mama's Sunday drinking glasses, she knew how she was going to do it.

A calm settled over Angel, one that drove back all the clamoring, teeth-jarring uproar in her soul and pried loose the demonic talons gripping her.

Soon she thought as her eyelids drooped shut, I'll be *free.*

It wasn't hard. Angel just upped her complaints of back pain and "excruciating" headaches, which increased the dosage strength. The pain capsules came on schedule. She faked taking them by holding them under her tongue until the nurse left. Then she tucked them away in a small white envelope and pushed them to the very back in her bedside table drawer. No one ever looked there.

No one suspected. Everyone trusted Angel to do the right thing.

But what was the right thing?

She didn't know anymore. God help her, she did not know. But the only time she felt calm was when she decided not to live. Was that not bizarre? She could almost laugh in a detached way. Then she panicked that even her detachment was off the wall.

Wasn't it?

Hell's bells, was she *pathetic* or *what?* She didn't even know what normal was anymore.

Didn't her psych doc once tell her, "There is no such thing as normal"? How about *that* little ditty? *Huh?*

So maybe she was searching for something that was *not*. Her head began to feel woozy again, like it was ridding itself of taunting thoughts by spinning her mind like a kid's top. Even that wasn't funny.

Nothing was funny anymore.

"Time to boogie, Angel."

Mark, the friggin' faithful therapist burst into her room and grabbed Angel's motorized chair from its corner parking space, then rolled it to her bedside.

"I'm not…going," Angel muttered. "Sick."

Mark snorted. "You are one lazy chickadee, if you ask me."

"Didn't…ask you."

"Well, aren't we the smart-ass today?" he said cheerfully. "You've missed – let's see – the past week of therapy. Not good." Then he shifted impatiently, waiting long moments for a change of mind. Shrugging, he placed the chair back in its resting place, singing, "Have it your way. Have it your way."

Angel listened to him leave, whistling the Burger King tune as he went. Relief flooded her when he shut her door, closing out the noise.

Shutting out the world. She pushed the button on her bed. "Yes, what do you need, Angel?" Nurse Cindy warmly responded.

"I need some p-pain…medicine for my…headache. It's bad this time," Angel haltingly muttered.

"Sorry, honey. Be right there."

Angel closed her eyes as that uncanny, surreal calm gripped her.

Soon.

"Something's wrong, I tell you." Liza had taken Charlcy into the little chapel to talk outside. "Angel didn't even care that you and I aren't helping her today with her bath. She's not even trying to cooperate with them. Just lies there like a zombie. What does that tell you?"

"Hmm." Charlcy's features tightened. "Yeah. That is so not like our little get-out-of-the-way-I-can-do-it-for-myself girl. I just thought it was temporary, y'know, all this *withdrawn* business? She's been through so much and all. But she has been mighty quiet lately." Liza could sense alarm set in on Charlcy, could feel it humming, harmonizing with her own.

"And tired," Liza added, worrying her lower lip with her teeth, arms crossed rigidly, pacing the chapel floor. "And come to think of it, I haven't seen her eating at all."

Liza pulled out her cell phone and began dialing.

"Who you calling," Charlcy asked.

"Penny." Pause. "Hi, Penny, I was just thinking about you. Haven't seen you this week. Are you sick?"

"No," Penny dragged out the word, then silence sizzled for long moments. "She sent me away, Mrs. W." Liza heard the catch on the last words.

"For goodness sake, Penny. Why?"

"I don't know." A long snuffling sound. Throat clearing. "She said she just wanted to be alone. Didn't feel like talking. So I told her to call me when she wanted –" Her voice broke again, then silence.

"Oh, Penny. I'm so sorry. I'm sure it wasn't anything you did or didn't do. Actually, I'm worried about her. It's not just you, honey. She's terribly withdrawn – from everybody and everything at present. Things are just not kosher with her."

Charlcy snatched the phone from Liza's hand and spoke into it, "Listen, Penny, you get your little arse back over here, y'hear? She needs you now more than she ever has. And that's orders from headquarters."

Liza took the phone back in time to hear Penny's near hysterical giggles, sensing a keen joy at feeling needed again.

"I agree, Penny," she said. "Now's not the time for any of us to jump ship. Come on back. We need you, too."

"Okay, Mrs. W. I'll come back. And...thanks."

"No, don't thank me. I'm sorry you were hurt. Thank you, Penny, for always being there."

"Angel?" Penny's voice woke Angel from the restless nap.

She stared blearily at her friend, a part of her rejoicing at the sight of the pale, lightly freckled face hanging over her. The brown-speckled hazel eyes, beneath the shock of spiked black hair stared intently into her features.

"W-what you doing here?" Angel asked more flatly than she intended.

"To see you, *beetle-brain*," Penny snapped, then grinned. "And this time, you won't get rid of me so easily." She dropped her purse on the floor and plopped into the chair she'd dragged up to bedside. "And by the way – I forgive you."

Angel frowned. "For what?"

Penny gave her a mock glare, crossed her arms, and stuck her nose up in the air. "*For what?* I cannot believe you just said that. You are so much smarter than that, Angel." She cut her eyes balefully at the ceiling and swung her crossed-over leg back and forth.

"Yeah," Angel said, acknowledging the obvious. "I'm sorry, Penny. Didn't mean...to hurt you."

"You were just being a knucklehead." She shot Angel another face-splitting Penny smile.

Angel felt a grin coming on. She let it happen. "Yeah."

"We all are at times," Penny said and Angel suddenly felt very, very blessed to have her friend back at her side. "The kids from church send their love, by the way. They can't wait till you're back."

Church? Angel felt so far from that world.

When had she become so detached? Where had faith gone? Or *had* it gone?

"Penny." She looked at her friend, heart in throat. "Do you think somebody who kills himself will go to hell?" She was careful to make the hypothetical character masculine.

Penny looked shocked for a moment, then shrugged. "Yeah. I suppose they would. The Bible says, 'Thou shalt not kill.' That would include killing yourself, wouldn't it?"

Angel sensed Penny's indecision and pressed on. "Heck, I don't know. What about people who... just can't get it together...anymore, you know?"

Penny scrunched up her forehead. "Jiminy, that's deep, Angel. Real deep."

"I know. I just sometimes wonder how f-far God's mercy stretches when...folks get so far out on a limb that they don't... know how to get back? I mean, like...total suffering?"

Penny looked real thoughtful. "I know that God's really merciful. Heck, look at all King David did. And God forgave him, didn't he?"

"Yeah. But David didn't kill himself."

"Yeah," Penny agreed and sighed heavily. "By the way, how did therapy go today?

"I didn't go."

"Didn't go?" Penny looked stunned. "Why? You never miss therapy."

"Sick."

"You look fine to me."

Mama and Daddy appeared just then. Penny and Mama hugged like they'd not seen each other in years. Daddy hugged her, too, making Angel feel even crappier for ever having sent her away.

Suddenly, the tiredness swamped her anew, picking up steam. Edgy and weary of nuances she could not grasp, Angel painstakingly maneuvered her body over to face the wall again and soon sank into restless slumber.

❧

"It's called Survivor Guilt Syndrome," Dr. Abrams told them all as Liza, Garrison, Charlcy, and Penny sat around the conference room table. "It's a good thing you all got your heads together to nip this in the bud. Angel was well on her way to a suicide attempt." He shook his head grimly. "A close call."

Liza was thankful that Penny had put a bug in her ear about Angel's suicide talk earlier today. Liza had found the capsules while Angel napped. She'd asked the nurse about them and figured out that Angel had been stockpiling them for days.

"I don't doubt that she meant business," Dr. Abrams said, looking gravely at Liza. "And I seriously doubt that she could have survived had she taken all those pain capsules you found. She's still too fragile from the accident trauma."

Penny spoke up. "Let me get this straight. You mean – she feels guilty that Troy died in the accident and she survived?"

"That's exactly what I mean. I've talked with Angel at length. From our conversation, I've gathered enough to sense that's what's happening. And though I've passed my suspicions on to Dr. Carlsbad, I've scheduled the actual therapy with Dr. Blair. Angel requested her. Dr. Blair will work her through this critical stage."

"Actually," Charlcy inserted, "I've been surprised that Angel hadn't shown these symptoms earlier. I mean, she went through the accident itself…losing Troy and learning the odds against walking again. All that should've made her a basket case. But she came through like a trooper."

"Too well," Dr. Abrams agreed. "She talked about some of the repercussions, but not about the current nightmares and such. She'd nearly drowned in it all by the time you all discovered the seriousness of her syndrome. I feel certain Dr. Blair will pull it all out into the open."

"Then she'll be on her way to complete healing," Garrison spoke confidently. "If there's one thing our girl is not, it's wimpy."

"You got that right," Charlcy said.

"She's the most fearless cheerleader I've ever known," Penny piped in. "Nothing ever, ever defeated Angel."

"Anybody who can hurl themselves into triple backward somersaults can whip anything," Liza declared proudly.

Dr. Abrams smiled then. A face-splitting one that altered his rather austere features. "We all agree, then. We have a winner on our hands."

$$\approx$$

"Hi, Angel." Dr. Blair drew her chair up to Angel's bedside. A wonderfully light floral scent followed her and tickled Angel's nose in the nicest of ways. She felt daggum *privileged* to have her request for Dr. Blair granted. And she found herself gaping openmouthed, in awe of the complete recovery this former paraplegic had made in so short a span of time.

Dr. Blair got right down to business. "Tell me about the bad dreams."

Angel began to share them. "They start out good. But they end up crappy and scary."

"They involve Troy?"

"Always. Sometimes even his mama and daddy. They're always sad or crying when they see me."

Over the next few days, Dr. Blair showed Angel things she'd not been able to see for herself. "You've been through so much, Angel. More than many others who suffer from survival guilt."

She had suggested that Angel remain in bed during their therapy sessions because of the sometimes stressful divulgences. "It makes it easier for you," she told Angel. So today, Angel watched her from her head-raised position on the white-tucked bed. However, now Angel was insisting upon wearing sweats and more sporty attire.

The lovely doctor continued. "In your case, you've weathered pure survival. Then you took on the task of overcoming paralysis. And note, I said, 'overcoming.'"

They shared a moist-eyed smile then, one that spoke of an affinity not shared by others. One that joined them in sterling trust, faith, and hope for the best.

"Then," Dr. Blair continued, "when you emerge from the protective shell of shock, you begin to realize all that's happened. Right?"

"Right." Angel gulped back a sob, surprised at its sudden advent, but glad to finally *feel* again.

"Tell me about the night of the accident." The request was mild and sensitive and Angel felt suddenly that she could finally talk about it.

She took a deep, rattling breath and began in her halting speech. "Daddy said I couldn't go…to the Vines concert that night because…the weather was so bad. He was upstairs… working. I went downstairs and told Mama that he was being an old fart and that —" She stopped and snuffled back tears. "T-that he'd said I was like her, tying to get my way by…manipulating, y'know? He didn't exactly say that but I…kinda lied to get my way."

"So what did your mother say?"

"Oh, it worked. She said to go on, to enjoy ourselves. We left and… went out into the rain."

"How does rain make you feel?"

"H-horrible! Like I want to d-die, y'know?" Angel felt a clutching pain in her chest and fresh tears stinging behind her eyes.

"What else do you remember?"

"Not much. Just talking. Troy teasing me about a…present he had for…me."

"Angel, how do you feel about Troy's death?"

Angel sucked in a deep breath and then erupted in the greatest weeping she'd ever experienced. It ripped at her throat and flooded her chest, making it hard to breathe. When she could she began to howl and wail and sob aloud, fists pressed to mouth as tears cascaded from the corners of her eyes, across her ears, and soaked into her pillow.

"It was my fault," she cried out. "It should have been me instead of Troy. Oh my God! I should have…died. He would be alive if not for my…selfishness."

Dr. Blair sat quietly while Angel sobbed and gasped and howled her grief, one that came from deep, deep inside her soul, one germinated that rainy night when the variables had sided for her and against Troy.

Finally, Angel's grief abated, leaving her breathless, boneless, and slightly hicuppy.

"Angel," Dr. Blair spoke softly, "that night was a no-fault occurrence. You did not invoke Troy's death. Nor your own serious injuries. The variables of that situation were many. No one has control over them. Nor can you predict what will happen. Hindsight is always twenty-twenty, don't you know?" Dr. Blair's smile emitted compassion and understanding.

Angel felt her mind begin to unfurl and begin tossing out some of the garbage it had accumulated. "Am I – weird to feel like this?"

Dr. Blair firmly shook her head. "No, you're not. Not by a long shot. Let me give you some examples from life. Did you ever see the movie *Schindler's List?*"

Angel nodded. "Mama and I saw it together on TV."

"Well, remember when Schindler had an agonizing breakdown? He'd spent many war years saving the lives of a small group of people. In this one particular scene he's being honored and thanked by some of the survivors. Remember?"

"Yeah. I remember."

"Rather than accepting their appreciation, Schindler apologizes. He gets distraught that he'd not saved all the people on his original list, some of the survivors' families. The gold ring on his finger becomes a symbol of his perceived selfishness, because he kept it rather than using it to save one more person."

"I remember."

Dr. Blair continued, slowly shaking her head "He can't see the good that he did. He can't accept the love and gratitude of the people he saved. He feels it's wrong that he lives when so many millions died so brutally."

Angel began to see things from an entirely different perspective. "But he did so much for others, he couldn't help –"

"Mr. Schindler had an extreme case of survivor's guilt," Dr. Blair interrupted, "It can happen in any national disaster, like 9/11, war, school shootings. Even in natural disasters like hurricanes, fires, and so on. The survivor goes on with life but –" She spread her well-manicured hands.

"But not really living," Angel added.

"Exactly. They don't allow themselves joy or happiness and feel even worse if they enjoy something even for a short time. Sound familiar?"

"Yeah," Angel said humbly. "Too familiar."

Dr. Blair went on to cite other examples such as Waylon Jennings's narrow escape when he gave up his plane seat to the Big Bopper on that fateful flight that ended in the man's death along with Ritchie Valens' and Buddy Holly's.

"Jennings says he suffered guilt over that for a long, long time," Dr. Blair said.

"I can understand that," Angel muttered.

"It's not your fault, Angel, this emotional crisis. Many, many people feel these unjustified reactions following traumatic situations. *Unjustified.* If you'd died, would it have saved Troy's life? I think not. So your guilt is unjustified."

Angel felt a trickling of hope, mixed with the dregs of despair she'd carried so heavily in recent days. "But I can't sleep lately. It keeps going over and over in my mind. I don't want to eat…or talk to anybody. What's…wrong? Will it stop?"

"There is treatment. That's why I'm here. Do you trust me?" She smiled and reached out for Angel's limp, cold hand laying across her chest.

Angel tangled her fingers in the doctor's and returned her smile.

"Absolutely."

"You know, you're lucky to have such a wonderful family and friends. I've never seen such rallying in all my life. To save you from yourself." She laughed then, a peal of pure humor. "I meant that as a joke, by the way. Partly. But you *are* lucky, Angel. Don't ever forget that rescue."

"I won't." Angel knew she never would as she returned the squeeze and felt her hand released. Dr. Blair efficiently recorded notes on her chart, making Angel's curiosity stir. What was she writing about her? But Angel knew that it didn't matter. A wonderful feeling of security came with the knowledge that she did trust Dr. Blair.

"I'm going to prescribe some medication to help you slide into a healthy sleep pattern and a mild antidepressant, temporarily, until you level out. I suspect you won't need either for long. Because you're already halfway there when you release yourself from the culpability."

"Do you think I'm gonna be okay?" Angel murmured a bit anxiously.

Dr. Blair's smile was dazzling. "I'm one hundred percent positive."

๛

Charlcy swiveled herself before the mirror and frowned. She and Raymond were going on a real date this evening, dinner and dancing, the whole shebang. Lordy, did they know how to have a good old time or what? Never a problem there.

She'd already heaped three outfits on the bed. None seemed right, including this one. She shucked it off and tossed it onto the growing pile. Charlcy wanted to knock Raymond off his feet tonight. She didn't want to analyze why, just wanted to do it.

She yanked from the closet a little pimento red sleeveless number she'd impulsively bought after melting away twenty-five pounds. She'd just begun her divorce proceedings and had craved a high from something other than chocolate, which had temporarily lost its appeal, as had most anything edible. The red dress had done the trick.

Tonight, she fluidly slid into it, glad she'd worn cutout sleeves and shorts for her daily outdoors run, allowing the sun to bronze her arms, legs, and face to match. *Nice*, Charlcy had to admit as she smoothed the form-hugging skirt over slender hips. Its hem didn't quite touch her knee-tops, baring more than Charlcy would have dared reveal a year ago.

For every day, she was a jeans and sweatshirt gal through and through. But dressing up was something that she could get into.

Charlcy slowly turned and studied herself from every angle. Even though the mirror screamed "gorgeous" she remained unconvinced of her appeal. The old familiar anger stirred deeply inside, accusing Raymond of assassinating her confidence.

From a closet shelf, she snatched matching pimento red sling heels, ones she'd miraculously found in a little Greek boutique, then plopped down on the bed to tug them on her feet.

Confidence? She huffed with dismay. When had she *ever* in her life entertained, to any degree, self-assurance?

Hello? She'd been too busy fighting. Running warfare had consumed her entire life. Only thing she'd developed was an armadillo shell behind which to take cover. And heaven help those who dared to get in her face, forcing Charlcy to tackle fear demons. Such unfortunates found themselves targets of unleashed volatile hostility.

No sir. She didn't take crap from anybody.

Furious, she strode to glare at her image in the full-length door mirror. Reflected were burning eyes, up-thrust chin, locked knees, rigid posture. oozing, festering hauteur.

Tall, lean, and mean glowered back at her. Amidst the glamorous trappings, rage flailed and thrashed like startled red birds loosed in an Eskimo igloo. It flashed like bullets from her eyes, stance, and demeanor.

Mean? Yeah. She was as mean as they came. It hit her upside her head like a steel mallet. *This is what Raymond came up against daily.*

In that pulse beat, the adrenaline high crashed. She felt her knees unlock and her chin cave. Her rigid bones dissolved. From the mirror her features stared back at her, emptied. *Poor Raymond.* And he'd always loved her anyway.

Hadn't he? A moment of uncertainty seized her.

The doorbell-peal hammered her nerves and she slammed the closet door shut. Leaning back against it for a moment, head hung, she felt herself reeling from the grasp of who she was. What she'd become.

A royal B.

Dear God. She squeezed her eyes shut for another second of shame. She had no right to send an SOS *there* because she'd even sent *Him* away. What a total waste she was. How had Raymond survived her for so long?

Charley rushed to the door and flung it open, feeling as lowdown as she'd ever felt in her miserable life. Raymond towered there, loose and lanky, a smile quirking his full mustached lip – until her appearance visibly stunned him. His mouth fell open as his hawk-focused eyes ran over her from head to toe and back again. He swallowed soundly, then gazed into her eyes, which she suspected were wary at best and mortified at worst.

Oh well. Hell or high water, here I am.

"God, sugarbabe. I could eat you alive," he husked and shook his head in disbelief. "You've always been the prettiest woman on the planet. But when did you turn into such a *glamourpuss?*"

Nearly melting with relief and humility, she shot a silent thanks to the Man Upstairs, then simply smiled from her very soul. Adoration gushed from Raymond's gaze, rode his rumbling basso voice, taking her breath away. Charley had never seen him so open and vulnerable.

Yeah. He was susceptible. How had she never seen it? For all his puff and cowboy toughness, he was gentle as mush when it came to her.

God help her, her anger had sent him away.

To drink. Into a stranger's arms.

Then she fast-video-replayed his guilt and anguish. And his vow of fidelity. And his attending regular AA meetings, which helped heal the body, mind, and soul.

Raymond meant business.

Betrayal would not happen again. Somehow, in her soul of souls, beyond doubt, she knew.

"Come 'ere, cowboy," she purred, tugging him inside, one slinky foot shutting the door behind her. "We've got some catching up to do."

He gazed down at her, eyes half closed, searching, weighing. "You know our divorce won't be final till next month and if we —"

"I know all that. Like I said, we've wasted lots of time."

He grinned then and sent his Stetson flying. "You got that right, sugarbabe. B'sides, we need to do some testing."

"Testing?" she murmured, sliding her arms around him and gently nipping his ear with her teeth.

"Yep. Gotta see if some fixtures still work."

Homecoming was a wonderful, exuberant event. Fifty-plus guests welcomed Angel back to her house late that afternoon. The early September weather was a comfortable warm and the humidity low. On the expansive lush lawn, the Byrnes cheerleading squad executed a three-tiered formation with Penny and teammate Cheryl atop, holding a three-by-six-foot gray banner emblazoned with royal-blue words. "CAN'T KEEP A GOOD GIRL DOWN! YOU GO, ANGEL! WELCOME HOME!

Angel's one moment of anxiety had been when she was being transported into the car for the ride home. Panic rose up like a tsunami, breaking out a sweat and hitching her breath into hyperventilation. Understanding, Daddy had gently lowered her back into the hospital wheelchair as she breathed into a paper bag to ease the buzzing in her head and hands and to reinstate a proper oxygen level.

This is stupid, she thought and held up her arms to her father. She was ready to go home. And though apprehension rippled through her while riding in the car, she now knew why. The flashbacks of that auto accident, Dr. Blair reassured her, would eventually subside.

As their car slowed to a stop, Angel's tears blurred the big sign's letters, but she got the message loud and clear. Her cheerleader teammates shared an affinity with Angel of which others – save close family – did not partake. It was the physical contact, teamwork nature of their affiliation that kept them intuitively connected.

A visceral thing. Angel felt it when each of them touched her and spoke intimately, from the soul, to her. She would always be a part of them and they of her. They had faithfully visited her in the hospital and filled her in on gossip and school happenings and remained steadfast that she would completely recover.

It was as though her renewal would be theirs, personal and intrinsic.

"Let's do our dove flight," her father murmured, leaning in the car to scoop her up.

When Daddy lifted her in his arms and carried her inside, all her loved ones closed in around her, laughing and poking good-natured fun at her and one another as though this party was one they'd anticipated for ages.

Angel felt like Cinderella, not a paraplegic. She could almost feel normal.

Almost.

Even Gramma and Grampa Wakefield had flown in from Florida for the celebration. They planned to stay three whole days, the longest stay they'd ever done before. Angel felt happy that she would have more time to get to know them on a deeper level. Tonight, they couldn't seem to say enough kind things about her parents,

Especially things concerning Daddy. Angel noticed how his eyes increasingly lit up when they shared little stories of his young days with the party guests. Angel appreciated this new facet of her grandparents.

Daddy's usual shroud of reserve when in their presence fell away tonight, exposing a wonderfully spontaneous, fun-loving man. He blushed with pleasure when they announced during a toast how proud they were of Angel's recovery, of Liza for her loving support to her family and also of their son and his productive life, both as a family man and as an artist

And Mama floated around during the gathering like a fairy godmother in her most nurturing role, as beautiful and graceful as the ballerina she was born to be. Angel still wondered at her mother's self-imposed exile from ballet all during Angel's young years. But lots of things in the Wakefield family's lives were changing.

Other guests included Aunt Charlcy, Uncle Raymond, and their daughter Lindi. Lindi's little five-year-old girl, nicknamed Tootie, captured Angel's heart anew.

"She's the spitting image of Aunt Charlcy," Angel declared, in awe of the cutie-pie, Tootie, who climbed up in a chair as close as possible to Angel's wheelchair, her tiny black patent-leathered feet dangling far above the floor. A little-old person by nature, Tootie divined Angel's every need, sliding deftly from her seat to scamper off for refreshments or drinks to replenish Angel's supply.

"But with a milder disposition, thank the good Lord!" Lindi countered Angel's observations, then burst into laughter when Aunt Charlcy shot a mock-glower her way from the sofa across the room. Uncle Raymond lounged beside her, absorbing multiple conversations from all sides.

Then Charlcy, too, burst into laughter. "We *can* thank the good Lord for that, huh, Raymond?" When he looked puzzled, she clarified, "That my little cookie-cutter-image Tootie's disposition is much sweeter than mine."

He reared back and angled her a mild look. "Now, sugarbabe, I wouldn't touch that with a ten-foot pole." He winked lazily at Angel and resumed eavesdropping on several nearby conversations.

Lindi, a replica of her father, seemed content with her husband, Chuck, a nice-looking, shaved-head, gold-ear ringed guy, who was quite attentive to his two females. Chuck's automobile-detailing business now flourished. He had several employees working for him. Angel again breathed a prayer of thanks that, despite Lindi's earlier trouble-riddled years, her cousin had gotten it all together.

"Thanks for visiting me in the hospital, Lindi," Angel said when Lindi gave her a big hug. "Having Tootie entertain me was some great medicine, I'm glad you decided to move closer to home. I really missed you all those years you were in Atlanta."

"Pshaw. I got tired of never seeing family." Lindi, tall and lithe and spunky as all get out also had a soft side. As she mellowed, the family solidarity leaning was emerging and Angel was happy to see it.

Lindi perched on the arm of the sofa as she chatted a moment with Angel. "We're just fifteen minutes from Mama's place – in Boiling Spring, actually.

"Imagine. *Us.* Seeing each other every day." She laughed boisterously at that, sounding so much like Charlcy that Angel's eyes grew moist. Funny how things like that hit her now.

"Mama likes it," Lindi whispered, cutting her eyes toward her mama who was talking with other family members. "But only because she'll get to see more of Tootie."

"Aaw, that's not so," Angel said as Lindi moved away, still laughing. Angel knew that, despite Aunt Charlcy and Lindi's personality clashes, they were tight.

Angel cut her gaze to Tootie, who was hanging on to every word. "Say, you wanna take a spin with me?" She wiggled her eyebrows and reaped a wide-eyed, ear to ear smiling face.

Tootie was aboard Angel's lap before she could say scat and off they went, round and round the house interior, from room to room, even up the elevator to a second floor, rambunctious tour. Folks scooted out of the way, laughing and cheering them on, eliciting Tootie's froggy belly laughter until she was exhausted, till she nearly fell asleep in Angel's lap later when they parked again in the guest of honor space in the downstairs living area.

Angel, too, was tired. But it was the good kind. The *living* kind.

Guests, including teachers and school friends, lingered until Angel felt herself crash and began to yawn. Then they dispersed, each pausing to give her a sound hug and words of encouragement.

Pity bled through at times. Not often, but it was there.

During those instances, outwardly Angel received their well-wishes with graciousness.

Inside, she recoiled.

She could handle most things.

But not pity.

The very next day, Angel began a journal. It was a gut thing, to keep the laptop handy and feed in happenings, both the good and the not-so-good. The journal was *her* thing. For her eyes alone. It began her list of things *she* now controlled in her life, under the heading of *self-reliance.*

This list was the most important thing in her life. Except for her faith and determination. But then, the iconic journal encompassed both. It defined who she was. And who she would become.

Her days began around eight-forty-five a.m. Though Mama stood by, keening to help, Angel insisted upon navigating herself into the kitchen and putting together her own breakfast, most of the time whole-grain cereal with fresh fruit and milk.

The new motorized chair was fantastic, turning on a dime, easily maneuverable in, out, and around any space. It was *the* conversation piece during younger friends' visits.

Learning to cope was actually an adventure. Some days, as exercise restored her appetite, Angel tackled cooking, careful not to burn herself when turning her own bacon or sausage and scrambling her eggs. Though always nearby, intuitively Mama refrained from hovering.

For that, Angel's gratitude knew no bounds.

Cooking was accomplished with an electric frying pan anchored to an adjustable countertop Daddy had installed especially for Angel's chair-positioned height. Bread was a cinch with the toaster oven. Her own coffee maker/hot chocolate machine resided there, too, as well as a restaurant-assortment of beverage mixes and herbal teas. Next to that sprawled a mammoth wicker goodies basket, perpetually stocked with granola bars and myriad other healthy choices. Fresh fruit magically appeared, never running out.

One evening a couple of weeks after her homecoming, Angel insisted upon making spaghetti sauce in her frying pan. That would be her contribution to dinner. Mama did the noodles and salad. Daddy had caught on quickly and had already added a spice turntable to a lower cabinet, within Angel's reach. Daddy designed a fancy plaque to overlook the entire section. It read, "DANGER: ANGEL CROSSING."

Those times were the great ones.

Her early treks to the hospital for both occupational and physical therapy helped Angel gradually advance her coping skills, especially in personal care. Now, her therapy sessions took place at home.

Those first days' bath time challenged Angel. At her adamant request, Mama visibly restrained herself from interfering to allow Angel time to learn to maneuver herself in and out of the specially raised tub. Exercise had strengthened the girl's arms and upper torso even more noticeably in recent weeks. Mama sensitively allowed her privacy and independence while Angel bathed herself and shampooed her own hair.

Sometimes, Mama helped Angel blow and dry her hair, considering it "mother-daughter time."

But mostly, Angel opted to do it herself, shooing Mama off in other directions. "Mama, you've got a life, too," she insisted, meaning it. "Let me do the things I *can* do. That's not only helping me, but it helps you as well."

Daddy had hired a medically trained caregiver from the get-go. Dixie came right after lunch and worked Angel hard until mid-afternoon. "These workouts exorcise spasms and avoid leg muscle atrophy," she kept telling Angel, garnering enthusiastic cooperation.

"That won't do," Angel was fond of retorting as she puffed her way through a series of muscle-strengthening workouts.

Dixie was deaf to the word "can't." She was great for Angel, her match in both determination and tunnel-vision expectations. She listened to, really *heard* Angel's hopes and aspirations. She never, in word or indication, doused Angel's hope.

Her favorite response was, "We are limited only if *we think* we are limited."

Yep. Dixie was just what the doctor ordered.

One day, Angel suggested to her mother, "Mama, why don't you get somebody else to come in a couple of times a week and give you a time-out? You need to do something productive." Then she got an idea. "Ballet! Go back and take some refresher classes."

At first, Mama resisted – but only halfheartedly. "Then you can dance for me!" Angel had tacked on. "I've missed your dancing, Mama." Angel had fought dirty and hard. Knowing Mama so well, she'd easily won.

But her battles had only just begun.

The church looked beautiful to Angel as she motored slowly down the aisle. Tears prickled against the back of her eyes as familiar textures in crimson, white, and oak beckoned to and flooded her with lifelong memories. Her parents trailed as she selected a spot at the end of a pew and expertly positioned the chair out of traffic's way. They filed in past her and took their seats.

Pastor Dill's text reading included one of Angel's favorite Bible verses. "Let us read aloud together Romans 8:28 from the King James Bible," he instructed the congregation.

"And we know that all things work together for good to them that love God, to them who are the called according to His purpose."

As Angel read the words aloud, they smote her. If "all things" meant even her accident and paraplegia "work together for the good to them...called," then it meant that her situation was in the greater design of things. A bigger picture.

Did that mean that she would not necessarily be restored physically?

Disappointment swamped her. *Is that what you mean?* she silently questioned.

Angel felt torn between two spiritual spheres, one in which she claimed by faith nothing less than total restoration, another in which she decided that "Thy will be done," whatever the outcome. Could she actually trust that completely? Even after her coma, and life-or-death survival, this thing facing her loomed like the Great Smoky Mountains.

This was like no other test she'd ever faced.

At service's end, she parked herself in the vestibule, out of the way, while her parents milled and visited with the pastor and friends. Her hopes of blending into the background to morosely vegetate were abruptly aborted.

Folks soon spotted her and migrated her way to chat and offer supportive platitudes. They came in all flavors, the well-wishers. Some were quite loving and sympathetic. Some were overly effusive, others perfunctory and insincere. Little kids were something else entirely with their nakedly curious gazes. Angel never failed to reap grinning responses when she quipped, "Wanna see me get a wheel?" and became a real person to them. Adolescent scrutiny was often baldly pitying.

Angel stretched herself to take the initiative when gazes accidentally collided, flashing a smile and sending a simple "Hi!" With that, she became real flesh and blood, not an icon for disaster. Her teen peers often didn't know what to say, so they avoided her. It was too painful to relate to her. Adult glances were more screened, but Angel sensed the underlying "how tragic" sentiments.

It all exhausted her. Wiped her out. She felt limp as a noodle.

On the drive home, she gazed into the clear blue sky and sought peace with what she'd experienced today. What she'd learned. Number one and most important, she realized that even though no one else outside her inner circle knew it, she'd come a long way in recent weeks. She'd grown in self-reliance, even staying alone in the house for growing lengths of time while Mama and Daddy were out – at her insistence – living their own lives. With the elevator and a drive-in shower stall upstairs, she was now fully mobile and independent, able to bathe herself and attend to most of her own personal needs. At least for limited periods of time.

It was workable and that was a big score for Angel.

Her journal daily talked back to her, measuring her successes. Monitoring and correcting her mistakes. It characterized her.

Angel felt a profound stirring in her heart. The question sprang from nowhere and everywhere. *What will I do if I never walk again?* It had hovered there in the periphery of her mind ever since she'd returned from the living dead. The ramifications of her answer drifted in and out as she weighed who she was and what she was truly capable of. Her will hovered there for long moments, weighing, balancing.

Staring her down. Daring her.

"I love you, Angel," Mama said suddenly, turning to gaze back over the seat, reaching to touch Angel's arm. "Just think; this time five months ago, you weren't even here with us. And look at us now. We've got a lot to be thankful for, haven't we?" Tears shimmered in her eyes as she squeezed gently then shifted herself to again face the front.

A word fitly spoken is like apples of gold in pictures of silver.
Wisdom.

Proverbs 25:11 was framed and flanked other favorites on Angel's bedroom wall. She rolled her eyes heavenward and whispered, "Yeah, I hear you."

Aloud, she replied, "Yes, we do, Mama." The words released a certainty Angel had never before felt. And she knew then that even if she did not ever walk again, she would consider herself blessed above measure to be who and where she was.

She could, if need be, blossom right where she was.

Above all, she now realized what was truly important in life. *Love.*

chapter nineteen

They came into their spacious, airy den. Its comfort embraced them. Seven months after Angel's homecoming, on her seventeenth birthday, in fact, she still marveled that her life had been spared. How easily she could have gone on like Troy had.

Troy. His love would follow her all the days of her life. He'd led her to the knowledge that she was the one who rescued herself. That she had it in her to be what she wanted to be. That the good things in life were hers for the taking.

Above all, he'd shown her that she could choose to live.

That did something to her. Something that made her feel invincible.

Angel's motorized wheelchair whirred and angled into the spot once occupied by an easy chair. Owing to the fact that everything in the house accommodated her needs, she no longer thought in terms of limitations. Her parents' love spoke eloquently, everywhere she looked. No expense had been spared in this gift to her. Expense with the renovations. Mama and Daddy called the renovations "renewals." They used that term a lot lately.

Mama and Daddy lounged on the sofa facing her. "You've come a long way, baby!" her dad sang with pride. She acknowledged him with a big grin.

"I have, haven't I?" She said this with not a trace of conceit.

She'd worked through the loss of Troy. Was slowly adjusting to his being gone. Not easy. She'd learned to lean toward the good memories, was aware that those times during the coma walk had helped prepare her.

Angel's cell phone rang. It was Aunt Charlcy.

"Hey, brat! Happy birthday! What you guys doing to celebrate?"

"Mama and Daddy gave me a choice: party or whatever else I wanted. I chose to just chill out together."

"Can't blame you, honey. You've had enough drumrolls and acclaim lately, haven't you?"

Angel laughed. "Enough for a lifetime." She rushed to add, "Not that I don't appreciate all the approval stuff. It's just nice to take quiet time, reflect on how far I've come. To enjoy where I am. Y'know?"

"Yeah, sweetheart. I do."

Angel heard the smile in Aunt Charlcy's voice. It was great hearing that because not so long ago, it had not been there. She knew its source.

"Aunt Charlcy, it was great seeing you and Uncle Raymond volunteering at the church soup kitchen. I enjoyed being able to help with the serving, too. I noticed you two at the church homecoming dinner last week. That man can pack away some food, let me tell you. Are you two gonna get hitched again?"

Aunt Charlcy laughed tightly. "Whew, you're just full of it, aren't you? Actually, it's a distinct possibility, hon. He's hanging out at my house, freeloading anyway. Might as well marry 'im and make him a dependent, doncha know?"

"I know Lindi's over the rainbow over her daddy being back and all. I talked with her last night and she can't stop crowing about it."

"Yeah. Knowing the truth about his shielding us from his illness and how facing possible death changed his priorities. Yeah, makes all the difference." A long pause. "Say, Angel, truth is, Raymond and I are still married. We – ah, called off the divorce awhile back. Didn't want you to think I was lying to you when you find out later on."

"That's great, Aunt Charlcy."

They rang off. Angel looked confused for a moment. "Mama, did you know Aunt Charlcy and Uncle Raymond called off their divorce? How do you call off a divorce?" She shrugged and rolled her eyes. "Duh. I guess they just moved back in together, huh?"

"Apparently so," Mama replied, raising her brow at Daddy. Angel saw a warm, knowing smile slide between her parents. She knew they celebrated the renewal in Charlcy's life.

So did she. Family was great.

Adjusting to her physical and emotional changes was another thing entirely. She supposed that, in cases like hers, it was to be expected. Her sense of self was constantly evolving, never hesitating long enough to grow static.

As though divining her thoughts, Mama gazed at the ceramic figurine of Scrounger, now nestled in a prominent perch on the coffee table, where everyone could be reminded of the dog's great spirit and courage. They shared a misty-eyed smile.

Overcome suddenly with melancholy and what-might-have-beens, Angel blurted, "I might not be able to rock 'n' roll, but there are other things I can do, huh, Daddy?" She didn't dare ask her mother. She'd always wondered since the accident, was Mama terribly disappointed?

But her mother replied. "Got that right, Angel. Daddy and I both want you to do what you want to with your life. Anyway," she grinned sympathetically and with a touch of knowing, "ballet was my passion. Not yours. I know that now."

Relief melted through Angel. Her smile was genuine and spontaneous. "Does that mean I can eat all the goodies I want, when I want?"

"Your call," Mama said, crossing her eyes and bucking out her teeth.

"Glory!" Angel shrieked. "Just kidding. I'm hanging close with my basic nutritional program. I only fudge when the cheerleaders come over. And at family celebrations. And church socials. And –" Mama burst into laughter, then Daddy.

"Gotta salvage what I can from bulimia nervosa damage." She sighed, turning more serious. "Mama, don't feel guilty. I could've spoken up, but I didn't. I chose to live my life the way I did." She shrugged and smiled. "We get over it. Right?"

Mama nodded vigorously.

Then Angel's face sobered. "I'm really looking forward to going to medical school after college. Not many medical students have been on the other side of the fence the way I have. I'll understand how to help folks who face impossible odds – you know, encourage them to see hope at the end of the ol' tunnel. And to help people who can't walk to see not an empty bucket but a half full one. To realize that there's still life after tragedy."

Then she grinned impishly, feeling a sense of purpose she'd never before felt.

"Hey y'all, there's still lots for this ol' girl to do." She looked at her teary-eyed mother. "For instance, I'll come watch you in your ballet performances, Mama." She wrinkled her nose wickedly. "Just think, something good came from all this. I have a perfect excuse not to take ballet lessons again. Ever! Whooee!"

Mama and Daddy both burst into laughter. "I hear you, honey," said Mama, impulsively blowing her a big old kiss. "I'm proud of you."

Angel felt herself blush and rushed on to divert attention from herself. "And I'll come to your art exhibit next June, okay, Daddy."

"Sure thing, punkin'. Oh! Speaking of which – let's all go upstairs. That's where your birthday gift is. It's time. I want to show you the finished painting."

Angel immediately struck up her motorized chair before anyone could rush to help her maneuver her way from the room. They all boarded the elevator and rode up to the studio where, since Angel's homecoming, the Wakefields had held court, Daddy painting while Mama danced.

Angel – well, she'd been doing her own thing there, too. Reading medical books was now a passion. Dr. Abrams, knowing of Angel's aspirations, had donated to her some of his precious early medical journals. They lined a library shelf her dad had added in the studio. The doctor and Angel had formed a pretty tight friendship during her renewal. His shared wisdom was now some of her most prized stored cargo, along with beautiful memories of her time with Troy during her coma-odyssey.

Daddy and Mama were proud and supportive of her decision to be a doctor. Most wonderful of all, she now had her father's undivided attention and affection. In recent months, since her awakening, he'd become the daddy she'd always wanted.

Today, she whirred into the studio and detoured quickly over to the corner, where a comfortably caged, orphaned kitten healed from a fractured leg. She fed it milk from an eyedropper, with Mama helping. Then she said, "We're ready, Daddy."

Angel whirred the chair into position before the covered easel and canvas and eagerly awaited the unveiling. Anticipation prickled over her. Not only for this unveiling but also for her own exciting secrets she intended to share with Mama and Daddy later.

She'd kept quiet so as not to give them false hope. At first it was the burning butt sensation, from perpetually sitting in the chair, that she'd begun to feel, and then the sense of wetness when the catheter leaked. But then, checking out the web's paraplegic chat rooms had revealed to her that other complete-spinal-severed paraplegics had experienced the same awareness, with no hope of regaining total functional recovery.

Angel had not been certain, had hardly dared to hope, when bladder and bowel sensation had slowly begun to develop, so she'd kept quiet, hugging the knowledge to herself, desperately wanting it to last. Then, she'd decided to wait until her birthday and surprise her parents with the news.

After all, Mama had early on succumbed to Angel's insistence upon self-reliance, no questions asked. So hiding her secret had not been difficult.

Then, almost simultaneously, the tingling in her legs had increased and feeling emerged in increments. Only Dixie, the therapist, knew. They'd worked together with advanced therapy techniques until Angel had been able to stand and to put weight on her limbs.

Today, she would show them that she could now stand on her own. Not only that, but she could take small, laborious steps with the aid of a walker, one she'd asked Dixie to place in the studio closet for today.

Not a big deal to some, but Angel knew that in her parents' eyes, she would be handing them the world.

She blinked and realized they patiently awaited her full attention.

It was Daddy's turn. He looked at her, his eyes alight with anticipation and slowly lifted the linen.

Angel gasped, "Oh...my...God!" She'd seen the painting in the hospital, through the post-coma smog that day upon awakening. But its vibrancy had not registered. Daddy had taken it home that day.

Today, it zoomed in with 3-D clarity.

The lily pond scene glowed on the canvas, where sunlight permeated every atom of life there. Sitting on a golden pine needle carpet were Daddy, Mama, and Angel. Their laughter and zest for life sizzled and spilled over into the studio.

Standing a little apart in the scene, lounged against the Love Tree, was Troy, ankles and arms crossed. Beside him was Scrounger.

Angel wheeled closer and trailed her finger lightly over the sixteenth notch in the Love Tree, then traced the intricately shaped letters spelling "G Loves L, Loves Angel, Loves Troy & Scrounger," trailing downward like a dripping totem.

A humongous heart wrapped it all, encompassing the original, smaller one – showing love's far-reaching capacity. Angel felt her eyes mist as her gaze connected with Troy's. From the canvas, Troy's luminous smile and eyes glowed like a beacon, the light from them splashing all over the room and filling her heart.

"Looks like he's cheering you on," Daddy whispered reverently. Beside Troy, Scrounger was as mangy and ugly as ever and ridiculously happy. From his grinning mouth, his tongue lolled lopsided.

Angel's released breath was half laugh, half sob. Through the tears, she gazed at her parents. "I saw this. All of this."

"Where?" asked her father. But he knew. So did her mother. She could see it in their faces.

"In my dream...in the coma." The three of them fought back tears, failing. They wiped their cheeks and basked in the sacred moment love had given them.

Daddy loudly cleared his throat and gestured to the painting. "Well, what do you think?"

Angel snuffled back tears. "I think you'd better not ever sell this painting."

Her dad visibly swallowed back a lump. "Money couldn't buy it."

"Know what else I think?" Angel grew even more solemn as she gazed at the painting, at Scrounger, who'd taught her the true meaning of courage.

"What, sweetheart?"

"He's the most beautiful dog I've ever seen."

Her smile grew and grew until it burst into laughter. "And now, I have a surprise for you."

Dear Reader,

My next book, *Flavors*, a novella, will feature twelve-year-old Sadie Ann Melton as she enters a life-altering season on her grandparents' South Carolina farm. She is dropped off there amid a passel of kids who closely resemble the silver screen's Ma and Pa Kettle's brood. Sadie Ann is a composite of us all. She represents a fascinating collage of inner-child traits nestled deeply inside each of us, regardless of age or gender. *Flavors* sweeps us along with her as this child-woman looks back on that 1950 summer that changes her life forever.

Sadie's odyssey is at once heartbreakingly tender and crushingly brutal. As she searches for herself and ultimately, her space, Sadie struggles with the juxtapositions of Heaven and Purgatory, good and evil. The epiphanies she experiences are both wonderful and horrific.

At times, she is her own worst enemy, drawing dark arrows of disfavor. At other times, she floats in the light, seeing beauty in others, even with their warts and warped psyches. Her ability to reduce the good, bad, and ugly down to flavors helps her keep a floatable perspective during this pivotal summer. At its worst point, this slice of time takes Sadie to an aloneness she's never before faced. A time when she's truly without a place .

Ultimately, the Melton women and men in Sadie's journey help shape her into the woman she becomes. They love, coax, and command her maturity into being. But it is Sadie herself who pulls it all together. It is Sadie who emerges her own woman.

I hope you get the chance to enjoy this evocative journey to renewal and beautiful self-discovery. *Flavors* goes on sale in March 2011.

Emily Sue Harvey